THE MIDNIGHT SWITCH

For Finn, Pip, Joseph, Zuzu, Gigi, Pax, Matthias,
Ignatius and those that are to come

First published in the UK in 2023 by Usborne Publishing Limited, Usborne House, 83-85 Saffron Hill, London EC1N 8RT, England. usborne.com

Usborne Verlag, Usborne Publishing Limited, Prüfeninger Str. 20, 93049 Regensburg, Deutschland, VK Nr. 17560

A CIP catalogue record for this book is available from the British Library.

ISBN 9781474970655 05603/1 JFMAMJJA OND/23

Printed and bound using 100% renewable energy at CPI Group (UK) Ltd, Croydon, CR0 4YY.

SAMUEL J. HALPIN

Chapter 1

The Yellow Eyes

Midnight, that was when the unusually large bird had come to visit. It hardly seemed to move as it perched on his bedroom windowsill. And the only sound came from the tip of its beak as it pressed expectantly against the glass.

Watching him.

"Fancy a walnut?"

Lewis blinked, the car flooding back into view around him.

They were whizzing along thc highway as dark peaks jutting out of tufted slopes flashed past. Woolham was now long behind them.

"Lewis?" Dad's hand was reaching into the back seat, rustling a small Tupperware container filled with walnuts.

"Er, no, thanks," Lewis croaked, shrugging his shoulders a little as he dislodged the memory of the strange bird.

"You sure?" Dad said, with another tempting rustle. "Lots of omega-3."

"Okay." Lewis took a walnut and checked the notifications on his phone.

As they were leaving he'd taken a selfie with Mum's favourite cactus – that was still strapped for safekeeping into the seat belt beside him – and sent it to his chess-club group chat, WoolyChessChamps:

Travel buddies 🌵 Loooong drive ahead. Any of u gonna come visit?

He looked at the selfie again.

How was it that of the two of them the cactus looked like the one that had done its hair that morning?

Lewis's hair was short and sandy with a longer bit at the front that had an agenda of its own.

He tried to flatten it a little with his palm as he locked his phone screen.

No one had replied yet in the group chat. Not even his best friend, Zia.

"I listened to a podcast that said walnuts are the *top* nut for brain health," Dad said.

"*You're* a top nut for brain health," Mum chuckled, as she tapped out an email on her phone. "Gah. Shoot! I just made myself type 'top nut' instead of 'dental probe'."

"Brain a bit foggy, June?" Dad grinned. "How about a nice walnut?"

Recently, Dad HAS been a top nut for brain health, Lewis thought, shifting his knees beneath the textbook spread across his lap.

Normally Dad would listen to podcasts about cricket and the top ten things all millionaires do. But for the past two months it was nothing but "hot study tips" and "best bites to beat a blurry brain".

As if walnuts are going to make a difference. Lewis sighed, his stomach going all lumpy at the thought of his scholarship interview tomorrow.

Elksbridge Collegiate School. Or the way Dad always said it: THE Elksbridge Collegiate School.

Lewis hadn't even got in yet: there was still the interview plus an exam in a few days' time. But for some reason Dad seemed to think it was a sensible idea that they move nice and close to the school anyway.

Away from Woolham.

Away from chess club.

Right across England to Barrow in the Snoring Broads.

The memory that arriving "home" tonight would mean arriving somewhere he'd never been before made a drifty feeling come across him. As if he were a helium balloon someone had lost above a school fair.

Lewis was not a big fan of sudden changes.

What about friends, for instance? Finding kids who liked the same stuff as you would take ages, and in Barrow he wasn't going to know a single person.

But in his mind's eye as the bird watched him again, Lewis remembered there was *one* thing he was happy to be leaving behind in Woolham.

He pushed his fingers into the gap between the seats of the car and squeezed the fake leather.

Lewis really wasn't that interested in birds. If anything, he found the way they flapped around the bins at the park kind of stressful. But for the past six nights, at just after midnight, it had seemed birds, or rather one unusually large bird in particular, had been interested in him.

The first time it had tapped on his window he'd tried not think about it and just recited Gramps's chess puzzle over and over to make himself fall asleep. The second time he'd brushed it off as a coincidence and watched a video on his phone about robots.

But on the third night, as nothing moved out in the street, Lewis had felt the sudden urge to open one of his eyes just a scratch.

There it was again. Silhouetted against the curtains in the orange street light.

When it happened for a fourth time and then a *fifth*, Lewis had used Mum's packing tape to seal the curtains to the windowsill. That way he couldn't see out, and nothing outside could see in.

But, like clockwork, only moments after midnight he'd heard a faint:

tchk,

tchk,

tchk!

Even in the stuffiness of the car, Lewis felt the skin around his ribs quiver as he remembered it tapping against the glass.

Its beak was too pale to be a crow's. He could tell it wasn't a raven because he'd seen loads of them up close on their school trip to the Tower of London. And there was nothing in the copy of *Flycatchers and Coal Tits: A Fascinating Exploration of English Passerines,* which he'd found underneath their coffee table.

But it wasn't the dark oily feathers, armour-like claws or even its size that made the bird seem so unusual.

It was the *eyes*.

Dad flicked on the wipers, as a sudden flurry of rain scattering across the windscreen made the towering crags passing the car look wild and hairy.

"Shall we play a game?" Mum asked brightly, twisting round in her seat. "Twenty Questions? Or how about a good old-fashioned round of I spy?"

But before he could reply, Lewis caught Dad's eye in the rear-view mirror.

"Do I detect some *revision* going on back there?" Dad asked, giving him a look that was halfway between surprised and impressed.

A guilty pang tucked into Lewis's stomach.

"Er, physics," he murmured, gripping the pages as his eyes darted to the textbook.

Dad nodded slowly. "Okay. Do you think maybe you should be focusing on biology? That's where you got let down a bi—"

"George," Mum said in a low voice. "Just...let him be, okay? It's moving day."

His biology results weren't his best, but they hadn't let him down...had they?

Dad hunched his shoulders slightly, as if he'd been told off. And in the silence an unwelcome thought that Lewis was far too familiar with burrowed like a woodworm through his head.

What happens if I don't get in?

He didn't care about it for himself. He couldn't give a hoot about going to a posh school. It was Dad he was worried about.

What would he say? Would he be all quiet and disappointed again?

Lewis hated when Dad was quiet. Because, even though for the past two months Dad hadn't stopped rabbiting on about "study planners" and how "avocados could help you focus", Lewis knew that Dad talking made him feel loads better than Dad saying nothing at all – which had been the case a lot since Gramps had died, six months ago.

"Dad?" Lewis asked.

"Yuh-huh?"

"There's..." Lewis began, trying to sound casual.

"There's loads of houses that you can sell in Barrow, aren't there?"

Mum gave Dad a very hurried glance.

"Oh. Yeah," Dad said with a dismissive little laugh. "Buckets of them!"

"Hey, and don't you worry about me either." Mum twisted round again. "Dentists always land on their feet, because there's always someone in every town on the planet that doesn't brush their teeth!"

Lewis forced a smile. Mum was always so jolly, with her crinkly eyes and short pixieish hair.

"And there's a school?" Lewis asked quietly as his fingers played with the lock on his door.

"A school?" Dad frowned a little. "You mean... Elksbridge?"

"No, I mean a normal school. Like, in the town."

"There is," Dad said slowly. "But it's just the local school where me and your aunty went when we grew up in Barrow. Why?"

Lewis stared out of the window again.

"I *could* always just go there, couldn't I?" he asked quietly.

In the front, Dad adjusted the little pine-shaped air freshener.

"If for some reason Elksbridge doesn't work out," Lewis added quickly.

"Hey," Dad said softly and Lewis's eyes flitted to the rear-view mirror once more. "You're *going* to get that scholarship."

Lewis pushed up against the headrest and let out a slow breath as his cheeks flushed.

"And if you don't," Mum added, "then I'll just think that Elksbridge is a ridiculous school, that they're nitwits for not seeing how brilliant you are – and that you're better off without them *anyway*."

"Oh, June, please," Dad sighed as if this were a disgraceful thing to say.

"If it's so great, why didn't you go to Elksbridge when you grew up in Barrow, Dad?" Lewis asked.

"Gramps worked as a cleaner at Marlow Hall, and he couldn't afford the school," Dad said, waving his hand dismissively.

"*We* could never afford this school," Mum reminded them.

"Then, why didn't you apply for a scholarship too, Dad?" Lewis asked.

"You remember how Gramps used to try giving the staff at his retirement home twenty pence every time they brought him tea? Gramps never accepted *anything* for free."

Lewis caught Dad's eyes again in the mirror.

"Hey. You've got this, Lewis."

The car felt suddenly hot.

Dad seemed so confident. As if victory was inevitable. Like he did before one of his cricket matches.

Lewis wanted to ask Dad more questions about Barrow, about the people there and what his school friends were like growing up. But he knew that, just like everything else for the past few months, Dad would somehow manage to steer the conversation back to Elksbridge.

Lewis opened a new browser tab on his phone and typed: *barrow snoring broads*

He tapped on the first result, a website called Visit the Snoring Broads.

Barrow – he tapped on the menu.

Photos of windmills, a strange fountain, wooden fishing boats and glittering rivers glimpsed past as Lewis scrolled. The pictures made it look kind of pretty. But maybe it was just in the same way Dad managed to make some of the terrible houses he sold look ten times better in pictures than they did in real life.

Lewis went on scrolling.

Thatched rooftops

Lakes

Marshy swamps

Waterbirds

Until from beneath his fingertips there was an unmistakable flicker of yellow.

The air seemed to thin.

A pair of familiar yellow eyes were peering out from the bottom of his screen.

Lewis's neck gave an alarmed prickle.

The bird, he thought to himself. *That's the bird.*

He dragged his thumb cautiously upwards and his feathery visitor from all those nights before came slowly into view.

His finger found the caption:

The East Snoring Rook.

An unusual residential subspecies of rook in the passerine or perching order of birds. Unlike its cousin, the considerably more common European Rook, the East Snoring Rook bears distinctive yellow eyes and lives only in the forested network of navigable marshes and rivers known as the Snoring Broads. In fireside tales, the East Snoring Rook is often depicted as the servant of the infamous Bogwitch of Barrow: Gretel Murk. Like other corvids they are highly intelligent creatures, are deeply fond of collecting shiny objects and have even recently been shown to have the ability to count.

Lewis's hand fell to his lap in disbelief. How was it possible? A bird that lived all those hundreds of miles away in the precise spot their new house was, landing on his very windowsill in Woolham?

In the front, Dad craned his neck. "I think this is it!"

Lewis scrunched up his sleeve and wiped the fog from his window. Peering through the rain, he could see a flattened landscape.

It was as if a great hot iron had once been taken to the rocks and trees leaving nothing but wild, marshy wetlands scattered with splotchy gaggles of forest. Reedy, twisting rivers and wooded lakes flashed past, as towering windmills stood guard over vast stretches of rust-coloured rushes.

"Yep – we're here," Dad sang out. "The Snoring Broads!"

Lewis's seat belt tightened as he wrapped his fingers over the headrests, leaning forward to get a better view as the car began to slow.

A thick rope was strung across the road, hooked from one post to another:

SEVENMILL BRIDGE CLOSED
Please seek alternative route
or call the number below...

Beyond the rope a raised wooden drawbridge suspended by rusted chains swayed in the wind.

"So, what happens now?" Mum asked distantly.

Lewis's eyes dropped back down to his phone.

Although not proven, some ornithology experts believe there is evidence to suggest that East Snoring Rooks may be prone to sensing changes in the weather, which would explain the proverb commonly recited among Barrow townsfolk: When rooks fly high, clear glass sky. When rooks fly low, strange winds blow.

Lewis's neck prickled again as those eyes, like two luminous egg yolks, watched him from the edge of his phone screen.

It's a coincidence, he tried to tell himself. *It's probably not even the same bird.*

But as he peered out of the window, Lewis spotted a mossy sign on the roadside:

WELCOME TO BARROW
Home of the East Snoring Rook
Population: 1,363

The rain danced in harrying drifts across their car, and Lewis knew: it wasn't a coincidence. Here in Barrow it seemed there was an even greater chance that the rook would visit again.

As if it knew I was coming here, Lewis Buckley thought, his shoulder blades twitching as he remembered the bird's beak tapping against the glass. *As if there's something it wants.*

Chapter 2
The New Old House

The minute the email had come through from admissions@elksbridgecollegiateschool announcing that, at the last minute, they had decided to award one additional place this year – and that he, Lewis Buckley, had been invited to a scholarship interview followed by an entrance exam – Dad had made a decision.

This was it. Yep. Absolutely. The sign they'd been waiting for. They were *finally* going to move back to his home town of Barrow. Just like they'd always wanted.

Why they couldn't have waited to see if he actually *won* the scholarship before moving all the way to Barrow, Lewis didn't know. But since Gramps had passed away, he tried to keep most of his thoughts to himself. After all, it had been the very same day they found out about his interview that Dad had come home from work whistling for the first time in months.

Lewis hadn't packed that much with him for the car journey. Just his waterproof watch, chessboard, textbooks and a bag of chocolate pretzels Zia had given him for his eleventh birthday. He was saving those.

Mum had brought a sensible overnight bag. But Dad seemed to think his postcard collection, ornamental cricket balls and golf clubs were far too precious to entrust to the whims of a removal van and he'd packed them lovingly in the boot.

As the Buckleys' car jolted over a pothole, drawing to a halt in front of the raised drawbridge outside of Barrow, Dad's golf clubs in the back gave a nervous rattle. And the thick rope slung across their path dripped and swung.

"Why's it closed?" Lewis leaned between the headrests.

"It's alright," Dad assured them pulling up the handbrake. "This is all perfectly normal. They raise the bridge for boats to pass through, or in this case when the weather's rough. Sometimes, when the river gets too high, they even set off the flood sirens. We just need to call that number on the sign and someone should pop out to lower it for a second so we can get across."

Lewis dropped back into his seat, defogging the window again with his elbow and flattening his nose against the cold glass as he peered out. He couldn't see the town properly. Just that it looked dark as the masts of the boats moored along the swollen river bobbed and jousted in front of it.

"No signal." Dad scowled, tapping the screen of his phone. "June, anything?"

"Emergency only," Mum said, poking her hand through a gap in the rolled-down window in search of reception.

Lewis checked his phone.

"I've got signal," he muttered disappointedly. No one had messaged back on his chess-club group chat yet.

"Well. Done. Lewis," Dad said triumphantly reaching back for Lewis's phone.

The door slammed shut as Dad slipped out of the car.

Lewis tried not to focus on how mossy and sunken the rooftops on the opposite side of the river looked, as the sails of an enormous windmill in the distance seemed to flash like whale fins above the bridge.

Mum reached round to give his knee a comforting squeeze.

A bell clanged from somewhere nearby.

Lewis squinted.

"Someone's coming," he murmured as a shape in an oilskin coat hobbled towards the opposite side of the river.

Out in the rain, Dad gave a jolly little wave and unhooked the rope. But the man, his hair lank and yellowing, didn't respond, just reached for a pulley.

"This is all a bit Dickensian, isn't it?" Mum chuckled.

The driver's door swung open.

"See?" Dad said cheerfully, lowering himself in. "What did I tell you? Easy."

From in front of them there was a clang as the chains swayed and the drawbridge's two halves thudded together. And with another jolt as it left the pothole, the car wobbled across the narrow bridge past the mottled-looking gentleman and into the cobbled town square.

Dad drew to a halt with a little "ta-da", grinning through the window as if he was showing them the Grand Canyon. Lewis's eyes darted back and forth.

From between the gloomy drifts of rain the township of Barrow emerged, like a drowned shipwreck risen from the river's murky depths.

In his stomach, there was an involuntary pinch of disappointment.

"Doesn't seem like anybody's about, huh?" Mum murmured.

"People in Barrow aren't just superstitious about the weather." Dad grinned. "They're *super*-superstitious."

Mum groaned.

"Lewis?" Dad asked softly. "What d'you think?"

Lewis opened his mouth trying to come up with something positive to say, but he became distracted as his eyes fell on a fountain at the very centre of the cobbled town square.

It was the statue of someone in a tunic, up to their waist in the greenish trough of pattering water. One bony arm was crumbled off at the elbow and the other raised triumphantly above the statue's head, clasping what looked like a cup, or some kind of goblet, as if they were about to take a drink.

"The cobblestones are cool," he remembered to say. "Medieval."

"There's the Wherryman's Windmill Inn." Dad pointed towards a windmill on the edge of the town square. "The pub Gramps used to go to. Gourdley's Cobblers where we used to get our school shoes. Oh, and the Wandering Eel Pie House. They always had the best fish pasties."

But although Lewis was listening, his gaze had fixed on a noticeboard with large interchangeable letters outside the windmill pub.

He squinted:

1 DAYS UNTIL
THE PEERING OF THE GOBLET
JOIN US TO CELEBRATE 97 YEARS WITHOUT
FLOODING IN BARROW

"Dad, what's...what's the Peering of the Goblet?"

"It's just some town tradition thing they do," Dad said as they pulled off again. "To forecast the weather for the year ahead. There's a town legend about some witch called Gertrude Perk...or something like that."

"You mean *Gretel Murk*?" Lewis asked. He'd seen that name on the Visit Snoring website where he'd found the rook.

"How'd you know about that?" Dad chuckled.

"Er, just read it somewhere," Lewis muttered as they swung past the tiny Barrow train station.

The shopfronts gave way to muddled rows of sleepy-looking houses, each of them tipped with creaking weathervanes. Until, with a putter, they drew to a halt outside number seven Orsman Road.

The white house looked limp and neglected in the smothered afternoon light. Snares of withered brambles spilled from the flower beds, fingering their way down the path and up over the windows.

"Now I know it needs a bit of work. But we can fix it up, eh?" Dad said eagerly twisting round in his seat. "Whaddya think?"

"Well…" Mum said clapping her hands. "It has a roof. That's a great start, isn't it?"

"And walls. Don't forget the walls," Dad added, poking her in the ribs as she climbed out of the car.

Lewis's gaze drifted upwards as he noticed an abandoned nest beside the chimney.

"So. What are you thinking?" Dad asked softly. "Lewis?"

Lewis swallowed.

I'm never gonna tell him the truth, he thought. *So I'll just say something else.*

"Was-was there…" Lewis murmured, "was there someone else living here before us?"

"Mr Smythe," Dad said heaving himself out of his seat. "But he passed away a few years ago. We bought the house from his nephew."

Wind bristled against Lewis's neck as Mum opened the boot. "You ready to explore then?"

He didn't want to explore. He just wanted to stay in the warmth of the car. The car still felt familiar at least.

Lewis reached over and stuffed his textbook into his rucksack. Digging his hand into the bottom of the bag he rooted around, and frowned.

"What's up?" Mum asked, hauling a bag stuffed with pillows onto her shoulder.

"My red bike light..." Lewis muttered in disbelief searching under the seat. "The one Gramps gave me. I always have it clipped on my rucksack. But it's gone. It's fallen off."

The ridiculous urge to ask Dad to drive back to Woolham so they could look for it came over him.

"Lewis," Mum said with a slightly warning tone in her voice that made him feel younger than he was. "I'm sure it'll show up. We'll have a proper look later."

Reluctantly pulling on his rucksack, Lewis hugged his chessboard close and swung his legs out of the car. His trainers squelched, narrowly missing one of the fat garden snails suckered to the driveway.

"We'll give it a few licks of paint." Mum squinted up from beside him. "Switch on the lamps. Maybe hang some photos, like that one of us at Loch Ness where we're all smiling normally. And before you know it, you'll forget you ever lived in noisy old Woolham."

Lewis squeezed the strap of his rucksack.

"You want to be first to open up?" Dad grinned, holding out a key.

Tucking his chessboard beneath his arm, Lewis climbed

the steps to the front door as Dad hovered behind him. Wedging the key into the enormous lock, Lewis fiddled.

"See this?" Dad pointed out as the key let out a resounding *click*.

At the very centre of the door just below Lewis's eye height was a large, rusted doorknocker ring. It wasn't detailed. If anything it looked a bit...home-made.

"That's a Barrow *tradition,*" Dad told them brightly. "It's a heritage regulation for every house in Barrow to have a doorknocker. The nice lady from the Barrow Historical Society told me she'd drop one by. Must have come before we arrived!"

Lewis glanced over his shoulder.

Dad was right. The houses he could see across the road seemed to have the exact same doorknocker.

"Ready?" Dad asked, ruffling Lewis's hair.

Lewis did his best to smile. But as the front door swung open, a sly wind gusted past him, billowing through the musty stillness and making the hairs on the back of his legs stand to attention.

As if, after a long time, the house was taking a deep breath.

Chapter 3
The Chimney and the Rook

Lewis stepped cautiously across the frayed carpet on the threshold of the Buckleys' new house, number seven Orsman Road. He breathed in through his mouth, trying to block out the smell of damp curtains and dewy cupboards. Was Mum right about the house?

On one of his open days when he was trying to sell a house, Dad once hired an actor to pretend they lived there and stand in the kitchen baking scones. Maybe it *was* just little things like photos and warm lamps that turned a house into a home and made it feel like it was yours and not somebody else's.

"Seems a bit empty, huh?" Mum whispered, lowering the suitcase in the front hall.

"Not for long." Dad swept inside proudly tapping a piece of vintage floral wallpaper that looked as if it was itching to be ripped down. Then he launched into a conversation with Mum about buying a special coffee machine for the kitchen that you could turn on remotely using your phone.

Lewis poked his head into the living room. It was much bigger than their old place, but not the sort of big that you wanted to tell your friends about. It was gaping and windswept, with loose scraps of paper gathering in the corners and a manky old broom leaning up beside some yellowing tins of paint.

The moving boxes, which had arrived before them, were stacked in a sprawling pile in the living room with their three bicycles leaning sloppily against the wall. It was as if the team of movers had dumped them and clocked off as quickly as they could.

Lewis slipped his hand into the front pocket of his hoodie and squeezed the soft material as he struggled to imagine himself in the room. Would it ever *really* feel like home?

Shuffling across the brown carpet, he peered through the heavy brown drapes. A dripping garden met his eyes, and through the overgrown bushes he could see a murky strip of river embroidered with lacy collars of lily pads and water weeds.

That's kinda cool. Zia would like that, he thought to himself, pulling out his phone to check his messages.

There was a ripping of cardboard from behind him and Lewis turned.

"You okay?" asked Mum as she scrunched some tape into a ball.

Out in the hall, the front door closed with a clatter.

"Dad's going out?" Lewis frowned.

"Just to pick up dinner," Mum reassured him. "I'm going to unpack a few things. And you –" she extracted his chessboard from beneath his arm – "are going to explore. No studying tonight."

With her free hand she unhooked his rucksack, like she used to when he was little and came home from school. Lewis slipped his arms out. It made him feel exposed.

"You know, Lewis…" Mum started in a low voice, hugging his backpack close to her. "All this scholarship stuff? All the study planners and revision lists?"

"Yeah," he murmured.

Mum sighed.

"Well…I know it can be a bit intense, but…your dad only does it because he wants you to have all the things he didn't have as a kid. You know that…right?"

Lewis swallowed. He knew Mum was saying it to try to make him feel better. But it didn't. He didn't want to think about tomorrow's interview, much less the exam in a few days' time. Especially when he hadn't been able to focus recently.

"I know," he croaked.

Mum gave him a searching look for a moment, then her phone went off. It was playing her signature ringtone – the theme song from *Jaws*. Apparently it was a dentists' in-joke.

"Good," she said answering her phone. "Now explore.

Get out of here! Oh, sorry, Judy. No, not you."

Mum winked and bustled back into the hall.

The kitchen, living room and what was going to become a study were all downstairs. Upstairs, the bedrooms poked off the corridor, which was speckled with darkened nooks and tongues of yellowed wallpaper that bubbled and peeled. There were no curtains in his room yet, but the movers had set up his bunk.

Lewis began filming a video to send to Zia.

"Thiiiis is my new room," he narrated as he panned around. "Got a garden view down to the front. And look –" he zoomed in on a moth-eaten slipper abandoned in the corner – "even comes with a nice free shoe."

Holding his phone out in front of him he continued filming out in the hall. "Mum and Dad's room is down there. Another weird little...nook thing. And this..."

He entered the room next to his. "This is the guest room. For when you come to stay. You can have a whole room to yourself. Oh. Smells a bit weird in here. Might suit you actually."

He panned slowly around and his phone camera found the only piece of furniture in the house that he hadn't recognized.

"Nice big wardrobe for you there," Lewis went on narrating. "Old owners mustn't have wanted it. Let's see if they left anything nice for us inside it."

He tapped the flash button so the torch light went on and pulled at one of the little brass handles. The wardrobe shuddered open with a squeak.

"Yep. We struck gold. I think that's an old hanky in the corner there" – he filmed – "a lovely half-used bag of mothballs, and—"

On his ankles, Lewis felt a gush of cold air coming from *underneath* the wardrobe. He stopped recording and took a sudden step back. Cautiously pushing his cheek against the wall, he peered into the gap behind the wardrobe. A garden of jostling cobwebs met his eyes, but through it, he caught a glimpse of something built into the wall.

Wedging his shoulder behind the wardrobe, he lay flat against the wall and pushed. With a squeak, it shuddered across and a blackened fireplace shrouded with cobwebs slid into view. There was no hearth or mantlepiece. Just a sooty opening from which a draught whistled.

No wonder it's covered up. Lewis shivered.

Crouching down, he flicked on his phone torch again and squinted up the chimney. It was dripping, smelled strongly of wet soot and, at the top, he could see a small sliver of light where the flue opened onto the roof.

"Lewis?"

He stood up too quickly, knocking his forehead.

"Ow. Ow. Ow," he muttered, slowly retreating as he collided with a mouthful of dewy cobwebs.

Mum poked her head into the room as he emerged awkwardly from behind the wardrobe.

"Your torch is on," Mum pointed out. "And you've got some—" She pointed at his forehead and he wiped it with the side of his hand.

"Just filming a video," Lewis blurted out, his head throbbing. "For Zia."

"It's cold in here!" Mum shivered folding her arms as she leaned in the doorway. "Dad's gonna get someone over to fill that chimney in. Get some proper heating installed."

Lewis nodded.

"You know, after all this scholarship business is over, Zia can come stay. If you like?"

Lewis looked up.

"Maybe after Moira's visit?" he suggested. "Not sure if she and Zia would...get along that well, you know?"

If he was honest, Lewis didn't really *know* Moira. Not properly anyway. She was Dad's friend Badger's daughter. Lewis had met her once when they were both six and her family had come to visit them in Woolham years and years ago. But all he could remember was Moira having a huge tantrum at the zoo and insisting Lewis play a game with her where he had to close his eyes and she got to hit him with a toy hockey stick.

"Dad didn't tell you?" Mum frowned reaching out to peel a cobweb off his ear. "He called Badger. Moira's not coming any more. We felt like it might be a bit too much with the new house, the scholarship and everything else."

Lewis felt a hopeful glimmer. "Where's she gonna stay then?" he asked, wiping some soot from his palm.

"I'm sure Badger will just end up taking her on holiday or something," Mum said. "It won't hurt him to spend a little time with his daughter."

It might if she's still got her hockey stick, Lewis thought to himself.

"Now, how about cod, chips and a nice dollop of ketchup, eh?" Mum said temptingly.

Lewis portioned out the paper parcels of fish and chips onto plates. There was no bulb in the living room light fitting, but Mum had found a rusty-looking lantern outside the back door and poked some tea lights into it.

They ate cross-legged on the floor beside the mound of bikes and boxes, and as the night drew in, the flicker from the candles grew stronger. And the hollow room became like a great cave, nothing more than darkened corners as Mum's and Dad's faces glowed in the rich orange light. Dad told them a story about how he'd once tried to sell a studio flat no one ever seemed to want because there was a huge painting of a clown holding a flower stuck to the wall. And Mum recounted an incident at her old clinic where a man who liked to be called Big Jeff had fainted not once but three times in the waiting room before a routine check-up.

Dad didn't mention that the oil which came from cods' livers was rich in omega-3 *once* and, in the candlelight, the house began to feel the tiniest bit friendlier. Cosier. Until one of the tea lights fizzled out and the lumpy twisted feeling returned almost at once to Lewis's stomach as Dad said, "Right, you. Off to bed. Big day tomorrow."

"How're you feeling?" Mum asked, narrowing her eyes a little.

Lewis glanced hurriedly at Dad.

"Fine."

"Course he's fine," Dad scoffed proudly. "Revised everything he needs to mention in the interview for *three* hours at the library yesterday, you know? He'll be unstoppable."

Dad elbowed him gently and Lewis forced a grin as the blanket of guilt seemed to suffocate him. He hadn't been revising at all. He'd watched and then re-watched a chess match between Magnus Carlsen and Jan-Krzysztof Duda. And now there was no time.

Scuffling to his feet, he skirted the pile of packing boxes until he managed to locate the one with *LEWIS BEDROOM BOX NO. 3* written across it.

Pulling back the tape, Lewis pushed his hand into the gap between the cardboard slits and felt around for his chess clock.

"What you after?" Mum asked.

"Gramps's old chess clock," Lewis murmured.

The clock was black with two bone-coloured clock faces. It didn't work any more, but if Mum was right about lamps and cushions, maybe having it next to his bed would make his empty bedroom feel a little more like home.

"It'll show up," Dad said, waving his hand dismissively. "Come on. Bedtime."

Yanking on his pyjamas upstairs, Lewis climbed onto his bunk and lay flat on his stomach. A few times he thought he was finally managing to doze off. But just as his eyelids drooped, he became distracted by the quietness.

There was no drone of distant traffic, no fire engines or police sirens. Just the quiet muttering of the rain in the street outside.

Reaching for his phone, he unlocked it, blinking as the light pierced through the murky darkness.

23:58

He could see Zia had already watched the video he'd sent her of the house, but she hadn't replied.

It was a Sunday night. Maybe she'd been out with their other friends from chess club or something. Or maybe that's just how it was going to be now they weren't going to see each other much. Maybe they'd drift apart. And then just forget about each other.

In the little gathering of cobwebs in the corner of his windowsill a spider struggled for a moment with an unruly piece of web.

Lewis propped himself up on his pillow and typed, *Just made my first new friend* 😎

Leaning out of his bunk over the windowsill, he pointed his phone camera at the spider, trying to take a clear picture. But it was too dark, and the image kept blurring on his screen. Lewis tapped his phone in frustration. It seemed to keep focusing on something flashing red in the background.

Blink! Blink! Blink!

His eyes flitted from his screen over to the spot where the light seemed to be coming from.

Lewis shot upright, his head spinning in the darkness.

Blink! Blink! Blink!

An enormous East Snoring Rook, its head cocked to one side, was peering directly at him through the glass. Its yellow eyes glinted in the red light.

Keep cool. Stay calm. There are loads of rooks round here, Lewis tried to convince himself. *There's no possible way it's the same—*

The thought was cut off.

Blink! Blink! Blink!

Lewis leaned as close as he dared.

His red bike light. The one Gramps had given him – the very one that must have fallen from his rucksack all the way back in Woolham – was clutched between the rook's pale claws.

And the certainty that this was the very same bird that had watched Lewis all those nights before settled over him in a glistening of cold sweat.

The rook blinked its yellow eyes.

As if it knew something Lewis didn't.

As if it finally had his attention.

His watch gave two feeble beeps.

It was exactly midnight.

Chapter 4
The Interview

"Remember to stay focused if the interviewers ask you anything unexpected," Dad told Lewis as scruffy patches of wetland crowded with lakes and wooded clumps flashed by the car in the brilliant morning sunlight.

"What do you mean?" Lewis croaked stiffly. "What kind of unexpected?"

The feeling of relief that had flooded over him when he woke in the early hours to see that the rook, along with his bike light, had vanished, quickly dissolved as his mouth became watery and his stomach anxious and hollow.

The interview was finally here.

Dad had been up since six, hunched over the ironing board, and when Lewis had come down to breakfast, his starched shirt, a blazer he'd worn to Aunty Jean's wedding, trousers and his black school shoes were laid out on a chair in the kitchen with a burgundy tie rolled up like a rosette on top.

"Dad?" Lewis asked again. But Dad was squinting through the windscreen at a sign up ahead.

"Here we are!" Dad sang out.

A set of tall iron gates had appeared, and soon they were shooting through them, and up a sweeping driveway surrounded by crisp hedges, rose gardens and a cricket pitch so manicured it looked more like a frosted-green birthday cake.

There were other cars too, and Lewis watched nervously as a stream of kids of about his age were escorted by harried-looking parents towards the turreted entrance of Elksbridge Collegiate School. He slowly unbuckled his seat belt, picking up his rucksack as if it was weighted with rocks before joining Dad on the gravel.

"Now, if they ask, are you going to play the Concerto in A or the excerpt from the Saint-Saens sonata?" Lewis heard a woman with flared nostrils say to her daughter, who was wielding a clarinet case.

The girl glanced at Lewis for a moment and he attempted a feeble smile.

How could he compete with anyone who carried a clarinet like it was a weapon?

He glanced up at Dad, who was smiling proudly as he marched towards the school. And the feeling it was all going to go horribly, horribly wrong nestled itself in the pit of Lewis's stomach.

As the prospective students lined up inside, they were

given a form to fill in by a lady with square glasses and asked to wait on benches for their names to be called. She was accompanied by a boy about Lewis's age with jet-black hair, dressed in what must have been the violet-and-silver Elksbridge school uniform. His skin was pallid, his eyes sunken and pinned to his blazer was a name tag that said:

Leopold
Student Usher

The hallway was polished and oak, with portrait after portrait of former headmasters and hallowed school alumni glaring down upon those lucky enough to pass through.

"There's so many people," Lewis whispered to Dad as he lowered himself onto the bench, trying not to wrinkle his shirt.

Across the hall from them, a boy with blond hair combed back in an icy wave sat with his mother. He wore a medal that said *National Under-15s 400 m Freestyle Champion*.

Lewis fished the folded list of interview talking points out of his pocket and swallowed as he stared down at them. He couldn't play an instrument and he wasn't champion of anything. He'd only come runner-up in the Woolham Regional Chess Tournament, let alone the national one.

"Five-Wicket George!" a shrill voice rang out along the hall and Dad seemed to stiffen.

A small woman came bounding towards them struggling with, to Lewis's surprise, something he recognized from robotics club as a large, home-made drone.

"Nice to see you again, Celia," Dad said, very properly giving the woman a polite nod. "This is my son, Lewis."

Celia had eyes that bulged enthusiastically, a lizard-green anorak and a frenzied head of hair that gave Lewis the impression she'd been walking along a blustery cliff.

"Well, hello, Lewis. Your dad and I went to school together, you know? It was nothing like Elksbridge, mind!" Her voice was like a drill. "Old George here was quite the accomplished bowler. That's how he got his nickname: Five-Wicket George. If I remember correctly, he also played a *very* convincing Bottom in *A Midsummer Night's Dream*."

Dad flushed a brilliant scarlet. And over Celia's shoulder, Lewis noticed Leopold, the student usher, stifle a giggle as if he'd overheard. Lewis grinned at him, feeling the room become a little less glassy.

Celia loomed very close to Lewis and squinted, as if he were an awful piece of art. "Well, you're not much like your father at all, are you?" she decided. "How are you feeling, Lewis? Confident? Jumpy? A bit green about the gills?"

Dad kept glancing anxiously at the people around them, making apologetic little smiles.

"I'm alright!" Lewis croaked, trying to sound chirpy.

"Good!" Celia said. "That's the spirit."

She bustled over to the bench opposite, nearly sitting

on the National Under-15s Swimming Champion, as she nudged him sideways with one of the drone's wings that had a red wire sprouting from it.

"Oh, where has Hereward got to? Hereward's my son, you see, Lewis. He's interviewing for a place at Elksbridge too. Look what he made. Isn't he clever? It's a *drone*. He uses them to film trains, despite my repeated warnings not to – it's quite illegal, you know, Lewis? Oh yes. But every time I try to tell him that, he sends one of them flying down the hallway after me... Hereward!"

A tall, gangly boy with hair so red it rivalled Lewis's sidled up to her. He was reading a battered copy of *Bradshaw's Handbook – Great British Railway Journeys* and paused only to rub his nostril with unprecedented ferocity.

"Hiya," Lewis said throatily.

Hereward gave him a flat smile and Lewis burrowed his head back into his interview points.

"So, George. Will the Buckleys be joining us at the Peering of the Goblet tonight to ward away flooding from Barrow?" Celia asked. Lewis's ears pricked up.

The Peering of the Goblet. That was the town tradition he'd seen the sign about outside the pub. The one that had something to do with Gretel Murk.

"Ninety-seven years and not a single flood, can you believe?" Celia marvelled to Lewis, who tried to look interested.

"I'm amazed they still do that," Dad mused, adjusting himself in his seat.

"Without *fail*!" Celia cried in outrage, her voice billowing down the hall.

"Shhh!" came a hiss from the lady with square glasses.

"It's tremendous, wonderful fun," Celia went on in a loud whisper. "The whole town comes out to the town square. And the singing, Lewis. Oh, the singing! We gather around Gretel Murk's fountain and then parade between the windmills wassailing away the shadows with lanterns and chanting to keep the Bogwitch and her feathery spies out of Barrow for another year!"

The sheet of paper in Lewis's hands crinkled a little.

"*Bog*-witch?" he mumbled. He had a vague memory that it had been mentioned on the Visit Snoring website.

Celia gaped at him. "Lewis, you're not seriously telling me your father hasn't told you about Gretel Murk, the Bogwitch of Barrow?" Celia hissed in disbelief.

Lewis shook his head and Dad straightened up a little.

"She's someone that *everyone* from Barrow grows up hearing about," Celia told him, leaning in mystically. "The ghost that lives beneath the cloudy waters of the marshes. The witch who tried to flood the town!"

The Under-15s Swimming Champion's mother rolled her eyes, but Lewis did notice that the other parents and children had fallen a little quieter, as if trying to listen.

"Skin as slippery as an eel with fingers like parsnips. Her hair protrudes above the surface in a spiny cluster. Which is why, to this very day, if you're crossing the marshes alone, you should steer well clear of any unusual-looking clumps of rushes, because it's likely to be Gretel

Murk herself, as she lies beneath those quiet waters, waiting like a snapping turtle to haul people down to her watery kingdom!"

Lewis noticed an unexpected chill catch him between the shoulders. "And what about those birds...those rooks?" he asked, trying not to sound like he cared.

"They're her *eyes,* Lewis," Celia said eerily. "The Bogwitch's eyes."

Lewis pressed his back up against the wall as his feathered visitor from the night before seemed to peer into his mind's eye.

"Because she cannot leave the marshes, she sends the rooks out to do her bidding," Celia went on. "To see things for her. They're fond of shiny objects, though, so whenever we walk our dog Cyril, I wear a big hat in case they swoop at me and try to snatch my hair clips."

Sends them out to do her bidding? What bidding?

Given how persistent the rook's visits had been, it felt coldly clear that he was, in some sense at least, being watched.

"L-Lewis Buckley?"

Lewis's head swung back into the room. Leopold, the student usher, had read his name from a list and, at the very sound of it, Lewis's mouth had become all dry and tacky.

"Remember," Dad said. "Confident, clear, focused. You've got this in the bag."

"Good luck, Lewis!" Celia smiled kindly. "You'll be brilliant, I'm sure of it!"

Lewis followed Leopold along the oak floorboards of the hall.

"Nervous?" Leopold asked.

"A bit," Lewis rasped hoarsely, catching up with him a little.

"Haven't seen you around here," Leopold commented as they turned a corner. "You from Reedmouth?"

"Woolham," Lewis told him, trying to take deep breaths. "We just moved to Barrow. Orsman Road?"

Almost at once Leopold seemed to stiffen and then quicken his pace.

Had he said something weird? Leopold only looked at Lewis oddly after he'd said Orsman Road. What was wrong with living on Orsman Road?

An imposing door appeared on their left and Leopold gave it two hurried knocks before scurrying back down the corridor, his sunken eyes catching Lewis's for a split second.

"Enter!" came a cheery voice from behind the door, and Lewis reached for the handle, his palm sweating.

An ornate library with glossy shelves and gilded book spines appeared as the door swung open. It made his old school library look like a garage sale in comparison. Behind a large desk in the very middle sat a man with a walrus-like moustache and a woman with a sharp fringe.

Lewis read the little placards in front of them.

Co-Deputy Head – Mrs Irene Chen

Co-Deputy Head – Mr Digby Saxon

He felt a tightness in his upper back, just below the armpits.

"Sit yourself down," Mr Saxon said in a pleasant yet instructive voice as he reached for an old-fashioned audio recording device on the desk.

Lewis did as he was told. The chair was hard. Cold.

"Just so you know, Lewis, *all* our interviews are recorded using a Dictaphone in the event we need to review them."

Mr Saxon pressed a button and the red light on the Dictaphone began to blink.

"Thank you for your application for the Marlow Family Scholarship, Lewis," Mrs Chen said replacing the sheet on her clipboard. "Now tell us, why does Lewis Buckley want a place here at Elksbridge Collegiate School?"

"I-I've—" he stammered in a croaky voice. "I mean, I'm eleven."

Mr Saxon listened.

"A-and at my old school I was in..."

Mrs Chen made a note.

Why was she making a note?

Mr Saxon's squint drilled through Lewis as his head fogged up like a car window, with looming visions of clarinets and swimming champions.

"Why don't you tell us about your interests?" Mr Saxon decided.

Lewis took a deep breath.

Confident. Clear. Focused.

"I love chess," Lewis said. "My gramps taught me. I was the runner-up in the Under-15s Regional Woolham Chess Tournament, and me and my best friend Zia started a chess club with our teacher Mr Assad."

They nodded, looking impressed as Lewis began to feel a glint of confidence.

"I was part of physics club and robotics club, and our team even competed in the Northwest Robot Football League last year. Which we won."

"A highly worthwhile pursuit," Mrs Chen said.

A sunny feeling seemed to fill Lewis. But then Mrs Chen's voice faded and a chill coursed through him. His eyes locked on the Dictaphone's pinhole of winking red light.

Blink. Blink. Blink.

Almost at once, the rook on his windowsill clutching his missing bike light came back to him in red flashes.

"Her eyes, Lewis," Celia's voice drifted into his head. *"The Bogwitch's eyes."*

She's not watching me, Lewis told himself. *She doesn't even exist.*

"Master Buckley?" came Mr Saxon's voice.

Lewis took a sharp breath as he became suddenly aware that the deputy heads were both staring at him expectantly.

"P-pardon?" he stammered.

"I was asking which subject you find the most difficult?" Mrs Chen smiled.

Think. Think.

"PE," Lewis blurted out.

"Really?" Mrs Chen frowned, glancing down at her papers. "It says here on your application that you played cricket for Woolham Comprehensive last year?"

A stabbing jolt twisted through him.

I didn't write that on the application, he thought quietly as a creeping panic set in. Dad had made him try out as soon as he'd turned nine. But he'd never made the proper team.

"No," he blurted out. "I mean...yes. I-I like cricket."

Mrs Chen looked up, narrowing her eyes shrewdly as Lewis's chest ticked and with a curt smile she said, "Thank you, Lewis. We'll be in touch."

Dad seemed fidgety as they climbed back into the car. Lewis tried to ignore him.

How could he have become so distracted by a fairy story about some stupid witch?

In the middle of the school's front lawn, Celia's son, Hereward, was taking his home-made drone for a spin, watching as it buzzed like an enormous insect around the turrets of Elksbridge.

"That was...quick, wasn't it?" Dad remarked. "Did they ask you any...any questions you didn't expect?"

"Not exactly." Lewis shrugged, feeling sure Dad was going to get a call at any moment telling him not to even bother bringing Lewis to the exam on Friday.

"But you feel good about it? Yeah?" Dad asked, inserting the key into the ignition.

Lewis nodded hastily. But it wasn't true. He'd imagined feeling a ballooning relief, but right now all he could feel was a mucky afterglow. A gloomy thought drifted into his head. *Dad didn't change the application before he submitted it, did he? Adding that stuff about cricket…*

Dad could sometimes bend the truth to make the houses he sold seem more impressive. Or take a photo of a room from an angle to make it look bigger. But surely he wouldn't…*lie*?

Lewis didn't want to think about it.

"You know that Peering of the Goblet thing? The tradition where they keep the flooding away?" Lewis asked, absent-mindedly tapping the lock with his finger.

"Uh-huh?"

"Did you and Gramps used to go…when you lived here?"

Dad checked the wing mirror.

"No," he said quietly. "We were never in Barrow in July. We couldn't afford holidays abroad, so Gramps sent me and Aunty Jean to Scotland every summer to stay with his sister, Great-Aunt Lynette. I used to be so happy to be leaving."

"You didn't like being in Barrow?" Lewis frowned.

Dad squeezed his lip with his fingers. "I loved Barrow. But Aunt Lynette had a big house by the sea and, you know…even when I was your age, Gramps and I didn't always…get each other."

Dad fell silent.

"Why not?" Lewis asked.

Dad ran his fingers back through his hair. "Oh, you know. He used to get impatient with me. Like when I didn't understand his chess puzzles. You remember that one he made you memorize all the positions for?"

"White: Ke1, Rf1, Qg1, Rh1," Lewis murmured. "Black: Bf4, Kg3, Rg2. White to move and mate in 5."

"That's it." Dad smiled faintly. "Gramps spent ages trying to get me to visualize the positions in my head. I could imagine one maybe, but then as soon as I imagined another everything else would just vanish. Your mum can do it. Says it's because she got used to visualizing which tooth someone was talking about at dental school. But I never could."

Lewis focused his eyes on the specks of the window.

Even I can't visualize all the chess pieces in the puzzle at once.

Had Dad and Gramps really never got on? He'd always just thought that was because they were so different. Dad liked cricket and being a little bit flashy. Gramps liked chess, reusing teabags and thought mustard-coloured blazers and whitening your teeth for an estate agent's poster were just about the most absurd things a human could do.

"You wanna go tonight? Keep the floods away at this Peering of the Goblet business?" Dad asked, sounding a tad more like himself.

"Yeah," Lewis croaked.

"Okay," Dad said, decisively tapping the steering wheel. "Let's go. We'll make it a Buckley family tradition, starting tonight. Lots of people from town will be there. Maybe we can make a few new chums?"

Lewis smiled. He liked when Dad was excitable and chatty.

The indicator blinked as they paused at the town square and Lewis got a proper chance to look at the statue of Gretel Murk, up to her waist in the water of the fountain. The neck was crooked. The fingers furrowed. And only the weathered suggestion of eyes and a nose appeared where the face was supposed to be.

Celia's voice and the flashing red bike light kept flickering through his head. *They're her* eyes, *Lewis. The Bogwitch's eyes.*

You don't believe in witches and ghosts, he told himself. *Everything can be explained.*

But whichever way he looked at it, something odd must have drawn the rook to him in Woolham. Something that had made it follow him all the way to Barrow.

To his house.

And Lewis was going to find out what.

Chapter 5
The Marlows and the Marking

As Lewis peered down from his bedroom window that evening, people began to emerge from the houses on Orsman Road and Barrow seemed to come to life a little. As if a dusky-pink glow were flushing through its cobbled cheeks. Children carried twinkling lanterns and parents untangled scarves as they jostled in a trail of boots and jumpers towards the town square.

Lewis tried to flatten his hair a little in the bathroom mirror, chose a fresh shirt, green jumper, his smart trousers and good trainers.

"Does this look okay together?" he asked Mum at the bottom of the stairs, showing her his outfit as she unpacked some of her tooth-themed ornaments onto the console beside the door.

Mum stood back to examine him. "Nailed it."

"Cool," Lewis muttered bashfully. He hated choosing what to wear.

Dad appeared from the living room in a smart coat, clutching a stack of flyers. On the front of the flyers was a picture of him in his signature mustard blazer with his arms folded. And emblazoned above his image in very large yellow letters were the words:

BUCKLEY'S ESTATE AGENTS
Find Your Forever Home TODAY!

"You got new ones made up?" Lewis noticed, lacing his trainer.

"Yep," Dad said proudly. "You think people will like them?"

"Definitely," Lewis lied, fairly certain that Dad had Photoshopped his teeth even whiter than usual.

"You coming?" Lewis asked, when he noticed Mum wasn't wearing any shoes.

"I'm gonna keep unpacking. You two go." She smiled, coming up behind him and placing her hands on Lewis's shoulders. "Boys' night out."

Lewis felt a pinch of disappointment, which wasn't helped by the fact that, judging by the look on Dad's face, Mum had mouthed something to him out of sight.

"Buckleys! Yoohoo!" came a familiarly shrill voice as Lewis closed the gate behind them.

"Brace yourself," Dad muttered under his breath.

Celia was battling towards them through the throng of people.

"I can't tell you how happy I am that you came!" she gasped, steadying herself on Lewis as if he were a fence post. "Where's June?"

Hereward appeared beside her, still reading his railway book and wearing a T-shirt that said: *Do you even train, bro?* with a picture of a steam engine on it.

"She's staying home to unpack," Lewis told her.

Dad's eyes were darting over the babbling stream of people in front of them. "Celia, do you mind if Lewis stays with you for a bit?" he said pulling out his wad of flyers. "Just going to go and...mingle." Dad gave a half smile and darted up ahead.

Lewis watched him, feeling slightly annoyed that Dad couldn't wait for just a little bit before he started schmoozing for new clients. But the two ladies Dad approached waved him off as he tried to hand them flyers.

It doesn't matter, he told himself, looking away.

Tonight wasn't about spending time with Dad anyway. Tonight was for finding out about why there were rooks watching him, and what sort of bidding it was that this Bogwitch got them to do.

Up ahead, the merry trail of people bottle-necked as they entered the town square. But as they passed the Barrow train station, people seemed to be pausing to give important little nods and bows to someone standing next to it. It wasn't until they shuffled nearer that Lewis caught sight of a tall, older man, dressed in a grey tweed suit leaning on a silver cane. His eyes were dark and small, and his head was topped with a thin cobweb of gossamer hair.

"Who's that?" Lewis asked in a low voice.

Hereward looked up for a moment and let out a barely audible snort when he saw who Lewis had meant.

"That gentleman is Sir Hector Marlow, Ninth Baronet and grandfather of the Marlow family. You call baronets 'sir', you see," Celia whispered from the corner of her mouth, patting Lewis on the arm. "He's the chairman of the Barrow Historical Society. They're the ones who organize this event. The Marlows live at Marlow Hall, just up the Sevenmill River."

"My gramps used to be the cleaner there," Lewis remembered softly.

"Yes. A lot of mopping no doubt. Grand old place. There have been Marlows in Barrow since…well goodness, even longer than we've had the Peering of the Goblet, which is many hundreds of years. You see it was Sir Hector's ancestor Lady Lucrilla de Marlow who, legend has it, is the one responsible for saving the town from the wrath of the Bogwitch: Gretel Murk! Sir Hector is a thoroughly important figure."

Lewis craned his neck over the trudging crowd, just in time to see Dad shaking hands with Sir Hector Marlow. Even the *people* in Barrow were connected to the story of the Bogwitch.

"George Buckley, pleasure to meet you again, sir," Dad gushed. "Er, Lewis?"

Lewis froze. Dad was beckoning him over.

"Sir Hector, this is my son, Lewis," Dad said, putting both his hands on Lewis's shoulders. "Lewis, this is Sir Hector Marlow. Of the *Marlow* family."

As Dad said it, Lewis suddenly realized what he was hinting at.

"I hear you've applied for the Marlow Family Scholarship, Master Buckley," Sir Hector said, his glassy black eyes latching onto Lewis, who shook the old man's papery hand.

From behind Sir Hector stepped Leopold, the student usher from his interview. His jet-black hair was combed back, making his skin look more pallid and his eyes more sunken than ever.

"I-I've still got the entrance exam in a few days," Lewis hurriedly told Sir Hector. "A-and I don't know how I did in my int—"

"He smashed it," Dad interrupted proudly, squeezing Lewis's shoulders. "Lewis is actually a *chess champion.*"

"Runner-up," Lewis added as he felt another pang of irritation.

Why is Dad being so presumptuous about the whole thing?

Sir Hector gave Dad a neat smile, which seemed to suggest that the conversation was now over, and Dad whisked out his flyers again.

Lewis caught up with Celia and Hereward.

"Hereward," Lewis asked when he was beside him. "Who's that boy? The one beside Sir Hector? Is he a Marlow too?"

Hereward looked surprised, as if he wasn't expecting Lewis to talk to him, but gripping the edge of his book he turned for a moment in the direction Lewis had indicated.

"*Leopold* Marlow," he said flatly, returning to his reading. "Sir Hector's grandson."

"His parents both passed away," Celia butted in, offering Lewis and Hereward a plum puff each from a paper bag. "Boating accident. So now he lives with Sir Hector at Marlow Hall. Must be lonely for him. Loneliness makes people do very strange things, poor lamb."

"There's nothing 'poor' or 'lamb-like' about Leopold Marlow," Hereward snorted without looking up. "He's more porcupine if you ask me. My TripAdvisor review would be: 'Steer well clear. One star.'"

Lewis tried to suppress a grin as he took a bite of his plum puff.

"What did I tell you about being snide, Hereward?" Celia sighed, rustling in her handbag. "Yes, admittedly, Leopold's a little…*tetchy*. But can't we all be? You get awfully grouchy when you haven't had your cinnamon milk before bed—"

"Mum!" Hereward hissed, flicking his eyes at Lewis.

"I-I like cinnamon milk," Lewis said tactfully and Hereward gave him a nervous sideways smile.

Lewis turned back to make sure Dad wasn't too far away, but his gaze quickly fixed on Leopold Marlow.

Leopold was staring directly at him. His eyes were wide; wary and yet somehow threatening all at once.

Lewis pretended to glance away.

Had Leopold overheard Hereward?

"Lewis?" Celia passed him a tiny lantern with an unlit tea light inside. "To keep the Bogwitch's eyes from flying too low," she explained as she lit the candle. "After all, you know what Broadsfolk say: *When rooks fly high, clear glass sky. When rooks fly low, strange winds blow.*" She glanced darkly up at the sky. "In fact, those feathery rats up there are flying a little too low for my liking. They don't usually come this far into town. Shoo! Shoo!" Celia brandished her lantern at the sky and from overhead there was a resounding *croak*.

Lewis looked up. A coven of rooks, ragged and dark against the turquoise sky, were circling the blades of the Wherryman's Windmill Inn, which rose up like a great chess piece at the edge of the town square.

Was it one of you that took my bike light? he wondered, his eyes peeled for a flash of red. *What do they want?*

"So just because some bird flies a couple of feet lower it means it's going to flood..." Hereward sighed returning to his book. "Oh puh-lease, mother."

"And there you go being snide again," Celia huffed. "It's all this non-fiction you read that makes you so... hard-headed! Why can't you just enjoy the drama and excitement of it all like Lewis? Lewis looks positively green with terror!"

Thankfully, Lewis didn't have time to respond as, just then, a throaty voice from somewhere near the fountain began to speak and a lone fiddle played.

"Gather round, gather round! That's it, nice and close."

Lewis felt himself being herded towards the front of the circle with some other kids as the crowd shuffled tightly together, a small sea of glimmering lanterns and glinting eyes.

"Welcome one, welcome all to this year's Peering of the Goblet."

Lewis swivelled on the spot, scanning the faces for Dad, but was interrupted by Celia's chin appearing over his shoulder.

"Do you see the goblet, Lewis?" she squealed with excitement. "With the strange marking on it!"

As Lewis looked up, the lanterns flickered on the faceless statue of Gretel Murk as her bony arm thrust menacingly towards the sky. But carved deep into the side of the goblet, Lewis finally caught sight of what Celia was on about. And although he knew it had to be the first time he'd ever laid eyes on the marking, it somehow felt strangely familiar.

So familiar, in fact, that he was sure that when he closed his eyes he could picture it just as clearly as if he had them open.

Lewis felt a distinct unease settle over him as the crowd fell deathly silent. As if even the very houses of Barrow were holding their breath. Waiting for something to happen.

CHAPTER 6
The Peering of the Goblet

The dusk had faded in the town square. And above the crowd gathered around the fountain, the rooks circled.

"Good show. Settle down. Thank you all for coming," a short woman with gingery hair and dressed in tweed called out. Loitering at her elbow was a timid old gentleman with a puff of white hair who was nervously rubbing his hands.

Lewis scanned once again for Dad, but in the lantern light it was difficult to see beyond the first row of flickering faces.

"Welcome, everybody, to this year's Peering of the Goblet hosted by the Barrow Historical Society," the lady with the gingery hair went on, her pale-blue eyes sparkling in the candlelight. "For those few of you who don't know me, I am Miss Gladys Putter, the society's treasurer. Would you join me in giving my fellow society members a round of applause for organizing tonight's proceedings and for their dedication to preserving the traditions of our fine town."

As a soft clapping filled the air, a group of eleven or twelve old men and women, all dressed in their country best took a bow almost in unison.

"But special thanks must be given to our dear chairman of the Barrow Historical Society, Sir Hector Marlow, Ninth Baronet, and his family for gracing us with their presence, and for their charitable contribution to the heritage of Barrow across the years."

Where was Dad?

"Those of you who are new –" Gladys Putter went on.

"That's you, Lewis!" Celia hissed, poking him in the ribs to make sure he was paying attention.

"– may not be too familiar with the story of the Barrow Bogwitch. It's an old legend from these watery parts that dates to the sixteen hundreds. In days gone by, Gretel Murk, the Bogwitch of Barrow, cursed our beloved town with a terrible flood that threatened to sweep away food and livelihoods. And as the clouds drew in and the river swelled, it seemed all would have been lost, but for the quick thinking of Lady Lucrilla de Marlow, ancestor of our very own chairman."

Gladys Putter gave a fond bow in Sir Hector's direction.

"Lady Lucrilla ventured bravely down to the witch's

watery lair at midnight and, climbing upon a high rock, she summoned the witch, who appeared in a flash of green light.

"As the flood waters swirled around them, Lucrilla used her famous cunning to flatter Gretel Murk into performing various feats of magical power, eventually convincing the witch that, if she could drink all the water her eyes could see, using nothing but a goblet, the villagers would finally bow down to her.

"Gretel laughed with glee and crouching at the edge of the rock she began to drink. She drank and drank until, after seven days and seven nights, Lucrilla seized the perfect moment to creep up behind the witch and push her in. Gretel sank to the river's marshy bottom, weighed down by the water she had consumed, until only her reedy hair remained visible above the surface. Thus the witch was vanquished and the town of Barrow and its people were saved from destruction!"

The crowd clapped gleefully as glints of yellow light danced on Gretel Murk's hooked fingers.

"But," Miss Putter went on, "rumour has it that, realizing she had been tricked, from beneath the water Gretel bade the rooks, her fellow inhabitants of the marshes, to become her eyes and ears in the outside world. And she waited. Patiently. For a flood to come and overflow the marshes so she could finally swim into Barrow and seek her revenge."

A murmur fluttered through the crowd.

Ridiculous. Lewis rolled his eyes.

But if he really thought that, it was difficult to explain the relief in the pit of his stomach when he glanced up to see that the rooks seemed to have been drawn off somewhere.

Gladys Putter continued.

"So on this day, the twenty-second of July, to commemorate the date of her undoing, we come here to this stone likeness of the Bogwitch herself and peer inside her scrying goblet to predict whether there is flooding in store for Barrow."

Another round of applause.

"We will commence the peering followed by the procession to protect the seven windmills shortly, but for now would you please join me in singing 'The Tricking of the Bogwitch' by Eugenia Bilge."

Celia had by this point whipped out a small stack of song sheets, plunging one of them into Lewis's free hand and dishing out more to those around her for good measure.

The fiddle began to play again and the villagers in the town square started to sing, half of them taking the part of Lucrilla, the other half Gretel.

As they sang, a man with a pouchy neck and mayoral chain appeared at the centre of the flickering circle. A wooden ladder was leaned against the statue and the mayor began to make his wobbly ascent.

When the song ended, a pin-drop silence followed as the town square held its breath.

The mayor steadied himself at the top of the ladder and peered gingerly into the cup.

"Half full!" he declared and a colossal cheer went up from the crowd.

"What does that mean?" Lewis asked Hereward.

"Half full is just enough rain for the year. No flooding. Apparently." Hereward sighed regrettably. "It's always 'half full'."

"But what about the rooks and the mark—" Lewis began, but Celia swept between them gripping Hereward by the arm.

"Come on, you two!" she squealed as the sea of lanterns began to form a line and shuffle across the square. "It's time for the procession of the seven windmills. A blessing to protect Barrow's grain and supplies from foul weather!"

"I'm just gonna find Dad," Lewis lied. "Catch you up in a second."

A breeze drifted over the cobblestones as Lewis lingered by the fountain, and the villagers trailed off towards the windmill at the edge of the town square.

Lewis leaned out over the edge of the circular trough, peering up at the stone goblet and the statue of Gretel Murk. It wasn't just that the strange marking seemed vaguely recognizable. It was *familiar*. As if he'd drawn it a hundred times over.

Was it something to do with the rooks? The lady from the Barrow Historical Society hadn't mentioned anything about it in the legend. Just the goblet itself.

Making sure no one was else still lingering, Lewis hooked his lantern on his pinky finger and whipped out his phone. Opening the camera app, he zoomed in to take a picture. Though he felt weirdly certain he'd be able to trace it from memory if he had to.

"Her marking! Her watery, nameless marking."

A nasty snare of surprise bolted through Lewis.

The voice had come from the other side of the fountain.

"He-hello?"

A battered umbrella appeared, followed by a snarl of silvery hair. And an old woman with round, milky eyes hobbled into view.

"They think they can stop her floods. Silly fools," she muttered, doddering around the fountain towards him.

Lewis took a step back, feeling a little unnerved by her strange appearance.

"Er – I was just heading off, actually. Sorry," he said politely turning to leave. "Need to find my da—"

But with eel-like speed the old woman lashed out, gripping him by the wrist.

"A flood *is* coming, boy!" she spluttered, drawing Lewis so close that he could see her mossy teeth. "Strange things will wash up with it. Others will vanish as it recedes."

"I-I need to find my dad. I need to go. Sorry," Lewis blurted out. He yanked himself free, the woman's yellow fingernails sliding down his forearm as he did so.

"Pompous imp!" she snapped, lashing out again.

Lewis stumbled backwards, his heart thudding as she swiped the hooked end of her ragged umbrella towards him. "You think it matters whether there's water in that goblet or not!? A flood is coming. Everything points to it!"

Lewis straightened his jumper and began power-walking in the direction of the Wherryman's Windmill Inn, refusing to look back. His whole body was shaking.

What was she talking about?

There was a shudder from the trees along the river as a powerful gust of wind made them bow. And behind him Lewis heard the woman still wailing.

"Oh, the Bogwitch has her watery ways!" she howled.

Not wanting to be there a second longer than he had to, Lewis broke into a run.

Raindrops began to patter on his hair.

Why didn't I just stay with everyone when I had the chance?! he berated himself.

His eyes flitted until, finally, down a winding alley, he spotted the glow of candlelight and the procession.

"Lewis!"

Dad.

Relief flooded through him as he dodged between people putting up umbrellas and buttoning coats as a misty flurry of rain blustered over the cobblestones.

"Apologies, all. Looks like we're going to have to call it a night for our remaining festivities," the gentleman with the puff of white hair announced.

"Storm coming apparently." Dad squinted as Lewis gripped the crook of his arm.

It felt safe.

The lanterns flickered out with a breezy scatter of disappointed mutters. And as the wind lifted even further still, the crowd began to head back towards the town square looking up with displeasure at the clouds.

"You ready?" Dad called out putting one arm round Lewis and clasping his coat together with the other.

Lewis tried to peer through the people to see if he could return Celia her lantern. But in the confusion, he could only see the strange woman. She was standing alone, still waving her umbrella beside the fountain as the goblet clutched in the statue's thin fingers overflowed.

"A flood comes!" she cried out. "After all these years, how did we never learn!? The Bogwitch lives on. Watch for her green lights! Hail her feathery eyes! For when her rooks fly low, strange winds blow!"

The rain began to blister down as Lewis and Dad made their way back along the road. People vanished hurriedly into houses, bolting their doors as weathervanes spun and letter boxes rattled.

Lewis leaned forward, hugging himself as he battled against the wind.

"Dad?" he called out. "Who was that lady?"

"JUNE?" Dad shouted and Lewis looked up. Dad was on his phone, his back facing the wind as his coat flapped. "June, I can't hear you! What do you mean!?"

There was panic in Dad's voice. "What…water?! Hold tight. We're coming."

Dad pocketed his phone.

"What is it?" Lewis yelled, the rain pummelling his cheeks.

But Dad was already charging down the road. "Hurry, Lewis!"

Lewis tried to keep up, his trainers squelching as the lantern swung darkly in his hand.

What was going on?

His lungs were on fire when he finally reached the corner of Orsman Road.

Dad had stopped dead in the street. Both hands on his head, an expression of pure disbelief plastered across his face.

Lewis's stomach gave a tense shrivel.

A huge colony of rooks had descended on their house. Some of them circled high above, their wings battering against the storm. But most of them seemed to be milling, flapping, spiralling like feathered ants around the chimney.

As if they were trying to get in.

A whirling panic churned inside of him. Why their house? Why him? What did they want? What were they trying to do? Then a far more imminent thought struck:

Mum!

His lungs still burning, Lewis staggered across the road, fighting his way up the garden path as the shrieks became deafening above him.

"Lewis, wait!" Dad shouted. But it wasn't until he grabbed the handle, and glanced down at the welcome mat that he stopped.

There was water pouring out from underneath their front door.

CHAPTER 7
A Stranger Blows In

"It all happened so suddenly – in just a few minutes," Mum told Lewis and Dad in disbelief. "I went upstairs to unpack the bathroom and when I came back down, there was water *everywhere*. I kept thinking that a pipe must have burst!"

Dad had shut off the electricity, then hunted along the fence line with his phone until he found the water main and switched that off too. The brown water had gushed past Lewis's knees out of their front door, swirling into the street as the drains threatened to overflow.

The carpets in the living room, the study and the hall were soaked through. And the wallpaper ballooned from where the water had gathered and burst it. To Lewis it almost looked as if the flood had come from within the very walls of the house.

To his relief the upstairs, including the bedrooms, seemed unharmed. Mum had moved most of the boxes from the living room before the water came. But the same could not be said for Dad's postcard collection.

"George. I'm so sorry," Mum said as Dad inspected their soggy contents.

"It's okay," Dad said bravely. "They'll dry out."

He gave a quivery little smile and began carrying them into the study.

"Where did it come from?" Lewis asked as he pulled his arm out of his sodden jumper and draped it over the banister.

Mum shrugged. "I tried calling the plumber, but they're out on another emergency call in Reedmouth. Maybe they can tell us in the morning. We'll have to wait until then to take showers, but there's filtered water in the fridge for drinking."

Lewis nodded. "A-are you okay?"

Mum broke into a smile.

"I'm fine. Just a little rattled. And –" she leaned into the living room to check Dad was still in the study – "feeling disappointed for Dad."

"The postcards will dry out, won't they?" Lewis frowned.

"I meant the house," Mum whispered, squeezing him on the shoulder. "After everything that happened just before Gramps passed away, he was so chuffed when he found it. I think he'll probably be feeling a little guilty that everything wasn't quite as perfect as he painted it." A look must have crossed Lewis's face, because Mum quickly scooped up a pile of towels from the kitchen and added, "Crazy about those birds, huh? Even in a storm like this. Hopefully they'll be gone by the morning. Thank goodness Her Majesty Moira Wigby-Polkinghorne isn't coming to stay: imagine what a night that would have been!"

For a moment, Lewis wondered if he should tell Mum. About what people said the rooks meant. About the strange shouty lady at the fountain. But when he really thought about it, he didn't know what he'd actually be trying to say.

That a witch from hundreds of years ago was sending birds to spy on them, and he didn't know why?

Can you hear yourself? Lewis sighed, pulling off his sodden trainers on the stairs.

He lay awake, gazing at the ceiling, listening to the pecks and scratches through the roof as the storm continued to rage.

Mum's wrong. They're not gonna be gone tomorrow. And if they are, they'll just come back again. And then what?

Lewis squeezed the hem of his duvet, his damp hair feeling cold on his pillow. Mum was right about one thing though. Dad *had* been really chuffed when he'd found the house, especially after Gramps passing away.

Swaddling his ears with the pillow, Lewis turned on his side.

It all started after Gramps had a fall and cut his lip. He was okay for a while. But when he fell again, Dad and Aunty Jean tried to convince him he'd be better off in a retirement home. The very next day, early in the morning, Lewis remembered waking up to a sound outside the front of their building. When he'd looked through the curtains, he'd seen Gramps. In his pyjamas. Outside their house. And for a reason Lewis really couldn't explain, he was hammering planks across their front door.

"Why'd you do it?" Lewis had asked Gramps on one of his weekly visits to play chess at Woolham-Goldenoaks Retirement Village, after Gramps had moved.

"I had a little nightmare, Lewis." Gramps had scowled dismissively. "Sleepwalking. Nothing more."

But Lewis wasn't quite sure if he believed him. People didn't just sleepwalk three blocks and hammer planks to doors. Did they?

"You're to forget about it, alright?" Gramps had grunted, placing his chess clock next to them on the table. "Now. Do you remember what we say to our opponent when we're cornered on the board, the seconds are ticking and we can't see any way out?"

Lewis had swallowed. "Not now."

"That's right, clever boy!" Gramps would say, inviting Lewis to start the chess clock and moving his first piece with his yellow fingers.

It was sad to think of Gramps's armchair at the retirement home with him no longer in it.

And for a second it felt like they'd left so much in

Woolham. So many memories, friends—

"CAW! CAW! CAW!"

I wish you'd been left in Woolham, Lewis thought, his eyes drifting to the ceiling. He jammed his pillow over his face, muffling his thoughts.

What do you WANT?! Why do you keep coming to my house?

The image of the rooks flapping and pecking like a feathery cloud of black smoke billowed through his head. It really *had* looked as if they were trying to get inside the chimney. As if they were trying to get inside the house.

Lewis stopped, and the pillow slid off his face.

The chimney.

What with worrying about his interview, he'd completely forgotten about investigating the fireplace on the day they'd arrived. Yanking off his duvet, Lewis slid down his bunk, then edging along the hallway he gently pushed the door to the guest room.

There was a brilliant sting of lightning through the window, as the rain crackled against the glass.

It'll take two seconds, he steeled himself, flicking on his phone light.

The scratching rooks grew louder. And for a moment the soles of his feet felt as if they weren't really planted on the floorboards, as if they were telling him he ought not to be there.

I haven't got a choice. For some reason his home was under attack and he needed to put an end to it. Once and for all.

Lewis wriggled into the gap behind the wardrobe, held his breath and ducked into the windy fireplace. The terror in his chest seemed to grip through his pyjama T-shirt as the rooks' shrieks bellowed down the flue towards him.

He closed his eyes, repeating Gramps's chess puzzle over and over to keep calm.

Reaching up, Lewis walked his fingers along the grimy ledge, his breath caught in his throat. *Cobwebs. Bricks. More cobwebs. Even more cobwebs.* Until, just as the stink of wet soot threatened to overpower him, his pinky landed on something smooth. Something metal.

He shifted his hand over.

The metal thing was round.

Lewis latched onto it. And, gripping the object, dragged it from its bed of cobwebs as he writhed out of the fireplace, elbowing past the wardrobe and onto the cold floor of the spare room.

Adrenaline thrumming through him, Lewis wedged the wardrobe across as far as it would go and, sliding back to his room, tossed the object up on his bunk.

The thudding in his chest seemed to slowly transform from one of terror to one of triumph as he buried his cold feet beneath the duvet. *Safe.*

But any satisfaction he'd felt from retrieving the object dissolved as he leaned back against the wall and held it up in his torch light.

At a glance, he would have thought it was a brass clock, but as his fingers brushed at the soot it wasn't numbers that appeared but words:

It's a barometer, Lewis thought twisting it to read the dial.

If he remembered correctly, the idea was that as the air pressure grew higher or dropped lower, the hand on the dial would adjust itself accordingly, predicting what sort of weather you might expect. Dad *had* said that people in Barrow were superstitious about the weather, and wasn't that what the rooks were supposed to be able to do? Predict the weather?

The barometer was about the size of a round biscuit tin, and beneath the soot, its needle, one end of which was shaped like a crescent moon, was stuck fast halfway between *Dry* and *Bone Dry*.

Must be broken, Lewis muttered as the storm battered at his window. *Why would someone hide a barometer in their chimney?*

But as Lewis flipped it over, his chest tightened.

A symbol was engraved into the brass.

It was the marking. From the goblet in the town square. Celia had said it was the Bogwitch's marking. But what did it mean? Who had put it there?

Lewis rubbed his thumb absent-mindedly against the engraving. There was a *click* from within the device, and he felt the back of the barometer give. A pale glimmer of lightning forged at his window.

And the rooks fell deathly silent.

Lewis held his breath, listening as the blood pulsed through his ears. But the creatures didn't make so much as the faintest of scratches.

As if they knew precisely what was happening inside the walls of number seven Orsman Road.

As if Lewis was doing just what they wanted him to do.

An uneasy ticking filled Lewis's chest as his trembling fingers twisted. And the back of the barometer came away like the lid of jar. There was little wonder it was no longer working. The place where its mechanism should have been was filled with folded squares of yellowed paper. Like names in a hat for a raffle.

Lewis pinched one of them out and unfolded it.

An address? In Barrow?

He retrieved another.

His fingers kept dipping as the blotchy scraps of paper piled up on his duvet, until one unfurled that looked slightly different from the rest.

Lewis's neck prickled. *Child No. 4?! Who was child number four, and why 1810?* His fingers went on unravelling.

Until *another* scribbled-out address appeared:

Child number 2? Addresses, dates and numbered children. What did it all *mean*?

Outside on the roof there was a sudden, ear-splitting flutter. Lewis's fingers gripped the edges of his bunk as he heard the scrapes of hundreds of claws launching. And through his window he watched as, like a huge ribbon of smoke, the rooks soared over the town and out towards the marshes as the lightning glimmered behind them.

As if their mission was accomplished.

But Lewis knew that his mission had only just begun. He needed to work out why there was a barometer hidden in the chimney of their new house. To find out what the strange slips of paper meant. To uncover what the barometer had to do with the Bogwitch and her strange marking and why the rooks had followed him and wanted *him* to find it.

There were answers hidden in plain slight within these slips of paper, he was certain of it. He just needed time to work it out.

From the corridor there were footsteps. And, stuffing the papers back into the barometer, Lewis prodded it beneath his duvet and seized a biology textbook, which was lying conveniently at the end of his bed.

He pointed his phone in the direction of the door, just in time for Dad to poke his head through.

"Thought I saw a light. Oof! That's bright!" Dad blinked. "Sounds like those birds have finally cleared off. Thank. The. Lord."

Lewis breathed through his nose as his heart thudded.

Dad gave him a squinty frown. "You're not *studying* are you?"

"Just a little bit," Lewis lied. He could feel the cold brass of the barometer against his leg beneath the sheets.

"Well...you know I love your attitude," Dad said, "but Mum saw light under your door and sent me to tell you to go to sleep. So...better call it a night."

Lewis flicked off his phone torch and huddled down beneath the duvet.

"Hey." Dad's voice cut through the darkness. "I'm... I'm really...nicely done...for all the hard work, Lewis."

Dad paused for a moment as if he wanted to say something else, but instead he pulled the door shut.

Lewis turned on his side, facing the wall as the guilt draped over him. He *hadn't* been able to study properly. Firstly, whenever he tried to really concentrate he just couldn't, then there was the rook and now...*this*.

Slowing his breathing, he tried to block out his burrowing thoughts and, pulling his eyes shut, recited

Gramps's chess puzzle. The positions of the chess pieces appeared one after another beneath his eyelids as he tried to draw up the board in his head, until, with a feverish flutter, Lewis slipped into a dream:

He was at a table in a dark room, with a stranger sitting opposite him. Between them was a chessboard and Gramps's chess clock was on the side.

Whilst the clock on the stranger's side was ticking normally, the hand of the clock on his side seemed to be moving anticlockwise.

Lewis stood up from his seat and picked up the clock. His left eye watched the clock on the left. His right eye watched the clock on the right.

And before he knew it, he could see nothing but clocks, one counting up, the other counting down, as their faces faded to yellow. Two luminous circles drawing closer and closer as the hands flicked.

Tick,

click,

click,

click...

The ticking in his ears grew louder and louder until—

Knock.

Knock.

Knock.

Lewis awoke with a dry gasp of air. It was pitch black and the rain was still pattering the windows. Jiggling his watch around, he pressed the side button as it illuminated and Lewis blinked.

Beep. Beep.

00:00

It was exactly midnight.

He sat bolt upright in bed itching his palm from a mosquito bite. He'd been dreaming. Something about chess. But he could have sworn that he'd heard…

Knock.

Knock.

Knock.

Lewis's spine prickled in the darkness as their doorknocker echoed through the house.

He managed to get along the hall as far as Mum and Dad's room before the knocking came again. From where he stood on the landing, he could see somebody shifting about behind the front door's frosted glass panel.

"Lewis?" came Dad's groggy voice from the darkness. "What's going on?"

Torchlight appeared.

Dad's hair was all tousled and Mum emerged from behind him, tying up her dressing gown.

"We heard knocking," she whispered.

"There-there's someone there," Lewis breathed, glad to have Mum and Dad beside him.

"It's midnight! W-who's there?" Dad wondered aloud, padding down the stairs.

The three of them waited, as the wind scurried through the keyhole.

"Can you hear me?" Dad called out again. "Who's there?"

Lewis swallowed.

"Just open it, George," Mum whispered. "It's probably just a neighbour."

Lewis stood back as Dad fumbled with the latch, and the door eased open.

A spatter of wind billowed inside.

"Oh my—" Dad gasped. "Are you—?"

He stopped.

"Moira?! I-is that you?!"

He pushed the door fully open and on the front step of number seven Orsman Road, the figure of a girl with chestnut eyes and a tangled bob of dripping hair emerged from the blustering gloom.

Chapter 8
A Cold Lasagne

The last time Lewis had seen Moira Wigby-Polkinghorne was when she'd come with her parents, Badger and Emerald, to stay with them in Woolham six years ago.

Badger, Moira's father, was Dad's best friend from when he was a kid. His real name was Arthur Wigby-Polkinghorne, and he lived in Berlin now, but he could have been called Snartley Snogbottom and live on Mars for all Dad cared, because whenever Badger called, Dad would do this funny little thing where he'd start to fizz with excitement and then call out, "June! Lewis! It's Badger!"

Lewis had never forgotten the Wigby-Polkinghornes' stay. Particularly the tantrum Moira had had on a trip to Woolham Zoo, when her mum had told her she couldn't throw sweets at the capybaras.

But now, dripping in the doorway, her hair tied with an orange ribbon that was strewn across her cheek, Moira looked different to how Lewis remembered her. Even from the last pictures Badger had sent Dad. Though, despite seeming ganglier and her nose a little pointier, she still had the same dark hair and unpredictable eyes as that girl who had clobbered his finger with her ever-present hockey stick beside the chimp exhibit.

"What the... But, but—" Dad opened and closed his mouth, as a string of stunned noises came out.

Mum hurried to the door.

"Moira, wh-what are you doing here?! Are you on your own?" she gasped, gripping Dad by the shoulders and hoisting him aside. "Come in, quick! Lewis, get some towels."

"Where are they?" he blurted out, still trying to understand how Moira Wigby-Polkinghorne had arrived on their doorstep.

"Cupboard in the hall – there should be a couple left," Mum said firmly.

"Are you alright?" he heard Mum ask as he fished out the last towel from the airing cupboard that hadn't been used to mop up the flood. "Oh, Lord alive, Moira. Let's get you warm and dry."

By the time Lewis scurried back down the stairs, Mum had installed Moira in the darkened living room, the postcards strung out to dry above her as if she were at some strange surprise party.

Dad was leaning on the frame of the doorway and looking utterly dumbfounded.

"George, don't just sit there like a limp Frisbee!" Mum hissed as she unravelled a blanket. "Candles! Light some candles!"

Dad scrambled into action.

Lewis laid the towel on the armchair as his bare feet squidged into the wet carpet.

"My goodness you've grown up!" Mum marvelled, wrapping the blanket round Moira's shoulders.

"Hi," Lewis said, feeling awkward. Moira looked up at him without saying a word.

"Moira, are you okay?" Mum asked, her eyebrows knitting with concern. "We'll call your mum and dad and let them know you're here safely. Don't worry. You must have been so confused when we didn't come pick you up. Did your dad give you George's number or something? We thought you were going with your parents to Switzerland?"

Lewis retreated to the doorway, and it was only then that he really had time to notice what Moira was wearing. Her dress was duck-egg blue with an enormous white collar. A sodden brown cardigan with pearly buttons was wrapped round her wiry elbows, and strung across her chest was an embroidered shoulder bag on a string.

"I s-saw –" Moira quivered faintly – "this house…the door with the—" She rapped her fingers as if imitating the doorknocker.

"Moira, could you sit tight for just one moment?" Mum asked, scooping Dad firmly by the elbow into the kitchen and closing the door.

Lewis gave Moira a weak smile, which she did not return. He could hear Mum and Dad's low hurried conversation coming from underneath the door.

"When you left that voicemail for Badger, to tell him it was going to be too tricky for Moira to stay with us..." Mum began in a low voice.

"Yeesss," Dad said slowly, sounding a little cornered.

"Did he ever call you back, or give you any indication that he'd received your message?" Mum's voice was firm, as if she knew exactly the answer Dad was about to give.

"Well, let me see..." Dad murmured sheepishly.

"Let you see what exactly, George? Hmm?" Mum snapped. "That poor girl's probably been waiting at the train station in the rain for us to come for hours! If I'm honest it's a complete miracle she's found her way here at all!"

Their conversation continued in low jabs until Lewis decided he ought to make their guest feel a little more at home.

"Can I...get you anything?" Lewis said, shuffling towards her.

Silence followed as Moira stared blankly at him.

He tried another tack. "Do you...still play hockey?"

"H-h-hockey?" Moira shivered, looking confused as the candlelight hollowed out her face.

"You had a hockey stick last time we met. You probably don't remember," Lewis said. Though he most certainly hadn't forgotten.

"Moira," she said slowly. "A-and...and you're *Willis*?"

Willis? Lewis felt confused. How could she not remember his name? Maybe she'd hit so many people with hockey sticks over the years that she couldn't keep track?

"No...not Willis...*Lewis*... *Lewis*," she repeated distantly.

There was another uncomfortable silence.

"Didn't you bring any luggage with you?" Lewis asked, glancing around in case he'd missed it.

Moira opened her mouth in what seemed to be bewilderment.

"You know...on the train?" he asked softly.

Her eyes grew so wide that for a moment he thought they were going to burst from her skull.

"I left it," she blurted out, "by accident."

Ferreting in her cardigan sleeve Moira produced a hanky that seemed to be covered in splotches of ink.

"What colour was it?" Mum asked coming back into the room.

"Lavender," Moira squeaked burying her face in the hanky and blowing her nose.

"Lewis can go with you and check at the station tomorrow. See if someone handed it in," Mum told her. "You'll have to borrow some of Lewis's clothes in the meantime though."

"Sure," Lewis said brightly, trying to sound helpful.

"Moira, I'm afraid there was a bit of a mix-up," Mum said with a crinkly smile. "We thought you weren't coming to stay any more, which is why we weren't there to pick you up." She raised her eyebrows questioningly in Dad's direction, and Dad pretended to examine the wooden frame of the door.

"But you're here safe now, and that's all that matters," Mum said, putting her hands together and sounding jolly. "So please make yourself at home. George, why don't we get that air mattress and set it up in the guest room upstairs? Lewis, can you make sure Moira's got everything she needs?"

Mum swept upstairs, Dad shuffled off, and there was an odd silence as Moira gazed at the dark screen of the TV.

"I can heat you up some food?" Lewis said suddenly, thinking of an excuse to leave the room. "We've got a lasagne. It'll be quick. You hungry?"

Moira didn't nod, but there was such a glint of eagerness in her eyes that Lewis was sure she meant yes, she most definitely was.

Ducking into the kitchen, he dug out the lasagne from the fridge, only realizing at the last minute that with no electricity the microwave wouldn't work. Using his phone light, he rustled up some crisps and a fancy yoghurt Mum must have bought and, prising a spoon from the drying rack, carried them into the living room.

Moira was reaching up and reading one of Dad's postcards, which dangled like bunting above her. But her hand recoiled like a frightened snake as Lewis dumped the yoghurt and crisps on the coffee table.

"You can start with these." He pointed to the stash

as he backed towards the kitchen. "Do you mind cold lasagne?"

There was a snapping voice from upstairs as Mum continued to berate Dad for not following up with Badger.

In the darkened kitchen, Lewis shovelled the lasagne onto a plate and stuck a fork in it.

"We haven't got any electricity at the moment," Lewis began, entering the room as if he were carrying a birthday cake. "But cold lasagne's just as—"

He stopped.

Littered around the base of the armchair on which Moira was sitting were the remains of the three packets of crisps and a yoghurt pot that looked suspiciously like it had been licked clean.

Lewis was in such a state of shock that he almost dropped the lasagne.

He'd only been gone for a minute at most!

Her cheeks flushing with embarrassment, Moira wiped the smearing of yoghurt and crisp crumbs from her mouth.

"It's alright," Lewis assured her, placing the lasagne on the coffee table and prising the wrappers from her clenched fingers. "I become a monster when I'm hungry too."

Lewis padded to the kitchen. Moira seemed…different to how he remembered her. Nicer…somehow.

When he came back into the living room, he half expected the lasagne to be demolished as well, but this time Moira was just prodding it lightly with the fork.

"Just pretend I'm not here," Lewis said, lowering himself cautiously onto the arm of the sofa. "Please. Eat."

"Now it's all a bit chaotic at the moment, Moira." Mum's head peered round the door. "We've got no running water and no electricity, so you'll have to wait until tomorrow for a shower. But you'll be cosy upstairs."

Lewis caught Mum's eye, and she smiled warmly at him. When he looked back, the rest of Moira's lasagne had completely vanished, leaving only a few dabs of red sauce on the plate.

Moira got shakily to her feet, her shoes squishing into the damp carpet. The shoes were leather and buckled, with giant stitches along the sides of the soles.

She paused for a moment, still wrapped in her blanket as she bumbled over to Mum. "Thank you," she said slowly and then added as if she were trying to remember his name, "*Lewis?*"

Lewis couldn't get back to sleep as the events of the night played over in his head.

The barometer in the chimney.

The rooks falling deathly silent.

The addresses with dates and numbered children.

Moira appearing out of the gloom to make it all even stranger.

Had she really not remembered him? Or was she just dazed from standing out in the rain when she was waiting at the train station?

Beneath the covers his palm itched.

And even though it was far from the most peculiar thing to have happened at number seven Orsman Road that evening, and he was yet to unravel the secrets of the barometer, there was one thought Lewis couldn't let go of.

The kids he knew had phones, sweet wrappers and maybe something rogue like a mini Rubik's cube in their pockets. Maybe it was just because Moira was posh, but never before had he seen anyone his age keep a hanky up their sleeve. Much less one covered in blotches of ink…

Chapter 9
The Missing Suitcase

"Voicemail. *Again.*" Dad scowled, hitting the *end call* button and plugging his phone into his portable battery pack. "How does Badger even know his daughter made it here safely?!"

"You'd think there'd be plenty of signal at the top of a Swiss mountain, wouldn't you?" Mum said with a mischievous little wink. Dad tiptoed across the squishy living room carpet to check his postcards.

"Is Moira awake yet?" Lewis asked examining his palm as he shuffled into the kitchen. The mosquito bite had left a dark spot on his hand, like the dab from a permanent marker, with another faint greyish splotch beside it.

"Out like a light. Probably best we let her rest as much as possible after last night. I think it might have been a bit traumatic for her," Mum told him, pausing to examine

Moira's duck-egg blue dress before adding it to the laundry pile. "Hmm, Emerald always did dress that girl quite unusually. Although I suppose this is the sort of thing you'd wear if your mum was a painter who changed her name from Susan to Emerald."

Lewis grinned.

Out of nowhere Mum gave him a "please, just for your old mum"-type look.

"What?" Lewis asked suspiciously, his grin fading.

"You couldn't take Moira down to the station today? Check if someone handed in her suitcase, could you? She said it was lavender."

Lewis gave a reluctant indication that he would, and Mum headed off to oversee the installation of some dental chairs at her new clinic. Dad had spread himself out at the living room table to "fire off some emails" whilst he waited for the plumber.

Splatters of bird poo and wet feathers flecking the windowsills served as the only remaining evidence of the rooks' visit. But the downstairs of the house was still sodden and grimy, with a film of plastery silt where the water had gushed through.

It was already Tuesday, which meant the final entrance exam for Elksbridge was just three sleeps away. But Lewis couldn't study. Not until he could look at the barometer again and read the paper slips. It wasn't just a coincidence that the very night on which the Bogwitch's floods were supposed to have been warded away, he'd come home to find water up to his knees pouring out of their front door. And he wasn't going to let it happen again.

A gargling snore floated out from beneath the door to the guest room as Lewis carried the biscuit tin and a slightly warm juice up to his room.

Sitting cross-legged against the post of his bunk, he set an alarm on his phone to remind him about Moira's suitcase. Then, digging through the moving boxes until he found one of his old chess scorebooks and a reliable-looking ballpoint pen, he shook the contents of the barometer out onto the floor.

"What secrets do you hold, eh?" he muttered to the curious little pile. And settling in with an alarmingly tough ginger nut, Lewis began to unravel the slips of paper, copying each of the addresses into the scorebook and numbering them as he went.

It was slow work, but the hours slipped by as he paused to read the scratchy, blotted script, cross-referencing the addresses online to make sure they existed, which most of them did. But there were a handful, like the Old Barrow Carriageworks, that he couldn't seem to find.

When he'd finally waded through all of them, just before lunch, Lewis stretched his neck as he stood back to admire his handiwork. There were 313 addresses in total, but only five of them were scribbled out with dates and a different numbered child on the back, like the first two he'd found:

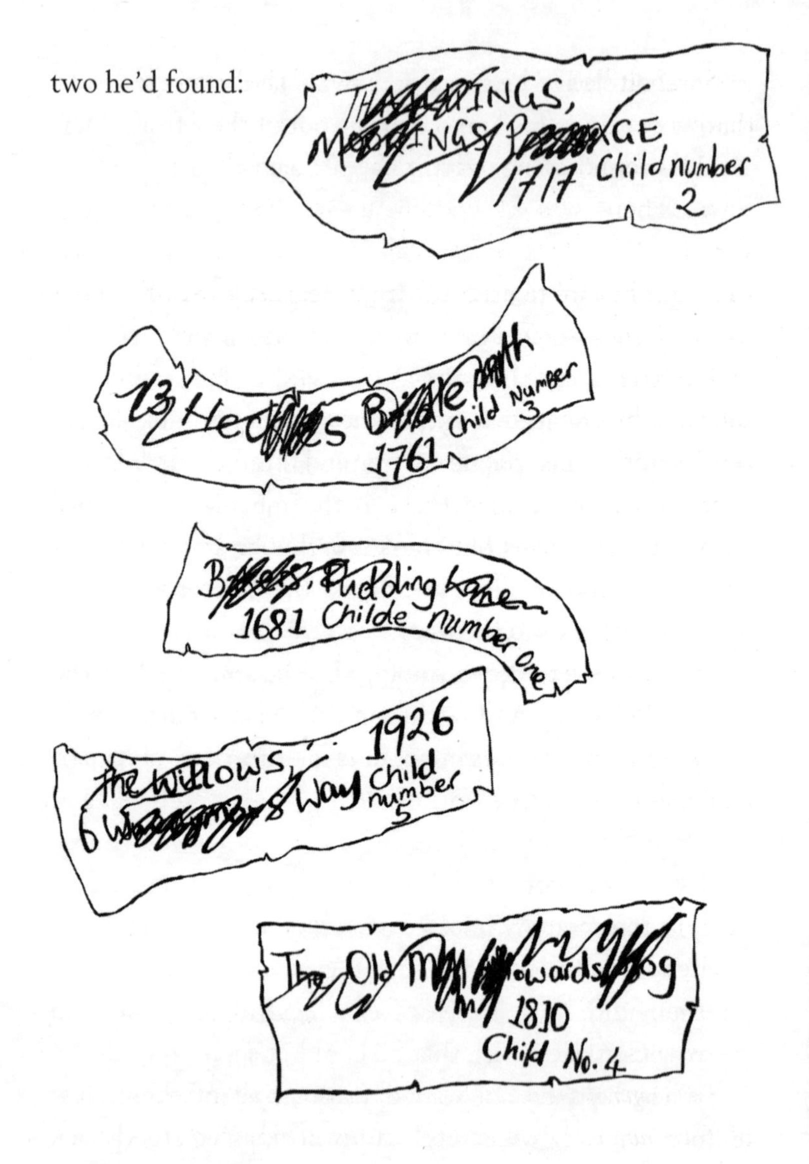

The addresses were all in Barrow. He'd even found a bunch that were on Orsman Road. Although, oddly, their house didn't seem to be in the mix.

Surely it had to be the five that had the numbered kids that were significant?

He'd found a "H*eckles* B*r*idl*epa*th" on the road out of town. There was a "P*u*dding La*n*e" just off the town square. "*H*owards *B*og" was out past the Dowsing Marshes. But there was nothing to suggest what "The Old M—l", "Th- ------ings", or "W----an's W—" was.

He tried again, typing years and "child number" followed by one to five, but that just came up with search results for some Netflix sci-fi movie about kids with supernatural powers.

As much as he didn't want to admit it, the Bogwitch seemed to link it all loosely together. The rooks, the marking that was on the goblet and the barometer.

Leaning on his elbows he searched again:

Bogwitch – paper bits – barometer – Barrow

Nothing but a scammy-looking list of phone numbers and street listings.

Rook – barometer – Bogwitch – paper slips

Gave him: *Did you mean:* Humphrey Rook and The Singing Barometer *by Edith Bagstitch?*

Barrow Bogwitch – marking – goblet – meaning

Brought up: *Origins: The Gretel Murk Story*

Lewis scrolled.

Versions of the origin story of Gretel Murk, the Bogwitch of Barrow, vary according to the teller, but it is most commonly believed that she was discovered by an elderly blacksmith when he was out gathering wood. The blacksmith heard a wailing coming from a rotten tree stump and, upon splitting it open, found inside there a most unusual child with reedy hair and skin as grey as eggshells. The blacksmith took Gretel Murk to his home, placed her by the fire and gave her food, unaware that she was no human child, rather a malignant witch grown from the cursed stump he had found her in. Gretel Murk bewitched the blacksmith, making him believe she was his real daughter and forcing him to smelt her a goblet to foresee things.

The definitive origin of the marking borne by the goblet at the fountain in Barrow's town square remains a mystery. One fanciful, but unlikely, explanation is that after the witch drank the floods for seven days and nights, she inflated to such an enormous size that, when Lucrilla de Marlow poked her seven times with a needle, the witch popped and shrivelled up like an old balloon. The needle's perforations form the seven dots of the marking.

Despite many differences of opinion, most versions of the tale agree that the Bogwitch, in some form or other, went on to haunt the marshes, waiting vengefully for a flood to come to Barrow. Appearing to wayward travellers as either a clump of unusually shaped reeds or a glowing green light, before she lured them to a watery death.

Why would the unusual pattern seem so familiar? And what was it doing on the back of a barometer hidden in a chimney in the first place?

On the desk, his phone vibrated. "Dad?" He frowned as he answered. "Aren't you downstairs?"

"Hi! Oooh! Ouch. Yep. Nearly caught my finger on the cheese grater," Dad yelped. "Don't want to miss the plumber. I've made sandwiches. And this new coffee machine I've ordered is out for delivery. Couldn't check if Moira's awake and wants some, could you?"

Lewis knocked gently on the door to the guest room. Surely by now Moira *had* to be awake, but from underneath the door a row of snores wittered out.

"She's *still* sleeping?" Dad marvelled, dropping a cheese and chutney sandwich onto Lewis's plate in the kitchen.

"Mum did say to let her rest," Lewis shrugged.

"Hmm, Badger's still not answering either," Dad added with a note of concern. "Tried him three more times. I hope everything's okay. I'll check in on Moira after lunch. How's study going?"

Lewis opened his mouth dryly, but a knock on the front door interrupted him.

"That'll be the plumber." Dad sighed, trying to wipe some chutney off his hands. "Why is it that *everything* always happens at once? Where's the paper towel?"

"Dad?" Lewis asked softly handing Dad the roll.

"Argh. And now it's on my trousers. Yep?"

"What was the name of that man again? The one who lived here before us?"

"Mr Smythe," Dad said flustering about until Lewis tossed him a tea towel. "Why? You find something of his?"

Lewis shook his head. "Just wondering."

"Coming!" Dad called out as there was another knock on the front door.

As soon as he was back in his bedroom Lewis prodded into his phone: *Mr Smythe Barrow Snoring Broads*

The search bar loaded. And a promising result appeared.

THE PARISH OF BARROW OBITUARIES
Mr Terrence James Smythe (1927–2011)

It is with great sadness that the Smythe family announce the passing of "Terry" Terrence Smythe. Terry will be fondly remembered by his friends at the Barrow Historical Society, which he served as secretary for over sixty-seven years. His cheese and spring-onion scones will be sorely missed. He leaves behind a nephew, Toby, and a cat, Janine.

Barrow Historical Society, Lewis remembered. They were the people who organized the Peering of the Goblet. The society that Leopold Marlow's grandad, Sir Hector, was chairman of.

The alarm on his phone went off with a cheery jingle: *Get Moira's suitcase from station.*

Lewis was kind of relieved Moira didn't stir when he knocked gently on her door again. At least it meant he could get the trip to the station over and done with and get back to his research without having to make polite chit-chat.

The station was only twenty minutes away according to Maps, but Lewis managed it in seventeen, power-walking.

At the station entrance, a crowd of six or seven people were gathered around the ticket booth. All of them looked thoroughly disgruntled, as a lady with pink hair in a high-vis vest shook her head through the hatch.

"Rail replacement bus service is just round the corner, departing in six minutes," she said without a smile as the small crowd shuffled off.

"Um, excuse—" Lewis began, approaching the booth.

"Come closer," she said, squinting belligerently. "You're not a megaphone. I can't hear you from all the way over there."

"Um, my…friend left her suitcase on a train that arrived from London last night. It's purp—"

"Are you trying *very* unsuccessfully to be funny, young man?" the lady said flatly, indicating to Lewis that there was another customer behind him.

Lewis turned and the man behind him gave a pert, but slightly impatient smile.

"Isn't there a luggage room or maybe lost property?" Lewis asked.

The lady leaned out of the booth and tapped the large temporary yellow sign on the wall beside it.

Rail Replacement Service
Due to Inclement Weather

"Fallen tree damaged the tracks from a storm in Snoring South. There've been no trains coming into Barrow for the past *two* days."

Chapter 10
A Highly Suspicious List

"Plumber said it was because of the gutters," Dad was telling Mum as Lewis pushed through the front door. "House had been empty so long that nobody cleaned them out. And the water leaked through."

On his way home from the station, Lewis couldn't stop obsessing. He did that sometimes, and Mum would have to remind him that there were some things you just had to let go. But he couldn't. He really, *really* couldn't.

There hadn't been any trains. How had Moira got there? Was it a rail replacement bus? Perhaps a cab? Maybe she left her suitcase in a cab? But why wouldn't she have just said that?

"Electricity's back on," Mum said brightly, unpacking a frozen pizza box from her shopping as Lewis shuffled into the kitchen. "Any luck with the suitcase?"

"No." Lewis began slipping off his sneakers and stowing them beside the door. "Kinda weird actually. The lady at the station said there hadn't been any trains to Barrow. Not for two days. They all got cancelled because of a fallen tree."

"Oh," Mum said and then added, as if she could tell Lewis was on the verge of proposing a theory about it. "She probably got the very last one or something, before it fell. We can ask her when she's feeling up to it."

"She's awake?" Lewis asked.

"She actually fell off the bed when I popped my head in to take her up some food." Mum chuckled as she handed Dad the pizza box and reset the clock on the oven. "Said she just wanted to read in her bedroom if that was alright with me. Poor thing. Must be a bit overwhelmed, or maybe she's a tad embarrassed."

"Actually, Badger did say a few weeks ago that Moira's been keeping to herself recently," Dad added as he read the heating instructions and then leaned in quietly. "Apparently there was a bit of trouble with some kids at school and Moira threw one girl's cello into the school swimming pool."

Lewis found it hard to imagine the squeaky, twitchy person he'd seen the night before hurling cellos.

Mum took up a tray Dad had prepared, of pizza, bananas, a spare toothbrush and some of Lewis's books, to Moira.

After dinner, Mum and Dad watched something called *Shocking Garden Makeovers*, and Lewis slunk upstairs to spread out on his bunk.

Using Maps to drop pins at each of the spots he estimated the dated addresses were located, Lewis worked out the most efficient route between them. If he started with Heckle's Bridlepath he could make his way anticlockwise round Barrow ending up at Pudding Lane. Hopefully he could find out what the dates and the numbered kids meant. And perhaps then he'd be able to work out how the rooks and the Bogwitch were connected.

At 22:30, there was a creak from the guest-room door, followed by the distinct sound of the tin tray Mum had taken up being slid into the hall.

Maybe she hitch-hiked? Lewis thought and then almost at once locked his phone and put it on charge.

He was being obsessive. And there were bigger fish to fry.

Why was it that the rooks had made such a din right up until the *very* moment he'd opened the barometer? And did the numbered kids just stop at 1926? Or were there more? Was *that* why the rooks wanted him to find it?

"Morning, Lewis," Mum said brightly from the kitchen the next morning as Lewis reached for the handle to the front door.

Caught!

Lewis had packed his rucksack the night before, and woken early so he could set out investigating the addresses before anyone else was up. He poked his head reluctantly into the kitchen.

"Have you seen my phone? Can't find it anywhere," Mum muttered, searching the top of the fridge on tiptoe as the frying pan sizzled.

"Er, I'll try calling it on my way out," Lewis mumbled, making for the door before she could say anything else.

"Good morning, *Lewis*," came a little voice.

Lewis peered round the fridge.

Moira was sitting at the kitchen table with both hands placed flat on either side of her bowl. She was dressed entirely in Lewis's old clothes: a pair of his school socks pulled all the way up to her knobbly kneecaps, with one of his baggier T-shirts tucked into an old set of striped football shorts and her little embroidered bag slung across her chest.

"Oh. You're awake. Hiya," Lewis croaked. "You sleep okay?"

"Yes. Thank you," she coughed, her chestnut eyes wide and her bob of dark hair tangled into a crest, making her look slightly like a chicken that had suffered an electric shock.

"Cool. See ya!" he said loudly.

"Hang on, hang on." Mum frowned, ducking her head out into the hallway. "Dad didn't tell you the plan?"

Lewis froze, rolling his eyes out of sight.

"I'm going to the library," he lied. "To study. Exam's in two days."

Mum gave him an apologetic grimace out of Moira's eyesight. "Dad's taking some meetings in Great Reedmouth today. He's going to drop you off at a bowling alley on the way. With Moira."

"Bowling alley?" Lewis said loudly, trying to disguise his irritation. Bowling was just the sort of thing Dad thought would be fun, but never was. What if the rooks returned before he'd had time to work it out or more scary stuff started happening in their house, like the flooding?

"*Sorry!*" Mum mouthed and behind her Lewis noticed that, for some inexplicable reason, Moira was shaking Dad's mini Bluetooth speaker over her cereal like it was a salt shaker.

The town of Great Reedmouth was thirteen minutes away towards the coast and Reedmouth Bowl was on the pier, which jutted out into the waves.

A cloud of seagulls milled above them, swooping every so often on a small boy smeared with ketchup, who kept hiding his chips beneath his shirt.

Inside Reedmouth Bowl, once Dad had paid, Lewis slipped off his shoes and slid them across the counter towards the spotty assistant and said, "I'm five and a half."

"You don't look it, pal." The boy winked, plonking a shiny pair of purple bowling shoes covered in hot pink thumbs-up emojis in front of Lewis.

"You ever bowled before?" Lewis reluctantly asked Moira, hoping Dad's meetings didn't take too long so he could get back to exploring the addresses he'd mapped out.

She gave a hurried shake of her head, before mimicking

Lewis and lifting her hefty buckled shoes to the counter.

"Sick kicks, man." The boy nodded approvingly as he picked up her shoes. "Very old school. My gran used to wear these."

"Er, thank you. Man," Moira croaked as he handed her an orange striped pair of bowling shoes.

"Write your names here," the boy told them. "You're in aisle seven."

Lewis scribbled his name on the piece of paper in front of them, then pushed it across to Moira.

She gave him a searching sort of look before cupping one hand and writing her name very slowly.

From behind them there came a thundering of polished balls on polished wood and the memory of exactly *how* bad he was at bowling came flooding back to him.

"Isn't that Leopold Marlow, Sir Hector's grandson?" Dad asked, squinting towards the bowling lanes as Moira examined the orange-striped shoes she'd been handed.

Lewis looked around. Leopold was hurling a large silver ball down the lane of aisle eight. The lane next to theirs.

"Let's go and say hi," Dad said, strolling over.

"No, Dad—" Lewis began, but Dad had already called out: "Hey there, kids!"

Lewis felt like he wanted to curl up into a ball and bowl himself down one of the lanes in embarrassment.

Leopold and his three friends gave Dad a look that suggested his interruption was about as welcome as a rat in a swimming pool.

"You remember Lewis?" Dad said beckoning for Lewis

to come over. "He's applied for Elksbridge. I'm sure he'd love some tips."

Leopold's hair seemed to recoil a little as he caught sight of Lewis and Moira.

"Well, I'll leave you guys to it," Dad said, raising his eyebrows hopefully at Lewis. "See you in a couple of hours. Bye, Moira!"

Lewis gave the group a feeble smile which none of them returned as he lowered himself into the booth beside them and pulled on his hot pink and purple shoes.

Moira followed suit, watching carefully as he laced up.

"A-a-re you all from Barrow too?" Lewis asked, tentatively.

"No," scoffed one of the girls. "We're from *here*."

Lewis grappled for something to say next as Moira huddled closely at his elbow, her shorts pulled up embarrassingly high.

"D-do you go to…to school togeth—"

"How was the interview, *Buckley*?" Leopold interrupted, bowling a frame. "Daddy proud?"

Lewis felt it pinch meanly in his chest. Why did Dad have to try making friends for him? This was just the sort of thing that happened.

Leopold imitated Lewis's open mouth.

"Don't get too comfortable around here, Buckley," Leopold sneered. "That way no one'll miss you when you don't get in."

The pinch bloomed into a sting.

Why would Leopold target him like that? Had it been

something to do with the scholarship? Or was it like Celia had said, Leopold was mean because he was just lonely? He didn't *seem* lonely. Especially with his trio of terrifying friends.

"C'mon," Leopold muttered to his mates, sloping off. "Let's play air hockey. No point *wasting* your time with this one."

Leopold had only started acting weird when Lewis had told him when he'd been for the interview that they'd just moved to Barrow. Maybe he didn't like newcomers?

Moira gave Lewis a weak smile. He felt hot with embarrassment. But to his relief he didn't have to say anything, because a little tune played on the screen in their booth and their scorecard appeared:

1. LEWIS

2. MUYRA

Is that how she spells it? Lewis wondered.

Who cares. Maybe she was rebranding herself a bit. He just wanted to get it over with and get on with researching the slips of paper.

It turned out Moira was as good at bowling as Lewis was rubbish at it. And once they'd got into a swing, the game wasn't actually so bad.

"You're really good at this," Lewis commented as Moira bowled a strike. And her eyes seemed to brighten a little.

Maybe she really has changed? he thought as his ball clattered into the gutter. She certainly seemed quieter than he remembered, and less stuck-up.

The rest of the game passed mostly in silence, except for Lewis reminding Moira every so often that it was her turn whenever she took to staring at the scoreboard.

"Who won?" the boy asked as Lewis returned their shoes.

"She did." Lewis nodded.

"Skills," the boy said coolly.

Moira did up her buckles and began plodding over to the door as Lewis wedged his toes into his trainers.

From nearby he heard the *Jaws* theme song start to play.

Lewis froze.

That's Mum's ringtone.

He felt his pockets. Had he taken her phone by accident?

"This yours?" The boy lifted up Moira's embroidered bag by the string.

Lewis felt his chest give an uneasy thump. The ringtone continued to play. Either Moira had the exact same ringtone as Mum. Or, for some reason, Mum's phone was inside Moira's bag.

He looked up just in time to see Moira jerking back slightly as the automatic doors closed in front of her. When they lugged open again she chanced her luck and bolted through.

The phone still ringing, Lewis fumbled with the clasp and prised the embroidered bag open. Inside was a mint, three hankies, a fork that was definitely one of theirs, a Buckley's Estate Agents Pamphlet, a pencil, a small notepad with something written on it and *Mum's missing phone*. Lewis fished out the notepad, flipping to its front:

- Muyra
- hockey
- train
- Suitcase
- badger?
- con-pewter
- cold lazzarnya
- Quail salad ??

It seemed Moira had been making some kind of list. An exceedingly strange one at that. But as Lewis glimpsed what was drawn at the bottom, the thundering bowling alley became distant and echoey in his ears.

Lewis felt a chugging in his stomach. *How does Moira Wigby-Polkinghorne know about the Bogwitch's marking?* Had she been snooping in his room and seen the barometer?

A car horn parped from outside, and Lewis saw Dad pull up. Ripping off the top sheet of the notepad, Lewis stuffed it into his pocket along with Mum's phone.

"You left this," he told Moira as they climbed into the car, dangling her bag by the string between the seats.

Moira's hand reached out and snatched it from him. "Th-thank you, Lewis," she breathed, clutching it close.

Lewis's thoughts circled as they drove back to Barrow. *Mum and Dad need to know. About the phone and about that weird list. They have to.* Not to mention the fact that he had been right and she probably was lying about the trains and how she got to Barrow.

But first he was going to find out exactly how Moira had come to know about the marking, and why exactly she seemed to be nicking stuff.

"Oh," Lewis pretended loudly. "Found Mum's phone. It was here on the back seat."

"Not like Mum to lose her phone, is it?" Dad remarked.

Lewis watched Moira. But she didn't even seem to blink.

When they got home, Moira excused herself incredibly politely announcing that she was going to "read in her room", after which she'd snatched up the instruction manual for Dad's new coffee machine, tucked it beneath her arm and scurried upstairs.

Dad had given Lewis an odd sort of frown before shaking it off. But Lewis *bubbled* with suspicion.

For the rest of the afternoon, Lewis patiently pretended to examine a biology textbook as he leaned against the post of his bunk. Listening. And waiting for Moira to emerge.

The only glimpse he'd caught of Moira all day was at 18:30 when Dad had called up, "Moira? Lewis? Dinner!" The guest-room door shot open and Moira scarpered down the corridor like a cat. As if she'd been waiting beside her door.

As they ate, and Moira struggled to spear her asparagus, he'd come very close to telling Mum and Dad there and then. After all, if Moira was stealing and lying then it could be serious. But he knew that if he did, they would most likely have a private conversation with her, Moira would be sent home and he'd *never* get to the bottom of why she had the Bogwitch's marking in her bag.

But Lewis *had* to work it out. Which meant that waiting for the right moment to confront Moira was his only option.

At 21:14 he excused himself to go up to bed, but instead of sleeping, he leaned on the post of his bunk, listening.

Through the wall he heard Moira's light flicked off at about 22:50.

And then at 23:32 the sounds of Mum's and Dad's electric toothbrushes echoed down the corridor. Until, finally, their bedroom door closed. And number seven Orsman Road fell silent.

It was time.

Lewis peered out of his room.

The coast was clear.

He tiptoed along to the guest room, balling his hand into a fist and working up the courage to knock.

But from behind the door, there was a *thump*, followed by a gurgling noise that sounded vaguely like the noise a blocked sink made.

Lewis pressed his ear against the wood.

Silence followed.

Then the thump came again, only this time, after the gurgle, there was a dim flash of green light from the crack beneath the door.

Lewis felt his shoulders tighten beneath his T-shirt. Placing his palm flat on the wood of the door, he pushed it open. And there snoring like a tractor, as her feet knocked gently against the wall, was Moira. Floating a good three feet above the bed.

Chapter 11
A Cold Shock

Lewis gripped the doorway as his head swam dizzily. He wanted to let out a shout or a scream, but he couldn't seem to gather a breath deep enough.

Moira was floating. *Actually* completely horizontally floating. As if the room was filled with an invisible water and she was drifting on top.

This can't be happening, he told himself. *No. Really. This. Cannot be happening.*

But the crackling fingers of electricity that glimmered around Moira's body like bolts of bottle-green lightning escaping from a drifting storm cloud suggested otherwise.

There was another snore, and a soft thump as Moira's feet clunked into the wall.

Lewis's stomach dropped through his legs as he watched.

Mum. Dad. I need to— But the wiring in his brain seemed to short circuit as the floating, flickering pile in front of him, wearing one of his old T-shirts, let out a startled intake of air. There was a snort, and Moira blinked groggily awake.

A strange moment followed as they stared at one another. Moira bleary and perplexed and Lewis riveted to the spot with terror. But when she realized what was happening, Moira's eyes bulged and she fell; from mid-air. The air mattress gave a springy little kick as she landed, catapulting her onto the floor with a pained yelp. The green sparks of electricity vanishing.

Lewis waited. Every muscle in his body refusing to move.

"Y-y-you-w-were—"

The room gave a sickening spin.

"I-I know how it must look," she whispered, raising her hands imploringly as her chestnut eyes filled with panic. "P-please-you've *got* to believe me, I'm just as flummoxed as you are!"

Lewis covered his mouth.

Was it a dream? A nightmare?

"I-I need to get Mum," he thought aloud, hardly able to bring himself to say the words as his stomach gave a nauseous churn. "Dad—"

He backed into the corridor, but within a split second Moira had vaulted across the room.

This was no dream.

With a firm yank, she hauled him back into the bedroom, then pulled the door silently shut.

"Y-you mustn't tell them," she whispered, cupping her hands together in pleading. "Please. Please, Lewis. I'm *imploring* you."

Lewis kept opening his mouth, but only a few croaky little sputters made their way out. Moira was speaking. Fluently. As if the nervous murmurs and scurrying around the house had all been a ruse.

"Y-you-were floating," he finally managed, pointing at her again. "You-were—"

"Would you just for *one* minute—" Moira snapped fiercely and then paused to compose herself. "Please, *please* keep your voice down!"

None of it made sense. None of it.

Moira fidgeted anxiously as Lewis tried to calm himself, but it was too much.

"Y-y-you lied!" he found himself suddenly stuttering at full volume. "There weren't any trains to Bar—"

With lightning speed, Moira snatched up the glass beside her bed, and Lewis felt a slosh of cold water knock him clean in the face. He let out a shuddering gasp of shock.

"Wh-wh-why did you—?" he gaped, his bottom lip quivering as the water trickled down the back of his pyjama T-shirt.

"Well what choice did you leave me?" Moira snapped, folding her arms guiltily.

Lewis blinked the droplets from his eyes.

"You mustn't, Lewis," she insisted, more calmly this time as her nose twitched.

"I-if you don't tell me what's going on right this *second*," he demanded. "Then I'll shout. At the top of my lungs."

"Alright, alright," Moira agreed.

His stomach was still churning, but somehow the sheer surprise of being cold and wet seemed to have cleared his head a little.

"Alright," she said again, letting out a slow breath and pushing her bob of hair back behind her ears. "But before I tell you, you have to *swear* to me that you won't become hysterical again."

"I'm *not* being hysterical!" he snapped, thrashing his arms bewilderedly in the air. "This is a perfectly normal reaction to seeing someone...*floating in mid-air*!"

"You're wailing about like an old hen—" she reared up argumentatively, almost as if she couldn't help it, then stopped and clenched her fist calmly.

Lewis waited for a moment. And when she didn't say anything, he took in a great lungful of air, ready to shout.

"I'm not who you think I am!" Moira blurted.

The air seemed to lodge in his chest.

"Wh-what do you mean?"

"I mean—" She paused with a frustrated flap of her arms before staring him dead in the eyes. "What I *really* mean is...*I* don't know...who I am."

Lewis felt his limbs stiffen, though it wasn't from the sodden cold of his T-shirt.

She went on. "Half the time I haven't the tiniest inkling what any of you are prattling on about. I don't know what my name is, what day it is, or where I am. And as for you...well...I'm sorry, but I really haven't got even the foggiest clue who you are."

The room fell silent.

"You're-you're—" Lewis stammered. "You're *not* Moira Wigby-Polkinghorne?"

The girl bit her lip and looked gingerly up at him as she shook her head.

"But...you...you can't be *no one*. You've got to be... someone?" he murmured.

"I-I can't remember," she said softly. "I just have these...flashes that feel like foggy dreams. Of a house. A nice house with nice people. But when I think about their faces, I can't tell who they are. It's almost as if, I *knew* them once. As if they mean home."

Her fingers seemed to contract involuntarily. "But there's someone else there with them. Another person. A stranger. A boy. I think. A sad boy. From a different place. And he keeps saying this one thing, over and over."

She swallowed. "'Quail salad. Quail salad. Quail salad.'"

"*Quail* salad!?" Lewis whispered, remembering seeing it on her list.

The girl nodded, pausing to swallow as if she were struggling to go on.

"Quail salad. And then after that, all I can remember is waking up in darkness. Surrounded by water and... and I shimmied, as hard as I could, to the surface until I came out."

"Came out *where?*" Lewis asked.

"In a marsh. It was dark and raining. And there wasn't a soul around. I felt –" her voice wavered a little – "I felt so afraid. But then I found a walkway. Across the water. I followed it towards a town. This town. And I wandered through the streets, calling out for someone to help. Anyone. Until."

She stopped again, gazing off into the distance.

"Until I saw this house," she said. "*Your* house. And I don't know how. But I knew, simply knew, that I had to knock on the doorknocker of *this* house. That I had to do whatever I could to get inside *this* house. And when your father seemed to think I was this other person, this Moira...I just...pretended. Too scared to say anything much in case you found me out."

Lewis's T-shirt dripped a little onto his socks and he shifted.

"That's why you wrote the list?" he said slowly. "You realized you must look a bit like Moira, so you pretended to be her?"

"I wanted to buy myself time. Noting down some of the things you kept saying," she whispered.

Silence fell again. That was why she'd called him Willis. She must have misheard Mum.

"You...you really don't remember anything else?" Lewis interrogated. "A-and this isn't a joke? You're not... winding me up?"

She shook her head. "Cross my heart."

Lewis crouched down to pick up the list from where it

had fallen from his fingers. "But what about that marking?" he asked, pointing to the drawing. "How do you know about that?"

She let out a breath through her nose.

Yanking up her sleeve, she turned her hand towards the pale light from the window.

Just below her thumb, on the inside of her palm, a small cluster of dark circles were clearly visible.

"I noticed these markings on that first night. But I didn't know if they were always there or if they were new. Just that they looked...odd."

Lewis felt a sinister cloudiness fog over him. Even though it was smaller, and two of the circles were missing, their arrangement was identical to the marking on the goblet. The one he had found on the barometer: the Bogwitch's marking.

"At first there were seven circles," she went on. "Then one vanished. And today one of the others started fading, until it vanished compl—"

She stopped.

With lightning speed, her thin fingers lashed out, gripping him by the wrist, and twisting his arm towards her.

"What are you—?!" He jerked forward.

But once more Lewis's breath seemed to leave him as he caught sight of what had so excited her.

On the inside of his palm he could see that the swollen redness of what he'd thought was a mosquito bite had faded leaving in its place two dark spots, where before there had been only one.

"That's them!" she spat, her eyeballs millimetres from Lewis's palm. "Those are *my two missing spots*!"

Lewis's mouth felt watery and, as he gazed down, the marking seemed to stare back at him.

"Almost as if...they've transferred somehow. From my hand over to-to you. As if you're *mirroring* the ones I'm missing."

Moira brushed his palm with her thumb.

"Two days," she murmured distantly. "Two markings. Yours are going up—"

"And yours...counting down," Lewis whispered back.

The sudden urge to attack the marking with soap and water filled him. But somehow he knew that no amount of washing would remove the strange pattern forming on his palm.

"There was only one there earlier today plus a faded looking splotch," Lewis told her hoarsely. "It's like it got darker."

As he twisted his hand, the face of his watch came into view.

00:06

"As if it filled out," he thought aloud. "Like ink drying. At midnight."

Everything happened at midnight. Moira's arrival. When the rook had paid its visit.

The girl swallowed and took his hand in hers once more. She looked almost happy as she stared at his mark. As if it were somehow a glimmer of hope. A sign that she wasn't alone.

And with a distant yet penetrating stare she looked up at him. "You saw the birds, didn't you?" she realized. "Black birds with..."

"...yellow eyes," Lewis finished off with a croak.

And the sensation that he was being swept up into something far stranger than he could possibly imagine prickled over him.

There was a creak out in the hallway, followed by the shuffling of footsteps and the bathroom light being slapped on.

"We need to tell Mum and Dad," Lewis muttered, trying to move past her. "They'll know what to—"

"No," she said unwaveringly, her arms outstretched.

"We have to," Lewis pleaded as he tried to push past her. "They'll be able to—"

"I said, *no.*"

Her hand shot out. Her fingers curled.

And from their tips, there came an electric spark of green light.

Lewis felt a charge stab through him. He tumbled over the air mattress, colliding with a half-empty packing box as he landed in a quivering heap.

"I'm sorry!" she scrambled across the room towards him. "I didn't—"

"H-h-how did you do that?" Lewis let out a winded gasp.

"I didn't mean it!" she blurted out wringing her hands hopelessly. "I don't even know *how* I can do that. I know it's not normal. It just starts to build...like a pot about to boil. Until I can feel it simmering into my hands. And then I release it and it…it makes things move…without touching them. I can make things happen."

She clenched her hands and gritted her teeth. As if she'd messed everything up.

But for a split moment, Lewis felt nothing save for a sense of wonder. The power he'd felt ricochet through him felt strange and volatile. But even as he stared at the girl across the room, she seemed to become just a small person once more.

Hauling the half-empty packing box towards him, he rummaged through the scrunches of newspaper until he found one of Dad's ornamental cricket balls. Lewis placed it on the floor and positioned himself behind her.

"Do it again," he murmured softly.

The girl gave him an uncertain look over her shoulder, but Lewis nodded encouragingly towards the ball.

"I-I-I can't…" She sighed with exhaustion.

"Just…try."

Although he could only see the back of her head, Lewis could feel her gaze locking on the object. And, reluctantly, her fingers stretched out once more.

From in front of them, there was a *spark*.

The ball gave a ghostly wobble.

And a wave of bottle-green electricity erupted across its leather surface.

There was a high-pitched ringing in Lewis's ears. The girl's fingers curled tighter as she raised her arm. And the ball lifted from the ground, floating just as she had, snared in a net of tiny lightning bolts.

Lewis was mesmerized as the green light flickered on the ceiling above them. It was like the plasma balls he'd seen at the Science Museum.

After a moment, the girl's arm wavered. There was a sputter! The electricity retreated. And the ball dropped. Moira's legs collapsed shakily from underneath her as she panted.

"I...I didn't mean to hurt you before...Lewis," she wheezed. "It's just...I haven't felt like myself. Even though I don't know what being myself feels like. And yet even just speaking out loud. Speaking properly to you now makes me somehow start to feel a little more like me. Like this person I used to be that I can't remember, but who keeps trying to come out in bursts. I don't have anything. Not even a name. And I'm—"

Her huge eyes began to glisten.

"I'm scared."

Lewis swallowed.

"Me too," he whispered.

"If you tell your parents I'm not who they think I am, they'll send me away or call for the police. And then whatever chance I have of working out who I really am, and how to get back to wherever I came from, will be gone."

The toilet flushed and there were more shuffling footsteps out in the hall.

Lewis felt the thumping in his chest once more. He couldn't lie about having a complete stranger in the house to Mum and Dad. Especially when this *stranger* didn't even know who she was. But then what about the marking? It wasn't just on her. It was appearing on him too. And when he imagined trying to explain it all to his parents – the rooks, the marking on the statue and the unknown guest who had now taken up residence in their spare room – the reluctant feeling that perhaps "Moira" was right began to settle uneasily over him.

In the corridor, Mum and Dad's door pulled shut.

Lewis let out a slow breath as he made his decision.

"If we're gonna do this you can't keep stealing stuff. Why'd you do that anyway?"

She gave a guilty shrug. "It piqued my curiosity. And how was I to know any of it was important, anyway? I thought it was just...a knick-knack."

"Have you got a pencil?" he croaked.

The girl scrambled for her embroidered bag on the bedside table and, tearing it open, she handed him a yellow pencil.

Lowering himself to the floor, Lewis began to amend the list.

- Loves horseriding (I think...)
- Lives in Berlin
- Dad = Arthur (banker) is friends with my dad
- Mum = Emerald (Painter, used to be called Susan)
- Parents are on holiday in Switzerland
- Spoiled

- Snobby
- goes to posh boarding school
- hit me once with hockey stick on finger
- My mum = June
- My Dad = George

"Here." He handed it to her. "If you're going to be Moira Wigby-Polkinghorne, then you need to know *something* about her."

She took the paper.

"And I'll have to call you 'Moira'," he breathed, hardly daring to believe the words were coming from his mouth. "You have to keep *being* Moira."

"I will," she said determinedly. "I'll be the *best* Moira you ever saw. I promise. You won't regret this, Willis… I mean, *Lewis*."

Lewis peered dubiously at her, almost certain he would.

"You know, you do *look* more like a Willis or maybe even a Willy than a 'Lewis'," Moira decided with a sniff.

"No I don't!" Lewis protested.

"You *do*," she insisted. "It suits your hair better."

Lewis had to force himself not to reach up and flatten his unruly bit of hair at the front.

"There's more I need to show you. Tomorrow," he said, choosing to ignore her. "But if you think of anything, or remember anything – write it down. We need to find out who you really are, why you were drawn here and how it's all connected." He looked down again at his own palm and the two circles there.

She gave a determined nod, followed by a toothy grin. But as he watched, her eyes flicked to the window and her smile faded.

"Look," she whispered, hardly moving, and Lewis turned slowly on the spot. "It's back again."

In the murky light one of the rooks, its yellow eyes more luminescent than ever, was perched motionless on the windowsill. The tip of its beak pressed against the glass. Watching them.

The two of them drew closer together. And the knowledge that there was a mystery in Barrow far stranger and more terrifying than the one he'd begun to investigate gathered closely around Lewis in the darkness.

"How long do you suppose it's been there?" the girl who was not Moira Wigby-Polkinghorne asked. "What does it want, Lewis?"

Chapter 12
A Surprisingly Old Shoe

Lewis had woken with a jolt. At first he'd thought it was a dream, but then he caught sight of Moira. Or at least the girl he'd thought was Moira.

She was standing on the ladder of his bunk, leaning over him with one finger outstretched, showing all the telltale signs of having just prodded him in the forehead.

"Morning, Willis," she beamed.

"What are you doing?!" Lewis blurted out, scrambling as he pulled the duvet up a little.

"Nothing," she whispered hurriedly, her finger recoiling. And then added, "You kept saying these letters and numbers whilst you were asleep. Letting out little squeaks every so often."

Probably Gramps's chess puzzle, Lewis thought.

"How long have you been stood there?" he asked, adjusting his pillows as he squeezed his fingers into his palm.

"Only about an hour."

"Wait...what?"

"I couldn't sleep a wink last night," Moira went on, ignoring him. "I was thinking about what you said. About trying to work out who I am. And just as I went to sleep, I had a brilliant little thought."

Producing one of her clunky buckled shoes, she plonked it in Lewis's lap.

"My bag was empty except for a mint, three handkerchiefs and a pen cap," Moira whispered as the two of them made their way downstairs. "Nothing you can tell from that except that I must sneeze a lot. But inside the shoe there's an inscription. Written on the sole. Do you see?"

"Gourdley's Cobblers, established 1872," he read, squinting into the shoe as they came into the kitchen. "That's *here*. In Barrow." Lewis remembered Dad pointing it out the day they'd arrived.

"Do you suppose we can go there? Sniff about?"

"I think so," he replied in a low voice. "Maybe they'll be able to confirm the shoes were made *here*. That way at least we'd know you've come from Barrow."

"Morning." Dad yawned groggily as he entered the kitchen.

Lewis slipped the shoe into his lap, his heart ticking.

Moira seized her moment.

"Lovely day for a *horse ride* –" she began, and then checked the list Lewis had made her underneath the table – "*George*."

"Yep," Dad agreed, looking a little perplexed. "Quite."

Lewis did a mental facepalm.

"Actually, that reminds me," Dad muttered as he pulled on his jacket and reached for his phone. "Need to try calling your dad again, Moira."

"He already called," Lewis blurted, as he gripped Moira's shoe, brimming with a sudden panic. He couldn't think of a better lie.

"Oh? Really?" Dad puzzled. "When?"

"This morning," Lewis flailed. "He left a message. Home phone. And I…I accidentally deleted it after listening to it. I meant to tell you."

"Oh," Dad said flatly. "Well…what did he say?"

Lewis hadn't thought that far ahead. "Um…well, he just rambled on apologizing for ages…said he lost his phone on holiday…let me see, what else…something about golf…and…yes, he said he'd call you to explain everything another time."

Lewis waited, praying the lie would work.

Dad gave him a funny look.

"I wonder how he got our new number? It only became active yesterday," he mused.

"Must be Google," Lewis said quickly, knowing Dad wouldn't question this.

Dad gave an interested sort of nod and toddled into the living room.

Lewis snapped into action, tossing the shoe to Moira. Diving for Dad's phone on the counter he tapped in the passcode.

0711

Lewis scrolled madly.

Badger

Block

He hit it.

Are you sure you want to block this number?

You won't be able to receive any calls or texts—

Yes

Dad appeared again from the living room with a stack of pamphlets. Out of sight, Lewis slid the phone back into position, his heart thumping.

"Lewis told you about his exam tomorrow, Moira?" Dad went on. "To get into Elksbridge, your dad's old school."

Lewis widened his eyes warningly at Moira, who so far had been trying to embody her character a little too much for his liking.

"He's a regular clever clogs, our Lewis," Dad said. "But I'm afraid he needs to keep his head down a bit today, studying. Home stretch though, right, Lewis?"

"Well, he's the cleverest clog *I've* ever met," Moira declared as if suddenly she had to fill every silence there was. "And *I* go to a posh…boarding school. *And* I'm very snobby."

Lewis gave her a warning kick but missed and stubbed his toe on the table leg.

"Yes," Dad said, giving Moira a dubious look. "TV's up and running if you want to watch something. And Lewis can lend you some books, comics whatever you like."

Once Dad had left and Mum was getting ready to head off to the clinic, Lewis slipped up to his room and began to toss things into his rucksack, including the chess scorebook and a pen with *Buckley's Estate Agents* printed on it.

As they headed towards town, Lewis told Moira everything he knew. About the rook that had flown to his window in Woolham, their strange new house and the barometer he had found inside the chimney. About the Bogwitch, Gretel Murk, the curious events at the Peering of the Goblet with the lady in the wading boots who had interrupted the proceedings as she wailed on about floods and rooks flying low, only for Lewis and Dad to come home to find the house covered in them and water pouring out from underneath their door.

Moira listened closely, taking larger steps to keep up with him and nearly tripping on Lewis's baggy old joggers she was wearing.

But as Lewis began to tell her about the slips of paper, Moira's face paled and he got the distinct impression that she too felt there was something sinister and altogether too close to home about the messages of numbered children.

"There were five addresses I found that had been scribbled out," Lewis explained, fishing out the chess scorebook to the page where he'd stuck the slips, and filled the gaps he'd already worked out in red pen: "Those are the ones that are marked with a date and numbered kids. I think they're the important ones."

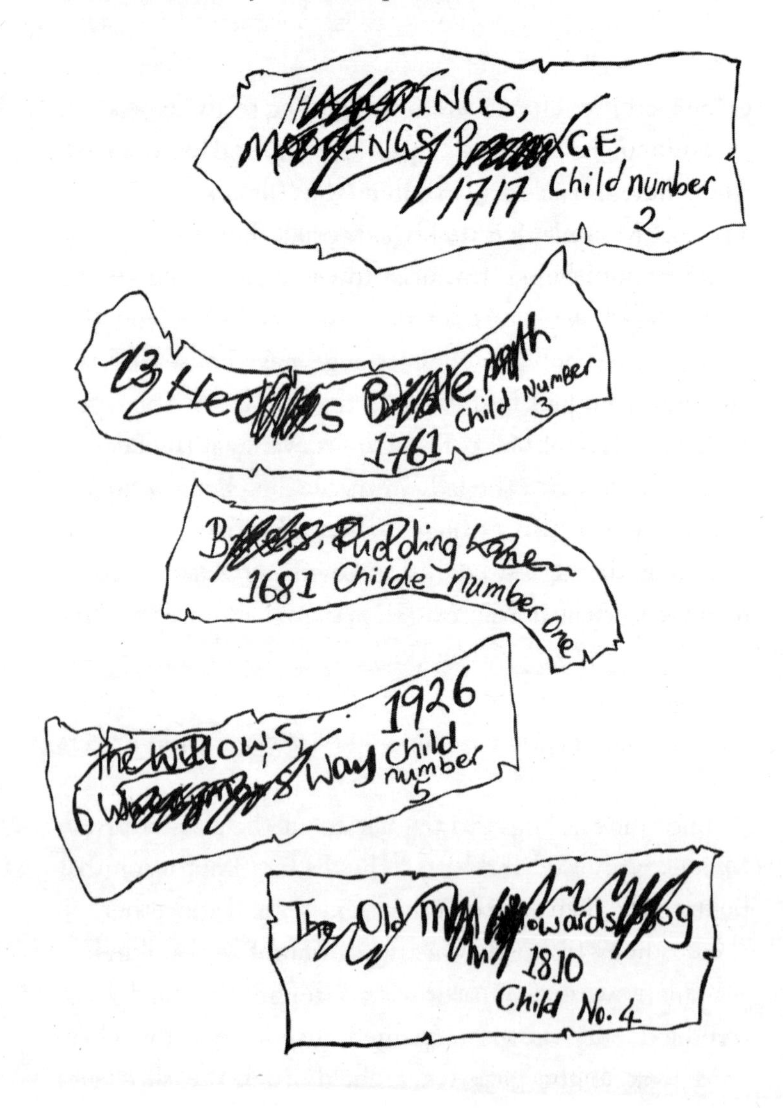

"*Th*-something-*ings, M*-something-*ings P*-something-*age 1717, child number two.*" Moira frowned, tapping her thumb on the edge of the book as she read one of them.

"Maybe these kids were at those addresses…in these years," Lewis pondered. "And something happened."

"Something? Like what?" Moira asked cautiously.

"I dunno. But we need to find out," Lewis determined. "The whole thing's so…odd, don't you think?"

"Yes," Moira added darkly as the shopfronts began to appear beside them. "Rooks. Addresses. The barometer. Even this sad boy I can't remember."

"The boy who kept talking about quail salad?" Lewis remembered under his breath.

"Yes. The sad salad lad," Moira muttered, "and that's without even mentioning…the marking."

Lewis felt a cold pulse in his gut. Whilst everything else, even the rooks, felt like part of some hair-raising adventure, the marking felt different. It was on them. Outside of their control. Tying them to the centre of whatever was going on.

At the train station a group of ladies all in red hats were crowded around the ticket booth as people muddled about on the high street.

Gourdley's Cobblers was tucked in beside a small alley with a large wrought-iron clock jutting out into the high street.

As they approached the cobblers' dusty glass door,

a bald, pigeon-like man bustled out, throwing a yellow silk scarf over his shoulder.

Flipping a sign on the door that read *Back in a twinkle!* he twisted a set of keys in the lock.

"Excuse me," Lewis said, as Moira hopped on the spot beside him wrestling with one of her shoes.

"We're closed," the bald man said, sweeping off down the street.

"It'll just take a minute," Lewis called after him.

"Don't they teach children to read nowadays?" he drawled. "*Back in a twinkle!*"

"We just wanted to see if these shoes were made here. Please," Lewis pleaded.

The man gave an exasperated little sigh and, swivelling round, snatched the shoe from Moira, who was steadying herself on Lewis's shoulder as she balanced on one foot.

His nostrils flared a little as he gave the shoe a hurried examination before handing it back to Moira.

"Well they're certainly a pair of Gourdley's. In good condition too I must say. But if it's a new pair you're after then I can't help you, I'm afraid," he said adjusting his spectacles and strutting off down the street.

"Why not?" Lewis called out.

"Because we haven't made any classic Mary Janes since 1928!"

Chapter 13
Tea-Chest Tabitha

"Well that wasn't at all helpful," Moira sighed, hopping on the spot as she pulled her shoe on. "But at least we know I'm well-shod."

"You don't think that's *weird*!?" Lewis gawped. "They haven't made shoes like that since the 1920s. That's almost…one hundred years ago!"

"One *hundred*?" She gaped. "But…w-why would anyone be wearing shoes *that* old?"

A ridiculous idea had begun to occur to Lewis. Yanking around his rucksack he fished out the ballpoint pen and his phone. "Do you know what *this* is?" he asked, handing her the pen.

"A pen?" She frowned, second-guessing herself. "Or an elegant sort of…writing implement of some description? Or is this one of those trick questions? Is it a hat?"

"And what about this?" he proposed, holding out his phone. "When you took Mum's one, what did you think it *was*?"

Moira shrugged. "Some sort of...contraption for looking at oneself. Like a compact mirror? Or a music box?"

Lewis felt his pulse quicken. "Don't you see?!" he blurted out. "*That's* the difference. You know what a pen is; but you've got no idea what a phone is."

"That's a *telephone*?" she gawked, trying to snatch it from him.

"You're missing the point!" he sighed exasperatedly and then lowered his voice as a man walking his border collie ambled passed them. "*You* didn't even know how to spell 'lasagne' until yesterday. Do you not think...you're –"

Moira craned her neck in anticipation.

"– from..." He could barely bring himself to say it. The idea was so absurd, so completely mystifying to him that he finished off in a whisper. "From...from a *long time ago*?"

Moira's face paled and her eyes began to flit questioningly back and forth.

"That..." she began with a feeble squeak. "That would explain a lot. Why some things seem familiar. And others completely...baffling."

A pulse thumped in his throat. It shouldn't and couldn't be possible. But the way she'd been gawking at the TV, her strange clothes, all of it seemed to suddenly fall into place.

He'd seen photos of Dad's great-granny who'd been born in 1915, but she'd always looked so distant. As if she existed only in a slightly fuzzy black-and-white world. Yet here Moira stood. Not sounding all that different when she spoke to kids he knew. A full living, breathing person with colour in her cheeks, a faint tickle of freckles on her pointy nose and something lost drifting in her eyes.

Moira looked down at her shoes.

"Goodness," she chuckled weakly. "That does make me feel...so very far from home."

Lewis felt a twinge of guilt for being so insistent.

"We'll work it out," he assured her, with an awkward pat on the shoulder. "I'm sure we will."

"B-b-but...but why would that happen?" she asked, bewildered. "How could that possibly...*be*?"

Lewis gazed into the street behind her, his head twisted and confused. But as his eyes eventually focused, he spotted Dad, standing outside the train station handing out Buckley's Estate Agents flyers, which no one seemed to be taking.

His heart shot up into his mouth and, lashing out, he grabbed Moira by the wrist and hauled her into the narrow alley beside the cobblers.

"Why are *you* so worked up!?" she demanded sulkily, as Lewis flung himself flat against the mossy brick wall. "*I'm* the one who's just discovered my shoes are old enough to be on display in a museum...I suppose you should just clip a sign to me that says *Come and see the hundred-year-old girl – one shilling a peek—*"

"It's my dad," Lewis hissed. "I'm supposed to be studying."

Lewis leaned against the alley wall, letting out a slow breath and closing his eyes.

When he opened them, the tip of Moira's nose was just inches away from his face as she squinted hard in the region of his left ear.

"What are you doing?" Lewis frowned leaning away.

"*M* –" Moira said, pointing to the right of him – "something –" she went on, pointing directly at his face – "*ing's P*-something-*age*." Her finger trailed off to the left.

"What?"

Moira gripped him by the shoulders and spun him round. "There," she declared proudly, pointing at the wall. On the spot his head had been leaning against was a low street sign, almost as mossy as the brick wall on which it was pinned:

MOORINGS PASSAGE

"*M*-something-*ings P*-something-*age*," she said again. "I remembered it. That was one of the addresses. In your little book."

Lewis scrambled for the chess scorebook.

"*Th*-something-*ings, Moorings Passage – 1717*," he confirmed as his eyes drifted down the narrow darkened alley, with a crooked church bell tower peering out over the sunken rooftops.

The gentle hum of the street faded as they counted the door numbers past the boarded shopfronts.

"Do you suppose *that's* it?" Moira wondered, nodding towards a slanting building just up ahead that had a great overhang of mouldy thatching. It appeared to have been derelict for some time. The door was bricked over and the shuttered windows were criss-crossed with boards.

"Can't see a thing!" She cupped her hands and peered between the cracks.

"Down here." Lewis noticed something, dropping to a squat as Moira crouched beside him. Screwed to the wall was a round plaque, engraved with the words:

"Lewis! The date is the same," Moira hissed. "*1717!*"

"There's more." Lewis nodded towards the adjoining information panel.

He pivoted on the spot and read aloud:

Tabitha Blight, or "Tea-Chest Tabitha" as she came to be known, was the daughter of a local cabinet maker, who lived in this house in the hamlet of Barrow, the Snoring Broads. Story has it that Tabitha's rather bothersome ability was discovered one hot summer's night after

Tabitha's mother left her window ajar. Tabitha was found the following morning, fast asleep, drifting over the Dowsing Marshes, her nightdress snared on a cluster of brambles. After this incident, each night before bed Tabitha would take a length of ribbon and tie one end round her foot and the other round a heavy tea chest. For many mornings after, Tabitha could be seen floating, like a kite, out of the top-floor window of this house. Little else is known about her, but according to some versions of the story, Tabitha became so fed up of people gathering outside this house on Moorings Passage to watch her float, that one evening she flung her window wide open, neglecting to anchor herself to the tea chest and was never seen again.

This plaque and others in Barrow are made possible by the kind patronage of The Barrow Historical Society.

The two of them gawked at one other.

"Doesn't that sound…" Lewis began.

"…Exactly like what happens to me…when I sleep?" Moira shuddered gazing darkly up at the Thatchings. "Remind me to shut the window tonight, won't you?"

"She was our age," Lewis observed from the date on the plaque.

"*Your* age, perhaps," Moira snorted. "But we've already established from my shoes that I'm old enough to use a walking cane and hand out cough drops to well-behaved children!"

Lewis felt his pockets for his pen.

"She must be child number two, then," Moira

pondered folding her arms. "And if she was able to float when she slept. Like I can. Then..."

Lewis looked up at her.

"If she's got a number. Maybe you have one too?" Lewis croaked. "Like you are *missing* from somewhere."

Moira shrank a little. And Lewis regretted saying it almost instantly as the marking on the inside of his palm that seemed to tie their fate together began to itch.

"We need to go to these other addresses," Lewis muttered, feeling his pockets again. "Find out who the other kids were and if there's more stuff like this at each of them. Maybe that way we can piece it together. Find out exactly why you arrived here...why it happened *now*. Hey, where'd my pen go?"

Moira clutched her little bag and squinted innocently up at the sky. Lewis gave her a knowing look and held out his hand. With a scowl she unclasped the button and handed the pen to him.

Pressing the chess scorebook flat against the wall, Lewis plotted in: *Tea-Chest Tabitha (floating girl) – 1706–1717, child two* and *"Moira's" shoes – 1927 (approx)*.

"I don't like the way you wrote 'Moira's shoes' just there." Moira leaned over his shoulder. "You make them sound like they're a suspicious object."

"Oh. Sorry." Clicking his pen, Lewis drew a little arrow and wrote "whiffy" between "Moira's" and "shoes".

"I *saw* that, Lewis." Moira narrowed her eyes at him as he grinned. "Don't you go forgetting I'm a hundred years older than you, you...insolent little whippersnapper!"

The two of them dashed across the high street to avoid Dad.

"We can start at Pudding Lane," Lewis told her, navigating Maps on his phone. "That's just near here, behind the station."

Hugging close to the shops, they headed towards the drawbridge and turned onto the town square. Over by the corner an old man wearing a fundraising tunic was rattling a donations tin as people passed him by.

"That's Gretel Murk," Lewis explained, nodding at the fountain.

They ambled towards the crumbling statue, Gretel's bony hand thrust high in the air, clutching the cup as the foggy green water rippled in the breeze round her waist.

Lewis crouched and ran his fingers over the weather-worn letters engraved beneath it:

GRETEL MURK – THE TERRIBLE BOGWITCH
OF BARROW
1628

"You think she's still out there then?" Moira asked, staring into the gloomy water. "The Bogwitch? And she's made kids go missing out of…revenge…because this Lucrilla lady drowned her?"

From above them, there was a flutter as a dark shape swooped down from the sky. Looking up, they were just in time to see an enormous rook perch itself on the cusp of the goblet. It pecked at the dank rainwater that had gathered inside it.

"Shoo," Lewis hissed feebly. "Shoo!"

Moira raised an eyebrow. "Lewis, it's not a moth. It's a bird. You're going to need to give it a little more *pep* than that."

"Any donations for the Flood Siren Fund?" came a wispy voice from behind them followed by the rattling of coins. The timid gentleman with his anxious puff of hair had appeared behind them, a badge pinned to his chest which read:

Mr Stanley Whiting
Barrow Historical Society – Secretary

"We're raising money to have one of our flood sirens replaced. Join in the quest to preserve Barrow's history and its people..."

"Er. No. Sorry," Lewis murmured fiddling with the straps of his rucksack as he and Moira backed away.

"Ah, pity!" The old man smiled, and went back to shaking his tin.

But for some reason, even as they hurried across the square, Lewis could feel Mr Whiting's eyes itching at the back of his neck.

They found the quiet little twist of street that was Pudding Lane just behind the station. But no matter how long they scoured around drainpipes, behind dustbins and under windowsills, there was no sign of another plaque or anything that looked even a little like a clue.

"Nothing here either," Moira sighed, replacing a large ginger cat to the top of a stack of wooden pallets once she'd checked underneath it, although Lewis could tell she'd just wanted to pick up the cat.

There were two short vibrations from his phone as a message came through.

It was from Mum:

Home for 16:00 please. Dad back around then.

You okay to offer Moira some lunch? Let me know if she starts being a you-know-what in the you-know-where.

Mxx

Lewis typed back while Moira leaned on her elbows, her nose touching the ginger cat's as it blinked.

Will do. Moira actually not too bad.

"Oi!" There was a squawk as Moira covered her nose, glaring at the cat as it licked its paw. "You know, you're not as cute as you think you are."

Lewis added another message as he grinned.

She's kinda funny actually.

He checked the time. *13:45.*

With the ten pounds he kept in the front pocket of his rucksack for emergencies he bought each of them a pasty and a Chelsea bun from The Floury Nettle bakery at the end of Pudding Lane, and together they followed the little red dot on his phone as they made their way to their next destination, Heckle's Bridlepath, on the other side of town.

But the walk was longer than Lewis expected. Not least because the bridle path seemed to be across two fields surrounded by hedges with a stile tucked deep between the brambles.

"There's no houses or anything." Lewis squinted along the unkept path as Moira extricated herself from a tendril of bramble by spinning on the spot.

They did spot a tumbledown sort of shed between the trees, but upon investigation it turned out to be nothing more than the sunken ruins of a coach house, littered with rotting wooden beams.

"Nothing. Again." Moira sighed.

Lewis checked the time as he swatted away a mosquito.

15:27. They needed to head home. Dad would be back soon.

"There's still *Howard's Bog*. And the other address that I haven't been able to locate yet," he reminded her as they trudged back across the fields. "Maybe we'll find clues there. We can go and investigate on Saturday. Day after tomorrow."

"The day *after* tomorrow?!" Moira repeated stumbling on a dry cowpat. "We can't wait that long!"

"The exam," Lewis told her, tightening the straps of his rucksack. "My parents think I've been studying and I need to—"

Moira gripped his forearm, twisting it over to reveal his palm.

"Do you see it? The third one – becoming more visible as another day passes by?"

Lewis felt his innards wince. He hadn't wanted to even think about the markings, much less look at them. But Moira shoved her hand in his face. "There were seven of them when I arrived, Lewis."

On Moira's marking there were now four. One less than yesterday. Lewis's eyes drifted across her fingers over to his palm where a third pale spot was looming into view.

"What do you think happens, Lewis?" she whispered darkly. "After seven days, when all the markings have changed. What happens to us?"

Chapter 14

Not the First People

"Blast!" Dad shouted holding Lewis's shirt up to the light the next morning. "Now I've done it, June. Maple syrup on the cuff of the sleeve. Must have brushed it against something. It's ruined, June. Ruined!"

"Okay, take a nice deep breath, George," Mum cooed. "It'll come off with some water. Just *relax*. Nice and calm. There we go."

Lewis reached quietly for the handle of the back door, Moira bobbing close behind him.

"Er, where are you two off to?" Dad asked, ducking his head into the living room.

"Just a quick bike ride. To the marshes. We wanted to do a bit of…sightseeing," Lewis said, casually adjusting his rucksack. His chess scorebook and some snacks had been stowed inside.

"With only five hours before your exam?!" Dad babbled incredulously. "No. You need to—"

"George," Mum interrupted calmly. "He's been studying for weeks. He studied all day yesterday. Let him have some sunshine. He'll be *fine*."

Lewis felt a bloom of relief and Moira gave him a congratulatory nudge with her elbow.

Outside the door, Mum pulled Lewis aside. "Be back here for twelve. No later. Okay? You've got your phone?" she said out of Dad's earshot.

"Yep." Lewis gave a hurried nod.

"Don't tell him I told you, but Dad's booked a table for dinner tonight. As a surprise treat for all your hard work."

Lewis felt his eyelid twitch.

"I know it's all a bit intense, but just –" she brushed something off his shoulder – "just try to remember what we spoke about, yeah? He only does it because he—"

"He wants me to have all the stuff he didn't have. I know," Lewis finished off, stuffing his thumbs impatiently into his pockets as Moira dawdled by the garden shed.

He regretted sounding a little snappy almost immediately. But he didn't want Mum to keep going on about it. Not when he hadn't really been studying.

"Okay," Mum said quietly and then pointed her finger at them both. "Helmets. Both of you. I've done my fair share of dental work on kids who didn't wear helmets and believe you me, a full arch dental implant is no way *near* as fun as it sounds."

As they'd cycled out of Barrow, the streets had ended, giving way to a country lane with faded white signposts pointing them feebly in the direction of the Dowsing Marshes.

"Well, I might have forgotten my name," Moira panted as they reached the boardwalk that zigzagged between the rotting thicket of rushes to the opposite edge of the marsh. "But at least I can remember how to cycle."

"It's scientifically proven that it's impossible to forget how to ride a bike," Lewis called out.

"You really are a clever little clog, aren't you, Willis?"

He glanced up as the wind played with her dark bob of hair. She was wearing his black *I've Got Great Moves* jumper with the picture of a dancing chess piece on it, the baggy sleeves as wide as trousers on her arms. And for a second he felt strangely happy.

He'd been half-expecting to spend these first days of the summer glued to his desk surrounded by heavy workbooks and Dad checking in on him every few minutes. Yet here he was. Going somewhere with someone.

He couldn't explain it, the expanding feeling in his chest. And for a split moment it didn't seem to matter what they were there to do, just that they were doing it.

"Do you actually think we'll find something this time?" she asked hopefully. "Another clue?"

"Maybe another story about a missing child." Lewis shrugged, ducking to miss a moorhen that had shot out from between the reeds across his path. "Like the one about Tea-Chest Tabitha."

The boardwalk ended and their bikes skidded to a halt in the mud. Tree trunks, dead and white, staggered out of the water and up into a boggy woodland.

Lewis scrunched up his face as he parked Mum's bike and consulted the map on his phone. "I think we have to go that way."

"How can you tell?" Moira asked.

"Maps," Lewis murmured.

"I thought that was a telephone?" she frowned.

"It's both," Lewis muttered impatiently.

Why did the arrow on his phone keep changing directions? Maybe his signal was just low. Lewis swivelled again, but out of nowhere Moira clouted his left ear.

"OW!" He jerked away from Moira. "What was that for?"

"Wasp," Moira said. "Don't worry, though. It's gone now."

Almost immediately a smile broke out across Lewis's face. It felt ridiculous to be so tickled at that precise moment. But it was something about the way she'd said it that had caught him off guard. As if she'd smacked his ear a thousand times before and it was just something she always did.

"I think I would've preferred being stung," Lewis muttered, massaging his ear and returning to the map. "It should be *here*. But there's no houses, no roads. Nothing."

In the corner of his screen he glanced at the time: 10:32.

"What was the address again?" Moira asked.

"The Old M-something-l Howards Bog."

The moment Lewis said it, something pale flashed between the tall reeds, just a few paces away.

"Lewis," Moira hissed, as they drew closer together. "Wh-what was that?"

Lewis held his breath. The silence was broken by the distant caws from the birds at the marshes' edge.

"Who's there?" Lewis called out. Crouching, he picked up a muddy stick and cautiously prodded the clump where he'd seen the pale something vanish.

Nothing moved.

"It could have just been a—" he whispered.

But as he turned to Moira, over her shoulder he saw a gaunt face with two milky eyes burst out from between the rushes.

Moira let out a muffled scream as a set of yellow fingernails clamped over her mouth.

Lewis stumbled in fright, his wellies sticking in the mud.

"What do you want with The Old Mill on Howards Bog!?" the old woman seethed through her mottled teeth.

She was wearing waders.

Carrying an umbrella.

Lewis's heart ticked. It was the lady from the Peering of the Goblet. The one who'd grabbed him by the arm before the storm came, and shouted blue murder about the Bogwitch.

Moira's eyes golf-balled with terror as she tried to wriggle free.

"W-we were just looking for information," Lewis babbled holding up both his hands. "W-we found this address...and w-we think it has something to do with the B—"

"Oh, you've come to torment me, have you?" the old lady warned, her fish-like eyes brimming. "Come to try and chase me from my home, eh?"

Moira let out a howl, and stomped the heel of her shoe into the old woman's wader boot.

"ARGH!" the gaunt creature shrieked, releasing Moira and snatching her umbrella towards them. "You poor wretches think it matters how much water there is when you peer into that goblet? Bah! No one commands the floods but she. The rooks fly lower than they have for nearly one hundred years! She has awakened. Everything points to it!"

"Please...please...we were just looking for information." Lewis tried to remain calm as the two of them huddled together. "We didn't mean to—"

"Be off with you! Scram!" the woman shouted. "I've been warning those townsfolk of her misty green candle for years. Her lantern, green as a garden pea that she uses to beguile and bewitch; to lure you into her murky waters like eels to bread! No one's believed me before, why would you believe me now!?"

"Because we've seen things that make us believe the Bogwitch is real!" Moira said stealing a hurried glance at Lewis as the old lady crept menacingly towards them.

"There are rooks trying to tell us something. And I can

remember a stranger – a boy. A sad boy," Moira spilled out. "And I think...*we* think, I'm from somewhere else!"

Even through the thuds from his heart, Lewis felt a jolt in his chest.

But almost at once the old woman's umbrella dropped.

"W-what did you say?" she rasped.

"We...we think I'm from somewhere else," Moira repeated. "Another time."

The old woman raised a trembling finger. "There's a marking on you, isn't there?" she asked in a terrified whistle. And Lewis felt a tingling in the soles of his feet. As if he were no longer anchored to the ground.

"Y-yes." Moira held her marked hand open, grabbing Lewis with her other. "On both of us."

"It's all true then. Everything he said," the old woman whispered to herself as she gazed at Moira's marking almost fondly. She looked up, and through her cloudy eyes Lewis could see her blue pupils.

"I'm Martha Godwit. I'm an amateur historian of this strange old town, and whatever your names are, you're not the first people I've met who bore the marking of the Barrow Bogwitch."

Chapter 15
Child Number Five

"He was my favorite uncle. Uncle Herbert," Martha explained as she led them between the dead trees rising up from the watery ground. "An unusual man. People always thought it. And when I was a little girl he'd tell me strange stories only I believed."

"And it was *him* who had the marking?" Lewis asked.

"Yes," Martha said. "But not that I ever saw. It was a long-buried memory that he suddenly discovered in his old age. A memory from when he was a boy."

When they arrived at the edge of a small lake surrounded by rushes, Moira elbowed Lewis sharply in the ribs, pointing wildly at the chipped sign that had appeared:

The Old Mill
Howard's Bog

"*The Old M*-something-*l, Howard's Bog*," Lewis repeated under his breath. The address they'd been searching for.

It took Lewis a moment to realize that Martha's home was actually a disused windmill, only missing its sails. An olive-green, three-wheeled car was parked out front and the sight of the white tower rising from the sunken edge of the lake made it look more like a chess piece than ever.

In the completely circular room that they stepped into, the enormous wooden cogs surrounding the pillar at the windmill's core lay silent, decorated with a collection of forks, doorknockers and fireplace tongs so rusted they must have been found out on the marshes.

Martha led them up a staircase inside the windmill, which came out onto a second floor that smelled like a charity shop, and was teeming with stacks of yellowed newspapers and battered books.

Lewis checked his watch. The exam was creeping nearer with every passing moment.

"You'll take tea?" Martha asked, removing a pouch of leafy white flowers from beneath her raincoat. "I'm afraid I only have white nettle. It shouldn't really grow on the marshes, but grow it does. Bountifully. Must be the nitrogen."

"Er...I'm fi—" Lewis began but Moira cut him off.

"We're *gasping* for tea."

"Nettle it is," Martha decided, stuffing the entire bouquet into a chipped teapot.

Once she'd handed each of them a cloudy-looking cup of tea, Martha hobbled across to the sunken iron bedframe on one side of the room.

"This is him," she said, pointing to a photograph on the bedside table. "Dear Uncle Herbert."

An old man with soft grey eyes seated in an armchair, with a blanket pulled across his legs, stared back at them.

Moira lowered herself to the lumpy mattress with a creaking of springs as she examined the photo, and Lewis perched himself on a mouldy pouffe whose spongy contents were spilling out at the sides.

"At first his parents thought it was amusing," Martha said, reaching up as high as her hunched back would allow and pulling out a red leather album from one of the shelves, "to have a son with such a vivid imagination. But when he started telling them that he thought he was from somewhere else. That he had another family from a different time. A family who lived in a windmill. Well, that's when things became more serious."

Martha laid the album on Moira's lap and Lewis shifted himself on the bed beside her.

A scrapbooked newspaper clipping was glued to the page. It was dated July 1926 and accompanied by a picture of a very sombre-looking boy with dark curly hair. He was wearing an enormous pair of fluffy earmuffs and performing a handstand in what appeared to be the middle of a cabbage patch.

Moira coughed out a great mouthful of tea onto the floorboards.

"THAT'S HIM!" Her eyes grew almost as large as Martha's. "The stranger, Lewis! The boy in my head. The sad salad lad!"

Lewis leaned in. The boy's hands weren't visible, but upon closer inspection it seemed that they were buried beneath the soil. As if he'd planted himself.

"You *knew* my uncle Herbert?" Martha said in a reedy voice.

"No," Moira panted with excitement. "At least. Not really. It's all foggy. But I remember his face. And that he was somehow near me!"

A fond smile crossed Martha's wrinkled mouth and her eyes softened at the edges.

Lewis extracted the album out from underneath Moira's elbows and read.

6th August, 1926

STOOP-ENDOUS

BY MERLINDA SPRATT

In this modern age of machines and aero-flight, if one speaks of strange events of the psychic or paranormal, one is likely to be greeted with a cynical smile. Not so for the Stoop family in the town of Barrow in the Snoring Broads.

For several weeks now, young Herbert Stoop has been wearing earmuffs and planting himself, hands-first, in the Stoop family garden. "It's like an electric humming in my fingers," twelve-year-old Stoop says loudly. "At first, I thought it was a wart coming on. But then, one day in the garden, I felt an urge to put my hands beneath the soil and I felt it shoot out like a lightning bolt."

Young Herbert, who claims these waves of electricity are accompanied by a high-pitched ringing, took to wearing his earmuffs and claims he won't take them off until science can give him an explanation for his extraordinary talent.

"We're quite proud of him," says his father, Edgar Stoop. "It's just a bit of fun, but the publicity's done wonders for the family business."

This from the boy's mother, Bernice: "It's all in his imagination, of course, but I have to admit, after the recent flooding, when he popped his fingers into the soil of a pot of geraniums I was having particular trouble reviving in our garden at the Willows, the plants suddenly took off. And now we have geraniums coming out of our ears!"

Lewis's fingers slid off the album.

Electricity from his fingers. Just like Moira. And what was more—

"The Willows," Moira read again, running her finger beneath the words. "Lewis. Wasn't that..."

Lewis dug out his chess scorebook, his fingers scurrying down the list.

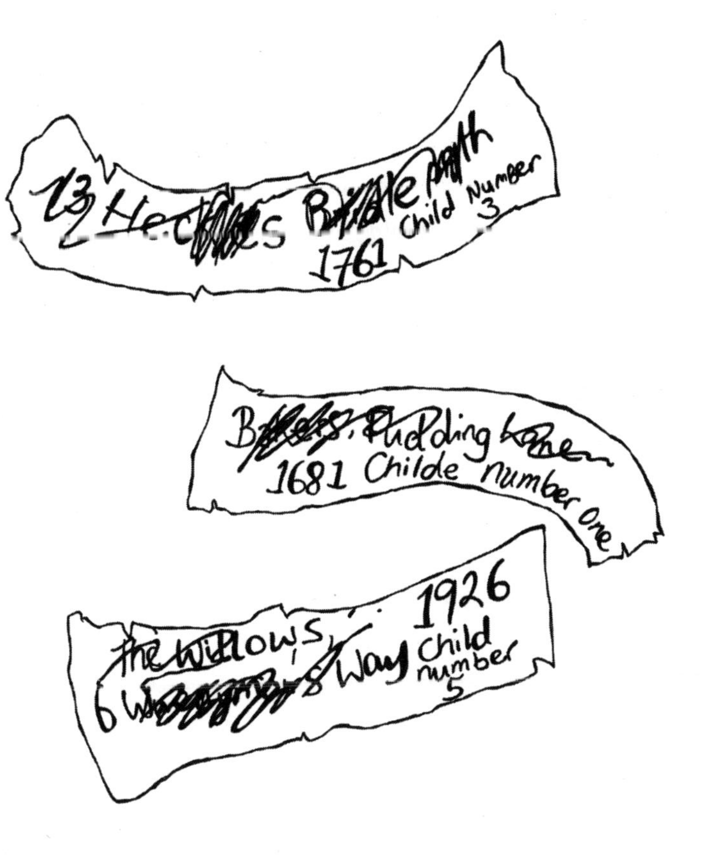

"Child number five," Lewis muttered under his breath.

"1926," Moira added pointing out the date above the article.

"His mother and father quickly changed their tune when he turned fifteen and started talking about memories they themselves had no recollection of," Martha went on. "Their doctor told them it was just a passing teenage fancy, and that he was acting out. But how wrong they were because, as time went on, Uncle Herbert began to remember more strange things. Until one day, when he was passing through the town square, he caught sight of the statue of Gretel Murk."

"The goblet?" Moira croaked.

"Yes," Martha breathed. "And the memory of the marking he once had returned to him."

Silence fell as the fire in the stove let out a crackle.

"What happened to him after that?" Lewis asked.

"As Uncle Herbert grew older he became increasingly reclusive. Superstitious. Withdrawing completely from other people. And whenever it rained, he would shutter the windows and sit in the very centre of the room inside an inflatable boat, waiting for the skies to clear."

"Because of the Bogwitch?" Lewis asked. "Because of her floods?"

Martha nodded darkly.

"With every passing day his convictions grew stronger. Until, after years of living in this very windmill, the windmill where he had strange, hazy memories of another life, in another time, Uncle Herbert passed on."

As Lewis scanned the room, he couldn't help but get the feeling that Martha seemed to have taken the same path her uncle had. And she didn't even have the marking on her palm. Moira had. And *he* had. Was *he* going to wake up without knowing who or where he was?

"Uncle Herbert spent ninety-one years digging and scratching and trying to discover who he was or might have been. And in the last years of his life he grew irritable and forgetful. But there was one thing he would say to me, *over* and *over* again."

Her glimmering gaze darted back and forth between them as they leaned forward in anticipation.

"Wouldn't recommend the quail salad," Martha said importantly.

Moira's eyes widened as she glanced at Lewis.

"It didn't mean much to me," Martha said, standing up and taking the album from Lewis. "That was, until I found this amongst his things."

She lowered the album to his lap once more. "I tried for many years to seek out the book from whence it came, but to no avail."

The page was completely empty, except for a tiny clipping that appeared to have been torn from the edge of a book...

C
y
h
ge hel
h
r
wouldn't recommend the quail salad.

"And on the other side," Martha said raising her eyebrows.

Lewis flipped the paper.

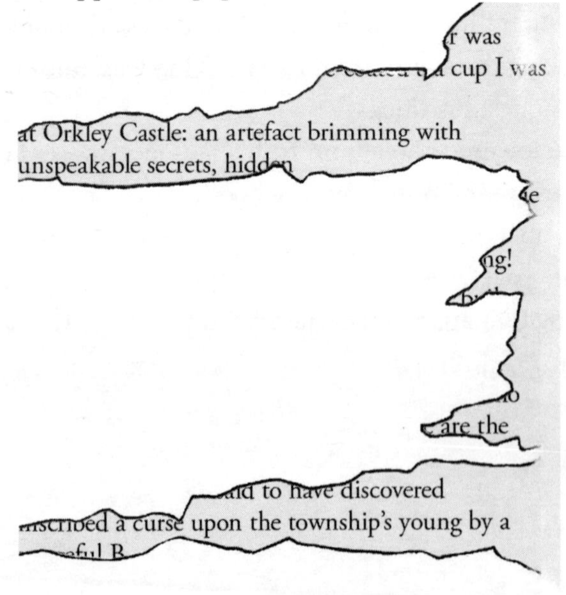

r was
cup I was
at Orkley Castle: an artefact brimming with
unspeakable secrets, hidden
e
ng!
are the
to have discovered
ed a curse upon the township's young by a

"Something – *at Orkley Castle: an artefact brimming with unspeakable secrets, hidden,*" Lewis read jarringly. "Something *discovered* something *upon the township's young by a vengeful* something."

"Orkley Castle," Martha repeated importantly.

Lewis looked up. "What about Orkley Castle?"

Martha gawked at him.

"Why, it's *their* headquarters!" she cried out.

"Who's headquarters?" Moira puzzled.

"Them ones that peer into the goblet, of course!" Martha snorted impatiently. "The Barrow *Historical* Society!"

Lewis and Moira exchanged confused looks.

"You mean…those old people from the town square?" Lewis asked. "You think…they *know* something?"

"Let me ask you this, my boy," Martha chuckled grimly. "Which bumbling local historical society have *you* ever heard of that kept a private archive, strictly accessible only to the chairman and the treasurer, eh?"

Lewis sat up a little. Mr Smythe, who used to own their house, had been a member of the Barrow Historical Society. Mr Smythe, who most likely concealed the barometer in the fireplace.

"So they're *hiding* something?" he asked.

Martha raised her eyebrows knowingly and Lewis reread the clipping.

"…at Orkley castle: an artefact brimming with unspeakable secrets, hidden…"

In his pocket his phone began to vibrate, and Lewis whipped it out.

It was Dad. And the time was 11:57. A wave of guilt crashed over him. They were late already. And Dad was going to be panicking.

"We *have* to go," Lewis said, hurriedly tapping *end call* and jerking his head towards the doorway as Moira got to her feet.

"Be wary as you cross, my dears!" Martha shouted from the top steps of the windmill as Lewis and Moira hurried along the edge of the broad. "Watch above the water for any strangely shaped rushes! The waterbirds nest in her reedy hair as she waits beneath the marshes!"

Her voice began to trail off, as Moira turned to give a hurried wave and the calls of the rooks echoed in the distance.

Lewis began to run as fast as he could manage with the rucksack clapping loosely against his lower back.

In his pocket he could feel his phone vibrating again.

"Both you and Herbert had flashes from a past life and were convinced you were from somewhere else. Both of you can shoot electricity from your fingers. Herbert was child number five."

Lewis hesitated for a moment. "What if *you're* child number six. And with the markings, you're passing it on to me. Like a cold. And I'll....wake up like you did. With my memories of *this* life all foggy...muddled up."

His jaw seized up at the thought.

"That clipping said there was *an artefact brimming*

with unspeakable secrets at Orkley Castle," Lewis wheezed. "We need to find out more about it. Is it something to do with the missing children? With what's happening to us?"

"But you heard what Martha said," Moira insisted. "Herbert spent his whole life trying to work out what was going on and couldn't. What if we're wasting time? What if he was barking up the wrong tree?"

But Lewis stopped dead in his tracks.

What had been a stretch of marsh this morning had transformed into a weedy lake. Only the tallest rushes were visible now, jutting like broomstick bristles from below the surface. On the other side, the end of the boardwalk seemed to float out across the water like a jetty.

"Lewis?" Moira asked.

Yanking his phone out of his pocket, he pulled back the zip of his rucksack a little and prodded it inside. There had been five missed calls from Dad.

"We'll have to wade across," he said, tightening the straps and scanning the water's edge. "There's no way round."

"What if I can't swim?" Moira wavered.

Lewis tried to ignore her, biting his bottom lip as he hesitantly placed his first welly into the murky soup with a wibble of bubbles.

"It's not deep," he called back, wading into the murk. "We need to get back. Now."

Reaching over his shoulder he hoisted up his rucksack

as the water rose to his waist. And he was glad he did. There was a jolt as his foot slipped and he let out a gasp as he dropped up to his chest.

Moira took in a huge breath, winced, and began to surge towards him, her arms stretched out to either side to balance her.

Lewis pushed on, trying not to think and doing his best to test the ground ahead of him with the tip of his foot. In his rucksack, the phone rang yet again. And a flare of irritation caught him off guard as the ground sank beneath him.

Why couldn't Dad stop? He was doing the best he could.

"You don't think," Moira began warily, "there are any eels in here, do you?"

But Lewis didn't respond. Something distinct had caught his ears. Only a little while before, the marshes had been echoing with the haunting cries of rooks and moorhens. But in the heavy air around them, the birds had fallen silent.

He pivoted as best he could towards Moira.

She hadn't seen it yet, but from behind her, through the limbs of the dead trees, an unseasonable mist was drifting towards them.

"M-Moira," he shuddered, pointing. She twisted herself, backing towards him as the mist reached its pale limbs across the water.

"What's happening?" Moira whispered, shuffling closer to Lewis.

The mist breathed past them, enrobing them in a grey cloak through which only each other and the faint outline of the twisted clumps of hairy rushes were visible.

Lewis turned slowly, squinting as he tried to see something, anything, through the gloom.

"Lewis?"

There was a vanishing flicker through the mist.

"What was that?!" he hissed.

"What?"

"There!" he spat, catching sight of it again as it glimmered beneath the water. "It was there." Lewis trembled, as his eyes darted back and forth between the tussocks of wiry rushes. "Just over there!"

"Lewis," Moira said firmly. "If you're—"

But before she could finish, her eyes widened and he felt her grip on his fingers.

One of the clumps of rushes protruding from below the surface was drifting straight towards them. As if there was something lurking in the waters beneath.

Chapter 16
The Rushes

The cluster of rushes glided silently across the water.

It's her. The thought drilled into Lewis. *Just below the water. Gretel Murk the Barrow Bogwitch.*

All of the whispered stories he'd heard. The legends of floods, and rooks and witches. Before it had seemed distant. Even with the inexplicable appearance of Moira, a girl who seemed to be from a hundred years ago, the stories had still seemed foggy.

But here in the mist it all became impossibly real, as the reedy clump drew to a halt just a few feet away.

"D-d-do you think you can swim?" he shuddered to Moira from the corner of his mouth.

But Moira said nothing, slowly removing her bag from across her shoulder.

"When I say go," Lewis whispered, his eyes fixed on

the wiry rushes. "We charge as hard as we can. I think the boardwalk's that way." He nodded his head towards the mist behind them.

Beneath the surface, Moira's fingers squeezed his wrist in confirmation, before releasing.

A billow of mist drew in around them, and for a second the rushes vanished.

"GO!" Lewis bellowed.

Moira shoved her embroidered bag between her teeth, and the two of them thrust forward through the water.

Lewis kicked off the ground, stumbling as his foot met with something jagged. But scooping with his free arm, he charged, lashing in murky sloshes.

Moira hauled herself alongside him, paddling and wading as best she could. There was a gasp as she slipped, plunging up to her neck in the water for a moment, but with a kick she was clawing after him.

"B-bo-oardwalk," Lewis choked as he heaved himself through the water.

It was up ahead. Emerging from the mist like a wooden lifeline.

He didn't dare look back, but just kept thrashing and scooping at the water as the sludge gave way beneath him.

"Moira?!" he gargled. "You okay—?"

"Just go! GO!" she spluttered back.

For a moment he felt his rucksack snare on something. A branch? Twig? Fingers? But as he twisted to free himself, he could see nothing.

With a final lunge, his palms slapped against the

wooden slats of the boardwalk as Moira wrapped herself round one of the submerged posts.

There was a scrambling of legs as the two of them flung their arms across the boardwalk, their fingers wedging between the cracks to haul themselves up.

With a heave, Moira lugged her foot out of the water, pivoting herself upwards until she collapsed gasping on her side.

But beneath the water, Lewis was still struggling to get a foothold as his toes slipped on the slimy post.

Moira snapped into action, scuttling towards the boardwalk's edge on all fours and thrusting her arm towards him. "Kick, Lewis!" she shouted, her eyes flashing in terror as the thing he could not see charged towards him. "KICK!"

Lewis latched his fingers exhaustedly around her forearm, his lungs aching as he drove his feet into the water.

Moira leaned backwards, hauling as he squeezed, until finally he felt his body begin to lift.

"Almost. Go. Go. Go!"

But directly beneath his scrambling feet, there was a bottle-green glow in the water.

The same as the colour that had shot from Moira's fingers. The same mesmerizing glow that clutched round her whilst she slept.

The Bogwitch's colour.

Lewis's eyes met Moira's, terror shooting through him.

And around his ankle, he felt a powerful grip.

He took in a great gasp, prickling fingers of fear creeping up his throat.

A sudden yank.

Moira's hand fell away in a murky splutter. And Lewis plunged below the surface as the Bogwitch hauled him down.

"Lew—!?" Moira shrieked.

The next thing Lewis knew, he was being dragged backwards; hooked like a fish along the marshy bed.

He was clawing, snatching blindly at the bottoms of the reeds and twigs – anything his hands could find to stop himself being hauled, as the mud scratched through his fingers, bedding into his nails. His eyes flashed open for a split second, but all he could see was a muddy cloud of water with his foot vanishing into it as the thing dragging him was obscured from sight.

A lung-crushing horror gasped through him. His head writhed like a bucket of worms.

The water grew deeper, his arms flailing helplessly as he kicked.

But the drilling, bony grip drew him relentlessly on.

A sharp pain stabbed across his chest as his breaths vanished up to the surface in a shimmer of panicked bubbles, and he felt his kicks becoming fainter, less powerful.

He was being squeezed of air. Like a deflating tyre tube caving in on itself.

Lewis slashed wildly in front of him, his fingers meeting nothing until, with a final desperate lunge of his weakened arms, his left hand wrapped around something solid, something wooden.

Tree roots.

A stump.

Lewis grasped with all his strength, grinding his teeth as the silty water floated into his mouth.

And as suddenly as it had appeared, the grip vanished.

His body drifted as he hugged the stump.

Too afraid to struggle. Too afraid to move, lest he feel its grasp once more.

But nothing happened.

And in the strange calm, Lewis could feel the murkiness swirling across his cheeks as the tall water weeds drifted like dreamy tentacles around him.

Has she gone? Is it over?

A flickering light. An orb of bottle-green light floated directly in front of him. It was mesmerizing. Beautiful almost. A shoal of tiny silver fish glimmering around it.

Greeeeeeeeeeeetel.

A thin, hiss rang through his ears.

Greeeeetel.

Lewis was frozen. Motionless.

There was a flicker; the fish scurried and the light darted through the murk.

Lewis felt his eyes sting.

A blinding flash followed.

And Lewis began to see things; glimmers in the ghostly light as it boomed with a terrible fury.

Someone trapped. In a dark place. Crying for help.

A goblet. Swirling.

Water thundering over cobblestones.

Rooks. A hurricane of feathers, wind and lightning.

Lewis lashed out, kicking and twisting in the water as he tried to close his eyes but couldn't. His ears filled with a strange wailing as the decaying weeds of the waterbed seemed to reach for him, wafting closer as their tendrils swayed.

Greeeeetel, came the voice again.

But from above him a jolt punched through the water, followed by another green light.

An electric bolt hissed past him.

Lewis looked up.

Moira.

He could see her arm thrusting about as her fingers curled.

And a panic welled up inside him, like bubbles escaping to the surface as his lungs threatened to burst. He kicked and scraped at the water, following the direction of the blurry, lightning-like bursts of electricity. Until, with a ferocious yank, he was hauled upwards, gripped again, only this time by the strap of his rucksack.

His head broke the surface and his chest expanded as he arched backwards, taking in an excruciating breath.

"LEWIS!" Moira bellowed. She was on the swampy bank beside him, pulling on his rucksack. "I was trying to help you," she babbled, "did I hurt you?! I was trying to scare it away!"

Lewis clawed his way onto land, kicking his heels as

hard as he could into the sludge, until he collapsed in a heap beside her.

"T-that was—" Lewis choked, panting desperately for air and sliding backwards as far as he could from the water's edge.

"It's alright," Moira said comfortingly, digging her arm round him and pulling him up to a seated position as he continued to splutter.

His head collapsed almost immediately on her shoulder. Not caring how he looked. Or what she'd think. Just that she was there. Just that she'd saved him.

"I'm here," Moira said firmly, as if she knew exactly what he was thinking, and he closed his eyes. "You'll be alright, Lewis."

His heaving breaths began to slow. And he swallowed.

"It was h-h-her," he stammered. "Sh-she showed me things. A flood. Some kid trapped somewhere. A cup… a goblet. As if she was angry about it. And she was…she was saying her name. Over and over."

Lewis looked up at Moira, his hair swept across his reddened eyes, as her face paled.

But before she could say anything, the sudden memory of the exam flashed through him.

Dad.

He twisted his watch round, his heart thumping painfully against his ribcage.

12:41.

Wrestling exhaustedly with his rucksack he heaved it off, snatching for the zipper.

Lewis wanted to be sick.

The zipper was already open, somehow having snagged beneath the water.

He rifled between the sodden flaps of nylon. But his phone, the chess scorebook – and all their research – was gone.

Chapter 17
Unspeakable Secrets

Lewis's watch beeped 13:00 as he dropped Mum's bike in the garden.

At that exact moment, a roomful of kids would be snatching up their pencils, one of them on their way to a scholarship at Elksbridge. But not him.

The car wasn't there. Dad wasn't there. Mum was.

"You're…soaked…a-and scratched?!" she gasped, the moment she saw them. "Lewis, what happened? Dad's out looking for you. Are you—?"

"We're fine…w-we—" Lewis began, glancing at Moira. "We lost track of time. And then our bikes. We fell in. And—"

A strained look crossed Mum's face. And Lewis could tell she was hurt. Not for herself. For Dad.

How could he possibly begin to explain it?

He heard the car pull up outside as his stomach squirmed, longing to sink into the floor. To be curled up in a tiny ball like a woodlouse that got smaller and smaller until it vanished all together.

The door opened. Lewis heard shoes wiping on the front mat. Dad appeared in the kitchen doorway dressed in his mustard blazer, his hair combed back, carrying a small gift bag and looking like an awkwardly tall kid who'd shown up overdressed to a birthday party.

"Saw the bikes out the front. What happened?" Dad asked quietly.

"Accident. Fell into the marshes," Mum mouthed to Dad.

"Either of you hurt?" he murmured without catching Lewis's eye.

Moira shifted on the spot in the corner of his vision.

"Dad, we—" Lewis pleaded, but Dad cut him off.

"Are either of you hurt?" Dad repeated firmly.

Lewis shook his head.

"You can go back to work, June," Dad said softly, gazing at the floor and squeezing the cord handle of the gift bag. "It's okay."

Lewis felt the drowning guilt rise past his chest to his throat. He'd do the exam six times over if it would make Dad feel better. What could he say to make him understand? Maybe he could tell him the truth?

But the four black spots gathering on his hand made a cold resolution fill him. He knew that he couldn't. Moira was right. They'd take her away. And he'd be alone, trying to work out how to stop himself waking up like she had, without any memories, as the spots moved closer to seven.

Mum played with her keys and Dad padded softly through the living room to the study carrying his shoes in one hand.

He hadn't expected they'd still be going out to dinner, and it seemed neither had Dad. But when Mum got home from work again, she'd ordered everyone to get dressed and marched them out to the car.

The Wherryman's Windmill Inn was almost completely empty save for a few people murmuring quietly in the darkest corners, where candles dozed and an ancient-looking sheepdog stretched out like a rug in front of the bar. Mum, who'd been trying to lighten the mood the whole way there, quickly spotted their table in the window. It was still littered with crumbs from someone's lunch and boasted a little sheet of paper that read:

TABLE OF 4 – BUCKLEY
Well done for all your hard work, Lewis
WE'RE SO PROUD OF YOU

She swept the sheet of paper up, stuffing it tactfully in her bag.

"Right. Moira, why don't you sit so you can see the river. George?"

Dad sat himself silently at the table. Lewis, who had his hands stuffed into the pockets of his hoodie, squeezed himself into the window seat, glancing across the table at Dad.

The circular walls of the pub were busy with dusty prints in bulky frames and, above them, hung old fishing nets and buoys. But Lewis could barely take it in.

He felt miserable. Miserable that he couldn't say or do anything to make it better.

"So," Mum said splitting the two menus at the centre of the table between them. "What are we all having?"

No one said anything.

"Dad got asked to sell his first property today," she said brightly. "Two properties in fact. Now that's something to celebrate, isn't it?"

Lewis looked up.

"T-two houses?" he asked hopefully. "Where are they?"

"One house," Dad said flatly. "The other's just the old gym at the Barrow School. They can't afford to keep it, so they're going to sell it off."

The fact that Dad had responded at all made his heart lift just the tiniest bit.

Mum ordered steak-and-kidney pie, Dad ordered boar sausage and mash, and Moira, who was looking slightly unsettled at the idea of being in a pub at all, just copied Lewis with his cod, chips and peas – not mushy.

"Sorry it's all been a bit strange, Moira," Mum said, sweeping some crumbs off the table and leaning on it with her elbows. "I feel like I haven't had a chance to properly talk to you. You seem a little cheerier though! How's your mum been? How's Badger?"

Moira glanced quizzically at Lewis.

"B-Badger is…well," she said slowly. "He sleeps a lot during the day."

Lewis tried to nudge her under the table.

"Oh? Is he unwell?" Mum asked.

"No," she said hurriedly. "He just goes out at night a lot."

Lewis felt himself pale, almost certain he knew what was happening. On the little cheat sheet he'd written for her, he'd completely forgotten to add Dad's nickname for Arthur Wigby-Polkinghorne.

"Does Badger *usually* go out a lot at night?" Mum asked, looking a little puzzled.

"He *only* goes out at night," Moira said as Lewis tried to warn her.

"I'm sorry, Moira, I don't know if I'm completely understanding." Mum smiled. "*Why* does he go out at night?"

Moira caught Lewis's gaze, but she was already in up to her neck.

"To look for food," Moira announced.

Mum frowned. "What food?"

"Er, mostly nuts," Moira blurted out. "Sometimes seeds, maybe fruit."

"Oh?" Mum asked. "Has he gone *vegan*?"

"I beg your pardon?" Moira asked as if Mum had said a rude word.

But Lewis butted across them.

"Are you gonna take on both properties?" he stammered loudly to Dad. "The school gym too?"

Dad gazed blankly at the little tea light at the centre of the table.

"Yes," he said flatly. "It'll be tough, but it'll be worth it. Because it will give me better opportunities in the future." He reached out and twisted the tea light a little with his fingers as everybody fell silent again.

Lewis squeezed his hands between his knees. He knew what Dad was trying to get at. And it was nothing to do with selling houses.

"Dad, I didn't mean—" Lewis began softly, but Dad spoke over him.

"I would have done *anything,* Lewis," Dad said, slamming his fist down on the table harder than he meant to, making the tea light and the little old lady at the table beside them both jump.

Moira straightened up in her seat.

"George—" Mum pleaded softly.

Dad let out a deep breath.

Lewis had never seen him like this. Stressed out or annoyed that something he'd ordered online hadn't arrived, maybe, but not like this. Not angry.

"When I was a kid," Dad said, trying to keep his cool as he dipped his finger in the wax of the tea light. "I would have done *anything* to have a shot at getting into Elksbridge. But I didn't. You want to know why? Because even if I did, Gramps wouldn't have been able to afford so much as the uniform. That was just how it was. And now *you've* had an opportunity placed right in your lap. And you've just thrown—"

He stopped, glancing up at Mum, who bit her bottom lip.

Lewis felt as if the wind had been knocked out of him. And suddenly his eyes blurred and became hot around the edges.

"Growing up comes around a lot quicker than you think," Dad muttered quietly. "And part of growing up is learning that you can't just run away from your responsibilities. Or from the things that scare you. You have to face them, head on. *Especially* when they affect people around you. That's all."

He fell silent again and went back to playing with the tea light.

Lewis felt his lip quiver. It was like being thumped in the stomach without warning. Humiliated. Ashamed.

"Two Cod and Chips?"

Plates were thankfully shoved in front of them by a short waiter with sensible hair.

The meal passed mostly in silence. Moira was making a huge effort to eat at a normal pace. Dad picked at his sausage and mash. And Mum talked far too much about how you could never have too much gravy.

Lewis moved the last of his chips around with his fork as he leaned on his fist. Out the corner of his eye, Moira kept trying to get his attention, but he didn't care. And for a moment, no matter how terrified he'd felt earlier that day, their investigation seemed almost silly. Childish.

There was a sharp *zap!* on his knee, which made his elbow jump off the table, and he glared across at her.

From underneath the table, Moira withdrew her finger, having no doubt just conjured a twig of the green electricity, like he'd seen her do before. She directed him with her eyes down to what little remained of her cod and chips.

"Do you want to see the pudding menu?" the waiter asked, whisking their plates away. Lewis was just in time to see that Moira had inexplicably rearranged the remaining peas on her plate into the shape of an arrow pointing towards the corner of the pub behind him.

"Er, no," Dad said as his phone started to ring. "Just the bill, please."

Lewis glanced quickly at Mum, who was rifling through her handbag, before swivelling in the direction the peas had been pointing. On the wall behind him was what looked like a large black-and-white bird's-eye view photograph of a lake, with a small inscription in the far corner:

Barrow from above

View of the Wherryman's Windmill Inn during the floods of July, 1926

Reprinted with the permission of the Barrow Historical Society Archives, Orkley Castle, Barrow

Lewis flicked his head back round at her and raised a puzzled eyebrow.

What was she trying to get at?

His eyes scrambled over the image, until, like a camera sharpening its focus, he spotted them.

Round shapes. Buildings…4, 5, 6, 7.

What did she mean? What were they—

Lewis stopped.

And like a Magic Eye picture coming suddenly into focus he saw it: seven windmills their tips emerging from the water to form a hauntingly familiar shape:

"It's just like Martha said," Lewis told Moira in a whisper when she crept into his room that night. "Her uncle lived in that windmill at Howard's Bog. It was one of *seven* windmills in Barrow."

Lewis shovelled aside a pile of laundry as Moira joined him.

"To keep out of reach from flood waters," she added, reaching for the unopened bag of chocolate pretzels.

"Oh. I was…saving those. Actually," Lewis said awkwardly. "For a special occasion. Like making friends at school." A pang of regret tugged inside him as Moira, who was poised ready to tear them open, placed the pretzels gently back on the floor with a little pat.

Lewis reached into his desk drawer where he'd stowed a chocolate honeycomb bar and slid it to her. Then, lugging his chess set off the desk, he placed it between them. Using the two kings, two rooks, a bishop and a queen, he started laying them out on the board in the shape of the marking.

"That must be what the marking means. It's what the Bogwitch tried to do in the first place: flood the town. When it floods, as the water rises and covers all the buildings. Until all you can see..."

He placed the last piece, the black rook, on g2.

"...is the tops of the windmills," Moira finished off distantly.

"Nineteen twenty-six was the year on that photo. The year there was a flood," Lewis told her. "And 1926 is the year that weird stuff started happening to Herbert. I *bet* you that if we still had the chess scorebook and we looked it up, there would have been floods in the years marked on those other slips as well."

Lewis prodded the carpet bitterly with his toe as he imagined his scorebook being pecked to pieces by a ball of eels.

"But if it's all really happening again and I'm child number six," Moira began slowly. "Then...that would mean...there really *might* be a flood...when the seven days are up."

Lewis sat with this thought. Dad and Mum's faces flashed through his head in watery swells. If only they could just leave this house. Leave Barrow and be done with it. But it was too late for that. The countdown playing out on their hands gave them no choice but to keep working it out.

Moira swung round her damp embroidered bag and rummaged inside. From where he sat, Lewis could see something that looked suspiciously like an old head from an electric toothbrush she must have swiped from the bathroom and a few cotton buds.

Reaching into the lining, Moira's pinched fingers withdrew a tiny slip of torn, damp paper which she lowered into Lewis's outstretched palm.

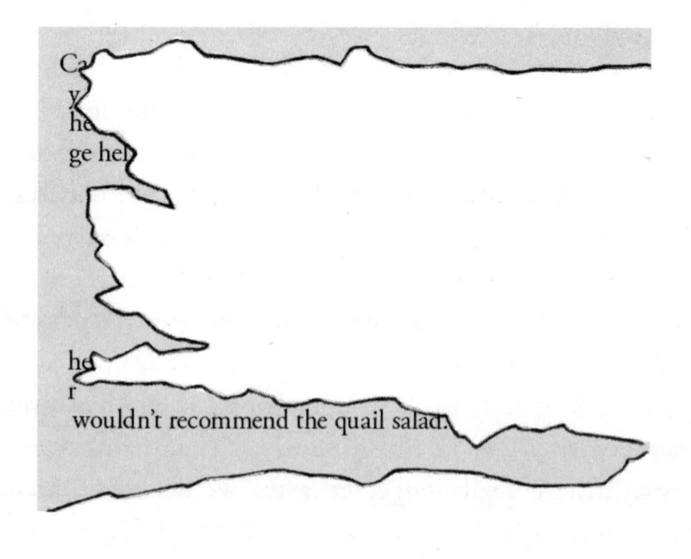
Ca
y
he
ge he

he
r
wouldn't recommend the quail salad.

He flipped it over.

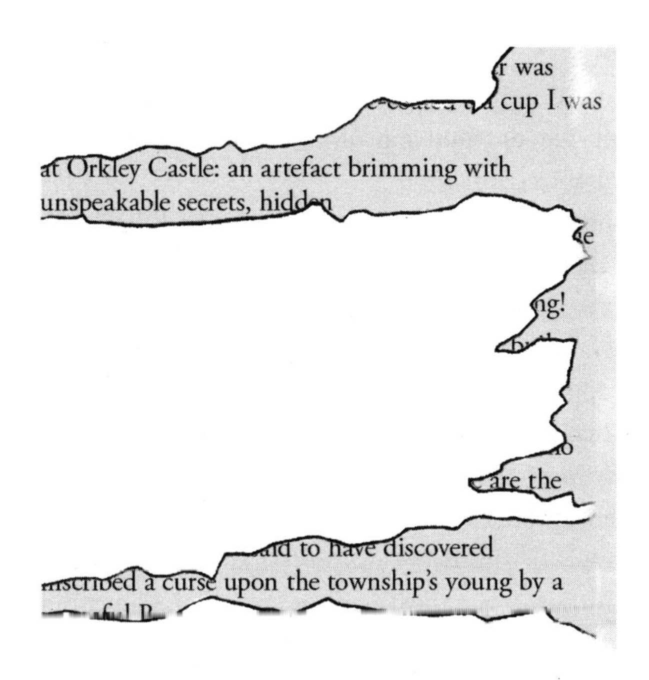

"How did you get this?" Lewis murmured in disbelief. "I didn't see you take it?!"

"*No* one saw me take it, Lewis," Moira told him and then pointed to the bottom of the slip. "This is all we've got to go on now. And I think you're right. We need to go to Orkley Castle, find the Barrow Historical Society's private archives and try to locate whatever this 'artefact' is."

Lewis let out a slow breath, feeling less confident than he had been before he was dragged beneath the marshes. "What if we get caught? What would we say then? What if Martha's right and the Barrow Historical Society are all…*in* on it?"

"I'm *highly* sneaky," Moira told him giving her embroidered bag a little rustle.

Lewis caught sight of the four black marks on his outstretched palm and almost immediately his fingers recoiled to cover them.

"Just three days left," Moira croaked, her wide eyes shimmering.

"You have to stop anything from happening to you. To your family, Lewis. And I have to get home. Whatever it takes," she whispered. "I keep seeing these faces. In my dreams. And I just *feel* it. Home. Like a song at the back of my head that I *know* I remember but I just...can't get the noises out. Except for *quail salad*."

Lewis felt his eyebrows soften as he smiled.

"Although the most curious thing," she murmured, "is that the longer I'm near you, the louder the song seems to become. And it makes me think that home isn't really a place...at all, is it? It's a feeling."

A warmth bloomed through Lewis's chest.

There was a knock on the door and Moira made a backwards dive for the laundry pile disguising herself beneath a pair of jeans.

"Only me," Mum said quietly as she poked her head in.

Lewis leaned back against the post of his bunk, gripping his left sleeve.

Mum sighed as she leaned in the doorway.

"Do you not *want* to go to Elksbridge? Is that it?"

"No," he blurted out. "It's just—"

"Then what's going on? Is it...Moira?" she whispered. "I know she's a bit...snooty."

The laundry pile protested a little.

"But not *everyone* that goes to posh schools is like that."

"I just..." Lewis pulled his knees up towards him. "Why does he have to be so intense about it?"

Mum sighed and leaned against the doorway.

"Let me tell you something," she said softly. "When I first met Dad, he told me that when he was about your age after his mum died and it was just him, Gramps and Aunty Jean, they had barely any money."

She pulled her arms closer together a little. "Dad used to go sit behind the bushes on the little slope at the edge of the cricket green and watch the boys from Elksbridge practise. Wishing he could join them. He watched them week after week, until one day their ball landed right in the bushes where he was hiding. And do you know who came to get the ball?"

Lewis shook his head.

"Badger," Mum said. "And when Badger saw Dad hiding there, embarrassed beyond belief, he didn't smirk, he wasn't judgemental. He just asked your dad if he wanted to come and play with them."

Lewis felt a lonely breeze blowing through him as he imagined Dad sitting on the hill by himself.

"I know he can be a bit full-on sometimes, and frankly there are occasions where he's a complete...goof. But ever since that day he first played cricket with Badger, he's always thought that schools like Elksbridge, where the kids all looked gleaming white and shiny in their cricket uniforms, meant being happy. And when Gramps suddenly moved them to Woolham, I think he might have felt that, despite Gramps just trying to do his best, your dad had had his chance of a life like Badger's – free of worry – taken away from him. I think that's why he wants it so badly. For you."

Lewis stared hard at his socks, avoiding Mum's gaze. Did Dad want it so badly for him that he was willing to lie on his application? But as Lewis remembered Dad's face as he'd arrived back that afternoon clutching the orange gift bag, his eyes seemed a little more tired and his shoulders not quite so broad.

How he wished Mum hadn't told him that.

"I'm not saying it to make you feel guilty," she added softly. "Just so you understand him a little better. If you can at least understand someone, I think it makes it easier when they're not at their best. If just for a moment."

Mum smiled and then frowned when she caught sight of the laundry pile.

She reached down. "Those shouldn't—"

"Don't!" Lewis blurted out and Mum started.

"*I* should take them down," Lewis told her, trying to remain calm as his heart shot up to speed. Mum gave him an approving smile as she left, pulling the door to, then Moira emerged from the laundry pile, a sock draped across her ear.

"I almost forgot to ask," she said, swatting the sock away. "Why are your family so utterly obsessed with *badgers*?"

Chapter 18
Orkley Castle

"Give Lewis a kiss, Cyril!" Celia yapped.

In the Winskis' lemon-coloured car with the peeling white stripe, Hereward was sitting next to what Lewis thought at first was an old bathmat. It turned out to be a puli dog with cord-like fur so matted it was impossible to tell which end of the dog was which.

"Give lovely Lewis a kiss!"

One end of the dog perched its paws lazily on Lewis's forearm and a tongue appeared.

He and Moira had planned the night before to go to Orkley Castle. It was their only lead. But as the headquarters of the Barrow Historical Society and, according to Herbert's quail salad clipping, the location of a mysterious *artefact brimming with unspeakable secrets*, the castle seemed like their best chance of finding out more.

Fifteen minutes after Lewis asked Mum for permission, there was a *parp!* from outside followed by frantic knocking.

"Who's that?" Lewis frowned.

"I've got to get to the clinic," Mum said. "And Dad can't take you. First viewing this afternoon with some potential buyers. So I called Celia."

"Just us! Just the Winskis! Yoohoo!"

Lewis groaned inwardly. It wasn't that he minded the Winskis so much. Just that he and Moira wouldn't be able to get on with their investigation in private.

Out of sight, Lewis couldn't stop checking the dots, which had grown in number like little spores of mould. There were four, with a fifth slowly appearing now. After today there were two days left. Two days before a flood would come. Two days before what Herbert must have passed on to Moira would be passed on to him.

"Hi, Lewis," Hereward said quietly as the Winskis' car coughed into action. One of his eyes peered out over a copy of the East Snoring Line train timetable. He was wearing a pair of sunglasses and a beige panama hat.

"Hi," Lewis mumbled back, not in the mood to make much effort.

"Hereward," Hereward said lowering his timetable as if it were a newspaper and reaching over Lewis to offer his hand to Moira.

"Moira," Moira coughed.

"Nice jersey, Moira," Hereward noted returning to his reading.

Moira's chin doubled as she looked down at her chest. It was one of Lewis's. A robot football shirt made to look like a real football jersey with *Buckley 07* written on the back.

A twig of guilt flicked through Lewis. Usually he would have been happy to talk about robotics club and the robot football tournament. But as Orkley Castle rose up on the banks of the Sevenmill River the moment seemed to have passed.

Once they'd exploded out of the car, they plodded towards the arching grate at the entrance to the castle where a large sign hung off a jousting knight's lance:

WELCOME YE TO ORKLEY CASTLE
A restoration project of the Barrow Historical Society Ltd.

"Say no to the B.H.S.!" came a raspy shout followed by the clanging of a bell. "Don't let them bully us!"

Martha Godwit stood to the left of the grated entrance of the castle, wearing a sandwich placard round her neck, which read:

Down With the B.H.S.
! FLOOD SIRENS ?
! DONATIONS ?
! CONSPIRACY ?

The timid-looking Mr Stanley Whiting appeared from the castle office. "Please, Martha, dear," he said, rubbing his hands together. "Won't you just give it a rest with the bell for a little while? Geraldine on reception has had to resort to earmuffs."

An irritated-looking woman with mahogany-coloured hair leaned through the hatch and glared at Martha.

"I won't stop hammering until the truth is exposed, Mr Whiting!" Martha said loudly clanging the bell right in his face. "I know you're behind every attempt to discredit me!"

"Martha," Mr Whiting said sounding a little more firm. "You know perfectly well that's because you were caught trying to climb in through one of the sewers at Marlow Hall!"

Martha hadn't mentioned that.

Marlow Hall was where Sir Hector lived with his grandson, Leopold. Where Gramps used to work.

Thankfully as Martha clanged Mr Whiting on his way, Celia swept them through the gate and over towards the ticket window.

Lewis had planned to peel off with Moira as swiftly as he could, but Celia had them quickly embroiled in a guided tour as Hereward seemed to hang unhelpfully close to his elbow.

"Gather round, gather round!" a man in a tunic called out over near the gatehouse. "That's it. Nice and tight. Good. Welcome to Orkley Castle. Built in the thirteenth century by the first Baronet of Snoring, Sir Hamelin de

Marlow, Orkley Castle served as a seat for five barons before it was abandoned, in favour of Marlow Hall, in the early seventeenth century and fell into decay. If you'll please follow me."

The group shuffled along behind him as he led them beneath the castle's ramparts.

Celia had burrowed right up to the front of the group and was now peppering the guide with questions. Lewis, Moira and Hereward hung at the back, trailing behind a little.

"Give it a minute," Lewis whispered from the corner of his mouth. "Then we can break away! Remember, if these archives are secret they may not be signposted. Look for anything remotely suspicious – dates, markings."

The tour group stopped just outside a spiralling stone staircase.

"These ironworking tools on display were discovered in the Dowsing Marshes by Reverend Timothy Wilks, an amateur archaeologist. Some suggest that because of the uncharacteristic white nettles found growing on the marshes, at some point, it must have been a site of human habitation."

The tour group followed the guide up the stairs and, letting Hereward press on before them, Lewis and Moira peeled off to the left, hiding themselves in a stony nook.

Lewis whipped out the folded map Celia had given him with his ticket and scanned across it, hoping to spot something that might give them a steer in the right direction.

"Lewis!" Moira hissed as she peered around the corner of the nook.

Just a little way along the covered castle walkway was a rope strung across a narrow entrance which read:

STRICTLY NO ENTRY

"Look." Moira nodded.

Sitting on a foldable chair beside the opening was a fierce lady with purple spectacles. She was knitting a large orange scarf, and kept pausing to scour the walkway with her pin-like eyes.

"She's *guarding* the entrance," Lewis whispered ducking back as her gaze swept towards them. "And she's got a Barrow Historical Society badge. Do you think the archives are down there?"

"Why else would they put such a ferocious little lady outside the entrance?!" Moira breathed.

There was a scratchy beeping and the lady retrieved a walkie-talkie from her waist.

"Marjorie reporting," she said into it, holding her knitting needles as if they were a weapon. "All clear on the Eastern Cloister. Over."

Lewis felt an anxious twinge in his stomach. How were they supposed to get past her let alone whoever else was down there?

"I'll handle this," Moira mouthed back, peeking round the corner again.

"What are you—?"

But then Lewis noticed her fingers. They were curling. Twisting. Summoning. And Lewis watched as a little net of crackling green sparks erupted over the ball of wool perched on top of the lady's carpet bag. Moira flicked her fingers. And the ball leaped in the air as it began tumbling merrily towards them, unravelling as it went.

Lewis held his breath.

The wool doddered past their hiding place, before veering left and bouncing its way down the steps the tour group had taken. After a moment, it went taut and Marjorie looked up as a suspicious frown crossed her puckered face.

Lewis and Moira flung themselves against the wall of the nook.

With a series of irritable mutters, Marjorie bustled past them.

"GO!" Moira hissed, snatching Lewis by the wrist. Sliding on the pavement, the two of them bolted towards the entrance, Moira leaping like a cat over the rope and Lewis clattering into it as he tried to duck beneath it. He let out a rattled breath, as Moira grinned at him in the darkness.

The spiral passage descended, and voices began to drift up.

"...and if I see you so much as *look* at those records without wearing gloves, Whiting, I'll have you out on donation duty again!"

Lewis stumbled, nearly tripping over Moira, who was crouching at the bottom of the stairs in the dark.

Light was bleeding up and when he peered over her shoulder a dimly lit sort of office with swinging table lamps and a leather-topped desk came into view.

Moira nudged him and pointed at the sign on the door.

The Barrow Historical Society
Archives & Chambers

Sitting at the desk was a slight old man. He seemed to be shaking and was copying out something from an ancient-looking tome using an inkwell and some white gloves.

Behind him, Gladys Putter, the lady with pale eyes and gingery hair from the Peering of the Goblet, was emptying a donation bucket of coins into a counting machine.

"Look!" Lewis hissed, pointing over her shoulder to a sign on a red door at the back of the study up a flight of three steps.

PRIVATE COLLECTION
NO ADMITTANCE WITHOUT WRITTEN APPROVAL
FROM THE TREASURER

"We need to distract them," Moira muttered.

Lewis's eyes darted around the room.

"I said *script* not *scrawl*, Mr Whiting!" came Gladys Putter's voice. She sounded different from before. Piercing and imperious.

Lewis was just in time to duck back as she loomed over Mr Whiting's shoulder.

"You call that an apostrophe?" she barked. Gladys snatched the pen from Mr Whiting, who scrambled aside, timidly clutching his fingers together. From round her neck she removed a set of keys, placing them on the desk and arranging herself above the sheet of parchment Mr Whiting had been copying the records onto.

"The keys," Lewis hissed, nudging Moira with his knee.

Gladys went on harassing Mr Whiting. "You've got to balance your forearm, you twit!"

There was a triumphant skip in Lewis's chest as he followed Moira's honing gaze and, on the desk, he watched as she conjured another snare of electric-green sparks which blistered over the inkpot. Moira's dark eyes flashed. There was a *zap!* And the inkpot flipped onto Miss Putter.

She let out a shriek, her face and cardigan dripping as the ink splotched over the documents.

"I-it wasn't me, Gladys!" Mr Whiting babbled.

"Sakes alive, Whiting, help me!" Miss Putter screeched. "A handkerchief!"

Mr Whiting fumbled in his pocket before leading Miss Putter, her face splattered with ink, out of sight.

Lewis and Moira ducked back, pressed against the wall of the staircase until they heard a door close.

Then Moira snapped into action, skulking across the room like a fox around a bin. Lewis followed closely behind, picking up the keys as quietly as he could and fumbling for one that looked as if it matched the lock of the door marked private.

He wedged the first one in.

It didn't fit.

"Stop jabbing me in the eye!" Miss Putter's voice echoed from down the corridor. "Do you want to blind me, Whiting?!"

"Quickly!" Moira breathed, wringing her hands.

He jammed a silver key into the lock.

There was a *click*.

"Go! Go!" Moira hissed and Lewis wedged the door open with his shoulder and plunged through. The door whooshed shut, and they collapsed in relief on the opposite side.

The room that met their eyes was a large sort of study. It was warmly lit, with a plush carpet and a small circle of six red velvet chairs at the centre. At the head of the circle stood an ornate wooden lectern, with a large tome opened out across it. It looked as if a meeting was about to start. Cabinets and shelves lined every side of the room, crammed with books, records, and boxes with little handwritten tags that read things like, *Porcelain Skull Figurine c. 1807* and *Miniature Callipers – early 16th century, unknown maker*.

"So," Lewis said under his breath. "We're looking for an 'artefact'. But that could mean almost *anything*!"

A photograph in a silver frame caught Lewis's eye. It showed six wispy people with their hands folded standing outside the castle in a neat row, with Sir Hector Marlow at its centre.

Serving Board Members of the
Barrow Historical Society,
1999

Squinting further, he read the names captioned at the bottom:

From left to right:
Miss Gladys Putter (Treasurer),
Mrs Bathsheba Musk (Member),
Leonard Boateng (Member),
Morwenna Stopes (Member),
Sir Hector Marlow Ninth Baronet (Chairman),
Mr Terrence Smythe (Secretary).

"That's the man who used to live in our house," Lewis told Moira, pointing at the thin creature with the hollow cheeks. "Mr Smythe."

"Speaking of which..." Moira breathed, and Lewis turned.

She was standing behind the lectern, next to a shelf laden with heavy tomes. But peering out from behind the books, Lewis could see what she'd spotted. Something brassy, like a clock, that seemed to be attached to the wall.

Moira heaved the books apart with a grunt. Lewis felt as if a cold pair of fingers had walked up his spine.

"Like the one from our chimney," Lewis breathed.

It was a slightly different shape, but the barometer displayed the exact same readings.

"The one in our house was hiding something." Almost instinctively, Lewis wrapped his fingers round the face of the barometer. He twisted. It was stiff, but with a rusty squeak, the dial came away.

Moira watched, her eyes wide as saucers and leaning forward the two of them peered into the dark hole that had appeared in the wall behind the barometer.

"Lewis," Moira whispered. "There's something in there!"

He rolled up his sleeve and reached into the opening, his fingers fumbling until they clenched round something metallic with a cup, and a thin stem.

There was a scrape as his hand withdrew and in the dim light…a rusted goblet appeared. The very sight of it made his arm twitch. *This is it.* The one he had been shown at the bottom of the marshes. The one from the legend, thrust high in the air by the statue of the Bogwitch in the town square.

Lewis let out a shuddering breath.

There was a tag tied round the goblet's stem:

Scrying Goblet

Thanks to the kind donation of Anne Pothecary from the collection of her father Faustus Pothecary.

He turned the goblet in his fingers. The Bogwitch's marking was engraved crudely into its battered side, but other than a large gash in the cup, which looked as if someone had once attacked it with an axe, it looked plain and ordinary.

Reaching into the hole, Lewis felt around again in case he'd missed something. Nothing.

"It doesn't exactly *look* like it's brimming with unspeakable secrets, does it?"

"Herbert thought it was important," Moira reminded him. "You said the Bogwitch showed it to you beneath the water. And, what's more, the Barrow Historical Society have been keeping it behind a barometer. *Just* like the one in your house. Barometers tell you when it's going to rain. And when it rains too much..."

"...it floods," Lewis finished off.

He tapped his chin.

"Those electric powers you've got," Lewis murmured, "you don't just randomly happen to be able to make inanimate objects tell you stuff by any chance, do you?"

"Not everything has to speak in order to tell you things," Moira reminded him darkly, taking the goblet and turning it by its stem. "If it was hers – the Bogwitch's – then I'd bet my last pennies it could tell us more than the *Encyclopedia Britannica* and the *Oxford English Dictionary* put together!"

At that moment, there was a rattle of keys from outside the door.

Lewis sprang into action, slamming the barometer shut and wedging the books back into place. There was a clatter and the pile of books split, sending a stack of them spilling to the left.

Moira floundered cluelessly, as the door began to open, before bowling the goblet across the floor.

Lewis's heart flew into his throat.

With a clang, the goblet clobbered into the table leg before spinning to a gentle halt.

But it was too late to run.

Someone about Lewis's height, their face obscured by the small stack of books they were carrying, appeared in the doorway.

Lewis watched, rooted to the spot.

The figure paused.

And a jet-black head of hair, and a pair of sunken eyes peered out from round the stack.

"H-hi," Lewis said with a feeble wave.

The figure scuffled, sending the pile of books flying out of their arms.

"W-w-what are *you* doing here?" Leopold Marlow

demanded crouching defensively. "You're not supposed to be here – this room is private… Can't you *read*?"

Lewis tried to think of something clever to say, but his throat was dry with panic and instead he blurted out, "We got lost!"

"*Very* lost," Moira added.

Leopold kept glancing furtively towards Moira. As if he were keeping an extra-close eye on her.

Why does he seem suspicious of Moira?

"You're lying," Leopold blurted out, backing towards the door. "This room's not for you. And when my grandfather finds out—"

"Oh? Finds out what?"

Through the door a silver cane emerged, followed by a tweed suit and a soft comb of hair.

Leopold swivelled, cowering as Sir Hector Marlow appeared before them.

"Th-they said they were lost," Leopold stammered. "But they've been snoop—"

"I've never heard of people becoming lost by wandering through *locked* doors," Sir Hector interrupted shrewdly.

There was an uncomfortable silence.

"Why don't you tell me what you're *really* looking for," Sir Hector said. "And if you're lucky enough, I might even be able to help you."

Lewis tried to catch Moira's eye, but before he could do so she blurted out, "We wanted to know about the Bogwitch."

Lewis felt his insides recoil.

"The Bogwitch, eh?" Sir Hector repeated, and for a moment he looked almost amused. "Nasty old creature, you know?"

"We're doing a history project," Lewis added hurriedly.

"What a load of—" Leopold began with a sneer.

"What did I tell you about the way you treat *books*?" Sir Hector butted in sharply, tapping his cane on the floor beside the fallen stack.

Leopold shrivelled as Sir Hector waited for an answer.

"'A-always treat other people's things as if they were your own,'" Leopold muttered and, hanging his head, he crouched down and began to pick them up.

"And don't sulk!" Sir Hector added. "You could do with spending a little more time around books!"

From between the table legs, where he was still gathering books Lewis noticed Leopold steal a fiery glance at him. And for a moment Lewis felt sorry for him. Dad and Mum would *never* say stuff like that to him in front of other people, especially other kids.

Sir Hector hobbled over towards one of the velvet chairs and seated himself on the edge with a groan.

"What little is known about the Bogwitch differs depending on who you ask, as I'm sure you've discovered in your investigations." He smiled, and Lewis felt his unease melt a little at the edges. They *weren't* in trouble?

"But history", Sir Hector continued, "is scattered with people who were wicked to their very cores, so I wouldn't be surprised if one such character had made their way to little old Barrow at some point in our past."

"So, *you* believe in her?" Lewis asked, hoping at least to get some sort of reaction from Sir Hector. "I mean the Bogwitch. *You* think she's real?"

Sir Hector gave him a look that was slightly surprised and disappointed. If it hadn't been for the frosty welcome from Leopold, Lewis might not have been quite so nervous. Sir Hector didn't *seem* terrifying. But from what Martha had told them, the Barrow Historical Society should have been chasing them through the archives right about now.

"I wouldn't like to presume, young Mr Buckley," Sir Hector said. "But if you're after proof that something paranormal is afoot, then I'm afraid I can't help you. Although this old town most certainly has its fair share of ghosts and ghouls. And as the weary passage of time creaks on, sometimes those ghosts become a little ragged at the edges. Their threads weave themselves together. And before you know it you have all manner of strange tales and the real truth so twisted out of shape that it becomes scarcely recognizable."

Lewis glanced down just in time to see Leopold glaring up at him as he reached blindly beneath the table for his last book.

Lewis froze. Leopold's fingertips were only inches from the goblet, propped against the table leg.

"You're...you're saying there *are* ghosts and...strange things here in Barrow?" he asked, trying to draw focus, and hoping Sir Hector would give away even just a little of what the Barrow Historical Society knew.

Sir Hector gave a papery smile.

"Ghosts are merely the things we hide in dark places," he said. "Things we want no one else to see. But every so often, these hidden things slip through the cracks. So in answer to your question. Yes. There are ghosts here in Barrow. Some of them hide in the walls and others stalk the marshes in the dark of night. Why, Marlow Hall is famed for our own little ghost that lives in the West Tower. Did you know? Oh yes. And sometimes, as I carry my evening tea up the stairs to bed, I fancy I hear it. A strange wind, blowing *inside* the walls."

Leopold watched them both as he carried the stack of books over to the shelf and, standing on a chair, began slowly replacing them.

Lewis glanced over at Moira, but her face stayed stony still.

"Am I correct, Mr Buckley, in thinking you were one of the applicants for the Marlow Family Scholarship?"

What is she staring at?

It seemed she was in a deep state of painful concentration.

"Y-yes," Lewis stammered.

From beneath the table, out of sight from Leopold and Sir Hector, there was a faint spark of green, and the goblet rolled lazily out from underneath the table to beneath the chair Leopold was standing on.

A triumphant punch filled Lewis's chest.

Sir Hector frowned. "I gave an address to the applicants before their entrance exam just yesterday and I don't recall seeing you there?"

Lewis tried desperately to focus as, over by the door, Leopold's eyes had begun to narrow suspiciously.

There was another green crackle over the goblet's metallic surface. And, catching on the leg of the chair with a *tink*, Moira raised it into the air and floated it towards the door.

"I-I missed it," Lewis said loudly, just in time to stop Leopold investigating the noise. "It was my fault. I was supposed to be there. But there was an accident and...I couldn't go."

As Leopold prodded the last book into place, his wary frown was replaced with what looked ever so slightly like a sigh of relief.

"Ah," Sir Hector said. "Now that is a shame. I do hate talent to go unused. Your grandfather had a very sharp mind too. Worked for me many years as a cleaner at Marlow Hall. I used to see him working out his chess puzzles on the chequered parquet floor of our grand hall, you know."

Lewis felt his heart rising to a piercing beat. A sheet of sweat had begun to form on Moira's forehead, and he could see her jaw clenching, trying desperately to hold her focus.

"We should be going," he said loudly.

"Are you sure neither of you need directions?" Sir Hector said, looking between the two of them. "Positive you won't end up in a cleaning cupboard thinking it's the car park?"

Leopold let out a snort and folded his arms, but his

grandfather gave him such a piercing glare that he shrivelled once more.

"T-that's alright," Lewis stammered, as he spotted the goblet spinning in mid-air behind Sir Hector.

Leopold's arms slowly unfolded and a look of pure suspicion seemed to creep across his face as his gaze drifted from Lewis to the back wall where the barometer was tucked away.

Lewis felt his nerve unravel.

"We should hurry," he blurted out, snatching Moira by the wrist and dragging her towards the door through which the goblet had just sailed. "Thanks, for your…help."

Lewis pulled the door purposefully closed behind them.

Moira gasped as she lost focus. There was a *zap*! The flickers of electricity seemed to retract. And the goblet toppled towards the floor.

Lewis dived, skidding on the flagstones, and with an awkward jangle it landed between his fingers just inches from the ground.

With surprising team skill, he tossed the goblet to Moira, who caught it clean in her little embroidered bag. And as his heart thumped in triumphant terror, the two of them bolted up the spiral steps, bursting into the sunlight.

"Excuse *me*!" Marjorie the knitting lady's voice came from behind them as they tried to power-walk past her. "How did you—?"

To Lewis's relief, a flustered-looking Celia barrelled

out from behind a dungeon-like grate.

"Lewis! Moira! Heaven's above, *there* you are! We're going for lunch."

Marjorie's suspicious gaze from behind her little horn-rimmed glasses followed them as they made their way across the lawn to the castle cafeteria.

Lewis and Moira waited by their table. Whilst Hereward and Celia scrutinized the menu behind the till, they had a moment to open the embroidered bag and gaze at the goblet a little more closely.

There were words engraved crudely into the blackened base:

For the truths ye seek within mine cup,
Reflect, place one finger, and look up

Lewis looked up at Moira, unable to suppress a grin, hardly daring to believe what they had found.

It looked identical to the stone cup on the statue in the town square.

The mysterious artefact brimming with unspeakable secrets.

The Bogwitch's goblet.

Chapter 19
The Shed

"And what was your favourite part of the castle, Moira?" Celia chimed, glancing in the rear-view mirror as the Winskis' car wheezed its way up the road.

"The, er...the stones," Moira said.

Lewis glanced nervously at Hereward.

As they'd eaten the rubbery serving of calamari and chips at the castle cafeteria, Hereward had fixed his eyes on Moira's embroidered bag where the goblet was hidden. And even when they climbed into the car, he wouldn't stop staring at it.

Did Hereward suspect something? Or was he just being...himself?

"How about you, Lewis?" Celia asked.

The car drew to a halt at the crossing.

A puzzled frown had crossed Hereward's face as he

folded and unfolded his sunglasses, still staring at Moira's bag, which she had tucked by her feet. Hereward's mouth opened and Lewis's stomach clenched.

"Oh, indicators!" Celia said, flicking them on. But just before she could pull out, and Hereward could ask whatever it was he was going to ask, Moira pulled the handle, kicked the door open with her feet and leaped out of the car.

Celia let out a shriek. The engine stalled. And Lewis, Hereward and Cyril the dog were flung forward with a jolt.

There was a sharp *bang* as the car backfired.

Cyril let out a mournful howl.

And Celia hit the horn with her elbow.

"W-wha...?" Celia murmured dazedly in shock. "Wha...Lewis?"

Lewis shovelled himself across the seat, his heart pounding, and scrambled onto the pavement after Moira.

What was she doing?!

Moira had already bolted down the street, her clumpy shoes slapping on the pavement. She skidded to a halt outside a low house on the right, before plunging through the gate, her shorts snagging on the latch for a moment. Freeing herself, she stormed up the steps.

Lewis hurtled after her, panting as he fumbled with the latch. Picketed in the scraggly front lawn was a large yellow sign:

BUCKLEY'S ESTATE AGENTS

And dangling on a smaller sign beneath that:

OPEN HOUSE!

The door was ajar.

"...Moira?" It was Dad's voice. "Sorry about this, Mr Saxon. Moira!"

But on the front door, Lewis had spotted something:

6

The Willows

This was the house Martha's uncle had lived in.

He flew through the door, his spine prickling, colliding almost instantly into something large and soft that let out a parp of shock.

The Deputy Head of Elksbridge Collegiate School, Mr Saxon, gazed hawkishly down at him. "Good *heavens*!" he blasted, his pouchy cheeks reddening as his walrus moustache quivered. "I thought you said this was a *quiet* street?"

The lady with him, who must have been his wife, gave a small scream.

Lewis tried to stammer out an apology as Dad gave him a look of complete incredulity.

"Lewis?! What's going on?"

But Lewis couldn't wait. Ducking past Mrs Saxon as she clutched her handbag to her chest, he ploughed through the darkened rooms of the empty house, his eyes darting back and forth.

He heard the squeak of a door opening from the back

and followed the sound until he came out into a glass conservatory.

Something white flashed out in the garden, and he caught sight of Moira, tearing across the tangled flower beds then stopping, absolutely still, in the middle of the overgrown lawn.

Lewis slipped through the door and picked his way over to Moira. Her eyes were wide, but they didn't look panicked any more. They looked calm. Almost as if something had suddenly made sense to her. Moira was gazing at a tiny wooden shed, its roof cloaked in ivy and twigs, that looked as if it might collapse at any second.

"Moira?"

But she ignored him and began to take great strides towards the little shed.

"Uh, Moira? That's not safe in there," Dad shouted from the back door of the house.

Lewis followed her, half walking half skipping to keep up.

What was she thinking?

Shifting the veil of ivy aside with her elbow, Moira twisted the wooden latch and wedged the door ajar.

The musty smell of compost and damp met Lewis's nose as he followed her inside, ducking to avoid the wafting cobwebs that had settled over the trowels and flowerpots.

"Moira?" he asked again softly. "Are you okay?"

Moira seemed to be looking at each of the walls, as if deciding which of them to choose.

"It was here," she murmured, dropping to her knees and heaving a stack of flowerpots to one side. "It was just *here*."

"What was here?" Lewis asked. "What do you remember?"

Moira felt her way down the wooden boards of the wall until with a *crack* she yanked one of them off. Her hands shot down into the gap between the frame of the shed and the boards and retreated clutching an assortment of items.

Lewis had the distinct sensation that he was seeing something stranger than anything he'd seen before.

A cracked compact mirror, an old cigar tin, a toy metal car, a used lipstick. All of them dusty and faded.

"L-Lewis," Moira squeaked, turning to him as if she were about to be sick. "I think I used to live here. That's how I knew that boy. Herbert. I used to live here. I'm sure of it. This was my house. The Willows. *This* is six Wherryman's Way."

Lewis swallowed, his neck twitching as he heard Dad apologizing again to Mr Saxon and his wife. He didn't want to rush her, but they needed to come up with an excuse for what had just happened and fast.

"M-Moira," Lewis whispered, reaching out to take her hand. "We need to—"

"Don't you *dare* try to tell me what to do!" she reared up, her fingers curling.

But Lewis held his ground, his eyes containing her flashing gaze.

"It's okay," he said calmly. "We just—"

"You're not the one who is *stuck* here, Lewis, not knowing who they are." Her lip quivered with rage. "This was *my* house. *I* lived here. I can see all these faces. These people. These nice people. And I don't know if I'll ever get back, and—"

Her eyes welled. Her arm lowered.

Reaching across, Lewis placed his hand on her heaving shoulder.

Dad poked his head into the shed.

"Lewis," he hissed. "What is going on?! Why aren't you at the castle?"

"Er, we were..." Lewis stammered, and then added quickly when a concerned look crossed Dad's face, "It's just Moira...she's...upset."

"You okay, Moira? Where's Mum?" Dad asked.

"Mr Buckley!" Mr Saxon's voice rang out from the back door of the house.

Lewis floundered, unable to summon so much as a single word.

"LEWIS! MOIRA?!" Celia shrieked across the garden, her keys jangling as she galloped. "Oh, Mr Saxon! Mrs Saxon! Afternoon!"

"I say, Mr Buckley," came Mr Saxon's impatient bark. "The wife and I are going to toddle off. Not sure if this is quite the spot for us. We're looking for somewhere that's less of...a public thoroughfare."

Dad closed his eyes softly for a moment, letting out a disappointed sigh through his nose.

After they'd emerged from the shed and were standing together, awkwardly, in the garden, Lewis had managed to cobble together a garbled excuse about Moira feeling carsick and Celia had swept them off whilst Dad stayed to close the house.

"Poor lamb! She must try holding a lemon on car journeys. Always works for me," Celia informed them. "Goodness, you don't suppose she's allergic to *Cyril* do you?"

Probably quite a few people are allergic to Cyril, Lewis thought.

When they'd pulled up at the house, Lewis had tried to help Moira, but without so much as a word she slipped out of the car and disappeared through the front door.

"Thanks. For the trip to the castle, Celia." Lewis tried to smile, closing the car door and hurrying towards the front steps.

"Lewis?" Hereward was clutching Moira's embroidered bag with one hand on top, one hand underneath.

Lewis's chest ticked.

The goblet.

"Please remember to take all your belongings with you," Hereward said flatly handing it over.

Lewis gave him a blank stare.

"It's what they say. On trains," Hereward explained.

"To make sure people don't leave their stuff."

Lewis waited praying Hereward wasn't about to blow their goblet retrieval operation wide open.

But instead Hereward said nothing at all.

"Thanks," Lewis croaked.

Once he was in the house, Lewis knocked softly on Moira's door. There was no reply. Just a gentle snoring, and when he peered through the crack, he could see she was floating like a lazy piece of driftwood about a foot above the bed. Smiling ever so slightly and dreaming, whilst green electricity glimmered and crackled around her. He couldn't begin to imagine how she felt. How terrifying and frustrating it must be all at once.

Maybe I won't have to imagine. Lewis looked at the collection of dark marks on his hand, trying not to let the thought sit too long.

"Celia called me," Mum whispered behind him, and Lewis wedged the door hurriedly shut. "Moira okay?"

"She's fine," Lewis blurted out. "Just. Er…drifting off."

"Is she really poorly? I really think Badger and Sus— I mean Emerald would want to kn—"

"She's just carsick," Lewis swallowed, trying to sound calm as he guarded Mum from the door. "Said she usually just…sleeps it off."

Lewis left his door ajar in case Mum tried to check on Moira again and sitting on the edge of his bunk removed the goblet from Moira's bag.

He ran his fingers across the gash in its side.

Maybe someone had once tried to destroy it.

The tag round its stem caught his eye as he turned the battered artefact in his hands:

Scrying Goblet

Thanks to the kind donation of Anne Pothecary from the collection of her father Faustus Pothecary.

Wedging out a dictionary from beneath his textbooks he flicked the pages through to S and inched his finger down the page.

Scry (v)

Gerund or present participle: scrying

Foretell the future or gaze into the past using a crystal orb, or other reflective surface.

Lewis read the engraving on the base of the goblet again.

For the truths ye seek within mine cup,
Reflect, place one finger, and look up

There was a creak from the hallway and he stuffed the goblet beneath his pillow. But from behind the door, Moira appeared. She was bleary-eyed, her hair looking as if she'd tried brushing it with a startled hedgehog.

"I'm sorry for running off. And for being angry, Lewis," she murmured, lowering herself to the floor and leaning against the doors of his wardrobe between the half-empty moving boxes.

"It's okay," Lewis told her softly, resting his toes on the rungs of his bunk-ladder. "I-I think it might be my fault. I think I forget that...that you must...miss home, wherever it is. And miss it badly. You must feel scared. And alone."

He was in his own time, with Mum and Dad nearby. His own things. His own clothes. Because although Moira was just a few streets away from the house she had once lived in, she was as far from home as any one person could possibly be.

Moira sat forward, leaning her elbows on her knees and playing with one of the chess pieces on Lewis's board. "I'm scared," she said. "But not alone."

Lewis watched his feet dangling off the edge of the bunk. The chessboard was as he'd left it the night before, the pieces arranged in the pattern of Barrow's windmills.

"Somehow, when I'm with you..." Moira struggled to summon the words. "Even though I don't know who this person I'm supposed to be is, I feel like I know *who* I am. Not my name or anything. Just *who* I am."

The corner of Lewis's mouth twitched. "Me too." He swallowed awkwardly as Moira smiled weakly up at him, but even without catching sight of her palm, the black markings seemed to imprint themselves across his vision.

Three spots on Moira, one of them quickly fading. Two-and-a-bit days to discover how they could stop it. Before a flood came to Barrow. Before the marking finished being passed on. Before he might wake up like

Moira and Herbert, without a clue who he or anybody else was.

And yet as he watched her, fumbling with the button on her embroidered bag, for the first time, Lewis felt a pinch of regret. What if they did manage to get Moira safely back to the Willows a hundred years ago, and he was left here without her? Without a friend in Barrow. It wasn't like his chess-club group chat from back in Woolham had exactly been rammed with messages to come visit or see how he was getting on.

He distracted himself by removing the goblet from underneath his pillow. "I think it shows you things. Magically," he explained sliding down the bunk. "The tag says that it's a *scrying* goblet. I looked it up and scrying means you can see into the past or future."

"You think that's why the Barrow Historical Society were hiding it?" Moira asked. "Because they know what's happened to these kids and they don't want people to find out?"

"Perhaps. Which means it might be able to show us *why* all of this is happening to us; why it happened to those other kids. And then *maybe* we can reverse it. So that we can stop it."

Lewis lowered himself opposite her placing the goblet on the floor between them.

Moira looked thoughtful for a moment then cleared her throat. "Oh great and powerful goblet," she said loudly. "Show us that which we wish to know."

Nothing happened.

"It says that to see the truth, you need to reflect, place one finger and look up."

"Reflect on what?" Moira wondered.

"On what we want the goblet to tell us maybe?" Lewis closed his eyes and tried to bring the thought to the front of his head. "One finger," he placed his finger in the middle of the cup. "And look up."

As his eyes opened, from in front of him there was a ferocious *bang*! A sensation like an electric shock pulsed through his arm and he recoiled, flinging his eyes open just in time to see the goblet shoot up into the air before clattering down in a smoky heap on the floor.

Moira let out a squawk, backing up against the wardrobe.

Lewis flailed, landing on his palms and scrambling backwards like a crab along the floor.

"That was *not* me!" Moira stammered. "I promise."

There was a knock on the bedroom door. Lewis's heart flew into his throat as he threw his hoodie over the top of the goblet.

"Only me!" Dad must have heard the bang. "Whoof! Smoky!" Dad coughed. "You two aren't setting off fireworks in here, are you?"

Lewis gawped, hoping that an explanation would come, but to his amazement Dad chuckled and jangled the set of keys hanging round his finger.

"After what I can only describe as a disappointing first open house," he said, sounding suspiciously chipper, "I was just putting away the keys in the safe downstairs when I got a very interesting call…from none other than *Sir* Hector Marlow."

Lewis felt his joints lock.

Sir Hector must have discovered by now that the goblet was missing.

"He said he ran into you today. At Orkley Castle." Dad smiled knowingly.

We're done for, thought Lewis. "I can expl—"

"Sir Hector told me," Dad carried on, "that he'd never met a young person with such an inquisitive mind and it would be a crying shame for you not to have a shot at the scholarship exam…"

Lewis's mouth fell open in surprise.

"So he's *personally* arranging for you to sit the exam by yourself on Monday before they make any decisions." Dad grinned at him proudly and Moira's wide-eyed gape dissolved into a sceptical frown.

"But—" Lewis began. He didn't understand. Sir Hector had caught them snooping through the *private* collection. Why would he then go out of his way to help Lewis of all people? He hadn't said anything particularly clever, had he?

"I don't know what you did," Dad chuckled, "but you must've said something right. Nicely done, Lewis."

He gave the keys another encouraging jangle before frowning at them. "Oh. Blast. Clean forgot to put the keys back in the safe with all the excitement!"

The door pulled to and Lewis and Moira gawked at one another in disbelief, as beneath the hoodie there was a sizzle and a taunting ribbon of smoke drifted from out of the goblet. As if it wasn't going to give up the secrets they sought so easily. As if it wanted them to try again.

Chapter 20
Scrying

"Three o'clock. It's the only day I can fit you in," Mum said firmly, holding Lewis's cheeks. "Nice and wide for me."

"Mum—" Lewis protested.

Moira was watching with great curiosity across the table.

"Do you *want* dentures aged thirteen?" Mum warned.

Lewis reluctantly opened his mouth and slipped his hands behind his back to hide the marking. With five spots now, it was growing more noticeable.

Mum used her phone torch and squinted in. "Three root canals," she sighed gravely. "Big ones."

Lewis jerked his head away scowling. It was Sunday morning and there were two days left. Two days before the marking transferred completely.

Mum bustled out of the kitchen and Lewis gazed through the window. The sky was a perfect cloudless blue, which made the idea that there was a witch out there cooking up a flood seem even more preposterous than it already was.

"We need to try using the goblet again. To get it to tell us the truth about what's happening to us. And why the marking seems to get passed on," Lewis said in a low voice across the table.

"What if it makes…another *bang,* and starts smoking again?" Moira whispered, as if the goblet tucked inside her embroidered bag could hear them.

"We need to find somewhere else." Lewis tried to think. "Somewhere no one can see."

"Tuesday, ten-thirty. Out the front. The Barrow School Gym, Pillwater Road," came Dad's voice from the living room. He was on the phone with someone arranging a viewing.

As Dad said it, a rogue idea drifted into Lewis's head. An idea he didn't much like. But before he'd had the chance to brush it hurriedly away, Moira gave him a shrewd look, as if the thought had occurred to her too.

At least it would be big and open, Lewis thought. *And with the summer holidays in full swing there'd be no chance anyone would be hanging around.*

Dad kept all the keys for the properties he was selling in a safe in his study, and the code to the safe was something

Lewis had known ever since he could remember.

0711. Lewis's birthday.

But that only heightened the sick feeling in his stomach as he unhooked the keys Dad had labelled:

Barrow School Gym – 11 Pillwater Road

Without a phone, Lewis looked up the route on Mum's laptop; it was only a short zigzagging walk away from the town centre.

The school grounds felt hollow and deserted as Lewis and Moira crept between the empty buildings. It looked just like his old school back in Woolham: ordinary, with faded wood chips in the flower beds and cracked asphalt out the front.

Out the back, it opened up onto faded playing fields with tired football nets. And across the tufty grass, Lewis spotted the dilapidated gym, quite separate from the rest of the school, tucked beside the trees.

Lewis wiggled the keys into the lock just beneath a large red sign taped to the door:

NO STUDENTS
OUT OF BOUNDS!

As they stepped inside the old gym, their footsteps echoed, and the beams above them fluttered with a huddle of pigeons.

A basketball court was marked up on the scuffed floor, and at the edges school chairs and desks were stacked in piles for storage beneath white covers. Bits of scenery from old plays jutted out of corners and dusty textbooks spilled from half-taped boxes.

Lewis placed the goblet inside the centre circle of the basketball court markings. It looked so out of place in the lonely gym. Something from long ago caught in a time to which it did not belong.

Lewis shuddered as he sat down next to the goblet.

"You're fretting?" Moira asked anxiously, sitting opposite him.

"No!" Lewis insisted. "Just...really don't like school gyms."

"It's not all that bad." Moira glanced at a lopsided cabinet of football trophies. "There's a...roof...and... pigeons...and most importantly it's private."

Moira reached out, gingerly placing her finger on the rim of the goblet. "Are you ready?"

Lewis let out a slow breath. Then, "WAIT!" he shouted, as a sudden thought popped into his mind.

Moira's hand recoiled in alarm.

Gripping the goblet with his sleeve, Lewis turned it over again.

For the truths ye seek within mine cup,
Reflect, place one finger, and look up

"How could I have been so stupid!" he realized.

"Scrying means to gaze into the future or past using a *reflective* surface. It doesn't mean reflect as in 'think'. It means reflect as in a mirror, or water."

"So?" Moira said slowly.

"This isn't reflective," Lewis told her. "You need something reflective in order for it to work. *Water* is reflective. It must show you the truths you seek in the *water*."

The tap in the gym toilets squeaked and spluttered with murky brown water as Lewis filled the goblet.

"Er, Lewis?" he heard Moira call out as he carried it carefully back. When he rounded the corner, she was standing at a distance from the centre of the gym, her hands her on her hips. "It just...waltzed on in through a broken window." She pointed and then whispered. "Do you think it's...spying on us?"

A rook was standing on the gym floorboards a short distance from her, its lidless yellow eyes gleaming.

"Caw!" It cocked its head at Lewis.

"Well then shoo it away!" Lewis whispered from the corner of his mouth.

Moira fidgeted. "Can't you do it?"

"I'm holding this, aren't I?" Lewis told her nodding to the goblet. "Use the broom."

Moira reached for the hefty industrial broom leaning on the wall behind her and pushed it gently across the floorboards at arm's length. The rook let out a squawk as Moira ushered it slowly in the direction of the door, its claws clacking on the floorboards until, with an outraged croak, it took to the air, landing on the ceiling beams above them.

"One finger," Moira muttered, reaching out with her finger once they were settled down again on either side of the basketball markings.

Lewis did the same, gritting his teeth.

In unison they leaned forward dipping the tips of their fingers into the water of the goblet.

Lewis flinched.

But again, nothing happened, and when he looked up, Moira had her eyes closed squintily as she wrinkled her nose. "You see anything yet?" she said loudly.

"Nope," Lewis sighed as nothing but a murky cup of water stared back at him.

Moira deflated a little. "One finger," she repeated.

Lewis copied her.

"And look up."

"Caw!" came a feathery rustle from above them.

At that exact moment, their eyes locked. The goblet gave a spluttering gargle, like a blocked sink, and the filthy water bubbled, before draining away to nothing.

But the two of them held their ground.

It sounded as if there was something bubbling deep down inside the goblet. Then, like a tap that hadn't been used in years, the sputtering pitch grew higher as whatever it was drew closer and closer to the surface, until—

Lewis braced himself and Moira took in a great gasping breath.

A dribble of water coughed out of the goblet.

“Do you think it’s—” Lewis began, peering cautiously over the goblet to see if anything had appeared. But almost as soon as he’d opened his mouth, there was a deafening crack and like a fire hydrant exploding into the air, a jet of murky water shot out of the goblet.

The rook shot off its beam with a terrified squawk and began to circle the room.

Lewis tried to topple backwards away from the stream, but his finger was glued inside.

“I’m stuck!” Moira shouted over the roaring din.

The tea-coloured water roared out of the goblet, splashing down in great sloshes as it splattered over the gym floor.

“Me too! Just hold on!” Lewis grunted, baring his teeth and fighting the urge to kick as the water quickly rose.

The gushing grew, thundering in their ears as the trophy cabinet shook and the photos of sports teams and captains shuddered on the walls. The water swelled. It was suddenly above their waists. As if an entire flood were emptying into the gym.

Lewis felt a thumping terror pummel through him. Textbooks bobbed on the surface like fishing boats. The rook, which was now perched on the tip of a punctured school globe, took off and swept past them.

With another surge, the water swelled up to their necks, crashing off the enormous windows as it continued to pour from the goblet.

Lewis’s heart throbbed in panic until a wave slapped against the back of his head. Moira inhaled. And suddenly they were underwater, as if plunged to the bottom of a stormy swimming pool that was filling at tremendous speed.

Lewis opened one of his eyes as his legs flailed out behind him, suspended in the water. In the glow from the windows, he could see trophies, books, play scenery and curtains swirling around him like the wreckage of a ship. Eels emerged through the flotsam and muddy fish darted about in shoals.

But their fingers were still lodged inside the cup of the goblet, and a pressure had begun to build like a gas canister in his lungs, until high above them there was a thundering *crack*, like two ships colliding at sea.

Lewis looked up just in time to see the surface of the water high above them rushing downwards as if it was an enormous bath emptying.

He flung his eyes shut, flinching, clenching until with a gargling *splat*, he felt his finger release from the goblet and he tumbled flat onto his back.

Silence followed.

And with his chest heaving, Lewis opened one of his eyes a scratch, trying to breathe slowly through his nose.

It was night. And, judging by the lumpy cobblestones he was now lying on, they were no longer in the school gym.

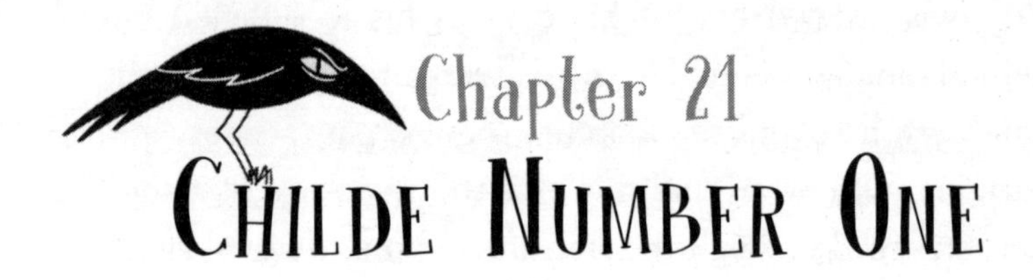

Chapter 21
Childe Number One

The air was damp against Lewis's cheeks.

Cobblestones. Dark windows. The smell of moss.

An alley? Or some sort of very narrow street?

The silver light of a cold moon scoured down from high above them.

"Wh-where are we?" Moira picked herself up and brushed her hands.

Lewis's eyes drifted upwards as a lone bell chimed. And from over the rooftops peeked a crooked church bell tower.

It can't be, he thought to himself.

"Lewis?" Moira whispered.

"I-I think...this is Barrow," he stammered, gathering his bearings. "That's the church with the crooked bell tower. A-a-and this must be Moorings Passage. Where

Tea-Chest Tabitha lived. But…" He crept down to where the alley ended and poked his head round the corner. "It's…different," he murmured gazing at the town square. "There's no fountain, no shops. And…there should be a sign here. Remember?" He pressed his hand flat against the stone wall as a realization came over him.

"Moira," he hissed. "This…this is a long time ago!"

The slapping of feet against cobblestones made both of them startle. A figure slammed round the corner of the alley. Moira gripped Lewis by the forearm and the two of them crouched. A small person, their face in shadow, was pressed against the wall of the alley, panting breathlessly. As if they were also hiding.

"H-hello?" Lewis croaked.

In the shadows the figure let out a whimper. Moira frowned at him in the darkness.

"Erm, excuse me?" she tried again softly, creeping a little closer. "Are…are you alright?" She waited.

"HELLO?"

"What-are-you-doing?!" Lewis mouthed.

"Lewis, I don't think they can hear us!"

Lewis waited, holding his breath. It seemed perhaps Moira was right.

"If the goblet shows us the *truth,*" Lewis murmured uneasily, standing upright, "and right now it's showing us the past, then the reason for why everything is happening must be somewhere in *here*. So, it's like a memory playing out or something. And the closer we are to knowing why, the closer we are to knowing how to stop it."

Moira nodded firmly in agreement. "So who do you think *that* is then?"

The small person peered round the corner, the moonlight catching their wiry rust-coloured hair.

It looked, to Lewis, like a young girl. Her dress was simple and coarse, like the tunics Lewis had seen in paintings of peasants working in fields. But nestled on her shoulder, as if it were as tame as a parrot, was a large black rook.

"Lewis," Moira breathed as the bird's yellow eyes blinked. "What's she doing? I thought the rooks were… evil?"

But Lewis froze as, from down the alley, drifted a hollow voice.

"Child! *Dear* child!"

The girl in front of them stifled a panicked whimper.

"Moira," he whispered hurriedly. "If we're right, and this is the reason everything happens, the flood, the kids somehow appearing years later... Then that must be the first kid it happened to. Child number one, the child from the first address. And maybe she's running from…"

"Sweet chiiiiiiillllld!"

The memory of the cold fingers clamping him round the ankle out on the marshes snared through him.

"T-the Bogwitch." Moira swallowed.

In front of them, the girl stretched out her quivering arm as the rook sidled onto her fingers.

"G-go to the blacksmith!" the girl whispered to the bird. "T-tell him. Tell him what's happening!"

There was a low warble and the rook shot off over the rooftops.

Which blacksmith? Lewis's head pit-a-pattered, but the piercing, guttural wail, nearer this time, interrupted him.

"*Sweet child!*"

And the girl scrambled past them, plunging down Moorings Passage.

"Follow her!" Lewis shouted as she charged ahead of them, pausing only to pound desperately with her fists on the doors as she passed them. "Help!! *Somebody*, please!"

But in the village nothing stirred.

"Anyone?" she shouted at the top of her lungs. "Help! She's coming for me!"

"Why can no one hear her?" Moira panted as Lewis wondered the same thing. "Why aren't they answering?"

The Bogwitch sang out again, and this time Lewis caught the flicker of lantern light out of the corner of his eye. Ahead of them the grassy churchyard, from which the bell tower rose, appeared.

"Where'd she go?!" Lewis babbled, his eyes darting back and forth.

"There!" Moira pointed, storming after the girl as she swung herself over the picket fence and staggered off between the tombstones towards the river's edge.

"I'm not going to hurt you, sweet child! You know what it is I want."

Lewis paused to help Moira untangle her oversized T-shirt, which had snared on the fence.

But up ahead, the girl had paused.

“Why’s she stopping?!” Moira blurted out. “She needs to run!”

But as they watched her twisting on the spot, the silver river glittering behind her, Lewis noticed a flicker between her fingers.

A green glow.

“Lewis,” Moira breathed as they drew slowly closer. “That looks like—”

The girl was whispering as her hand crackled with tiny forks of lightning.

“Do you think that’s—?” he began.

But there was no mistaking that it was the same stormy magic that glimmered inside of Moira.

Lewis felt his spine prickle in the darkness. Taking a deep breath the girl blew on the handful of green flickers. For a second they glowed like fireplace embers, before puttering out and vanishing in a twist of white smoke.

“What’s she doing?” Lewis asked as he drew to closer to Moira.

But Moira remained silent. And the white smoke drifted towards them. Billowing. And growing.

Lewis took a single step back as the cloud wrapped around them, moving like watery ink through the air.

“I-it’s mist,” Moira quivered. “She’s using mist. To hide herself.”

The Bogwitch’s voice rang out from the churchyard. “*Greetel!*”

Lewis swivelled.

Gretel?

He gripped Moira's forearm. But Moira had heard it too.

"Lewis. I thought..." she began slowly, drawing close to him and gazing at the lantern drifting towards them across the churchyard. "Gretel was the Bogwitch's name... So if that's not the Bogwitch, then..."

The two of them slowly turned towards the river.

"*She* is," Lewis breathed.

In front of them, Gretel Murk withdrew a familiar object from the pocket of her tunic.

"The goblet," Lewis murmured.

Misty fingers twisted between the tombstones, breathing and swelling until they were surrounded in a milky labyrinth.

"Lewis," Moira shuddered. "What's going on? That's *Gretel Murk*. *She's* the Bogwitch! But...she's...she's just a girl. She's just like us!"

Lewis's head tumbled. *None of it makes sense. None of it.*

"No need to use those tricks, dear Gretel," the voice from the hooded figure behind them rang out. "You know what it is I want."

"Where'd she go?" Moira squinted and Lewis turned just in time to see Gretel's rusty hair vanish into the fog.

"There!" he hissed, leaping over the tombstone nearest.

Splash!

Lewis's shoe landed in water.

The river.

There was a slosh from nearby, and he caught sight of Gretel crouching between the rushes. She pressed the goblet to her face and closed her eyes. "Keep no secrets," she murmured breathily. "Whomever seeks truth within your cup, tell them what really happened."

In the corner of his eye, the lantern from across the tombstones drew closer. In the distance there seemed to be other lights behind it. More people.

"Where arrrre you, Gretel dear?"

Moira grabbed Lewis's wrist and hauled him behind the nearest tombstone as they crouched, the water lapping. "Lewis. Her *hair,*" Moira mouthed, her terrified face inches from his. "Did you see her *hair?*"

There was a crackling of dry reeds as the hooded figure reached the water's edge.

Lewis peered out from the tombstone.

Gretel's wiry hair was poking out above the water, almost completely disguised against the rushes except for the bubbles wibbling to the surface beside it.

It doesn't make sense, Lewis kept repeating to himself.

"Greeetel!"

Lewis ducked back, pressing his cheek against the mossy grave, watching the reedy patch of water where Gretel was hiding.

Silence followed.

And a thin hand appeared as the cloaked figure waded into the water.

"Ohhhhh, Greeeetel!"

Its fingers were outstretched, just above the rushes.

"Lewis!" Moira squeaked in terror.

With a shriek the hand plunged beneath the surface.

Lewis flinched, and a sudden deluge of dark water came from above them. Everything went black and foggy as the misty churchyard melted like a rainy reflection. And Lewis felt himself tumbling. Plunging downwards as the water receded. Books and chairs flashed past him in the chaos until there was a deafening gargling sound and the soup around them spun.

Light flooded in as the windows of the school reappeared. Desks drifted and water spiralled into a swirling drainpipe. With a hard thud, Lewis felt his body find the floor of the gym, sliding to a halt beside Moira in the water as it poured back into the rattling goblet.

There was a sucking sound, like a noisy straw at the bottom of a milkshake, and the water vanished. The goblet spun like a coin, clattering to a halt at the centre of the circle.

Moira let out a groan from beside Lewis.

"I'm glad we didn't try doing that in your house. Your father would have had a fit."

They were dry again, and the gym was just as it had been before. Undisturbed.

Lewis lay still, his palms ringing from just having slapped the floor. "I don't understand it," he muttered in disbelief. "*That* was the Bogwitch? She's just a kid. And she was…*terrified*."

Moira thought for a moment. "You don't think…she's trying to trick us, do you? The Bogwitch?" Moira suggested. "Showing us things that didn't really happen? It is *her* goblet after all."

Lewis analysed what Moira had said, but somehow it still didn't seem to fit. It had all felt too *real*. Too specific. "Why would she have been so *scared*?" he pointed out. "She was *evil*, wasn't she? Why didn't she just use that electricity or her flooding powers to blast whoever was chasing her?"

They had so little time. Why couldn't things just be clearer?

"Do you think we were right then, about the Barrow Historical Society wanting to keep it hidden? Because they didn't want anyone to see the truth?"

"I don't know any more!" Lewis huffed, rubbing his eyes.

"Lewis," Moira said firmly. "Don't be crotchety. We only have today, tomorrow and then at midnight that's it. Maybe I'll be stuck here. Or maybe *you'll*—"

"I'm not *crotchety*!" Lewis reared up. "I'm scared, because what we just saw makes everything even more confusing and I feel even further away from solving this... mystery than when I—"

Lewis froze.

As the two of them lay recovering on the floor of the school gym, there was a buzzing sound, and high above them a home-made-looking drone hovered.

"Well. That was weird," came a familiar voice.

Lewis and Moira sat bolt upright.

Standing holding the remote control of his drone, with a small name badge that read *Junior Librarian* pinned to his chest, was Hereward Winski.

Chapter 22
The Junior Librarian

"Wh-wh-at are you doing here?" Lewis blurted out as Hereward raised a smug eyebrow.

He was wearing his panama hat and a baggy T-shirt that read, *Keep Calm and Full Steam Ahead.*

"Me?" Hereward scoffed patting his badge. "Oh, I have *every* reason to be here. I come in on weekends to upgrade the cataloguing system at the school library whilst Mum does her holiday tutoring. The *real* question is, what are *you* doing here?"

He had addressed the question specifically to Moira.

"M-me?" she stammered. "I'm—"

"Mum told me that you arrived on the twenty-second of July on an evening train from London," Hereward said matter-of-factly.

Lewis froze.

"And then I got thinking," Hereward rambled on, his panama hat making him look far more adult than he really was. "That day I was trainspotting at Hogweed Bridge, just outside of Barrow, and I didn't see a *single* train."

Lewis swallowed and Moira threw him a terrified glance as it felt like part of their game might be up.

"There was a rail replacement service due to inclement weather," Hereward said, the look of a self-satisfied detective about him. "So, Moira, just how did you get here?"

They didn't have time for this. They had what remained of today and tomorrow before the marking was transferred completely from Moira to Lewis. Before he forgot everything and perhaps even woke up in another time.

Lewis squeezed his fingernails into his palm. "Cool story. W-we should be going. Dentist appointment," Lewis stammered, pulling his rucksack up as Moira stowed away the goblet and skirted around him. "Good seeing you again, Hereward."

"Faustus Pothecary," Hereward blurted out. "I can show you something. Something about him."

Lewis reluctantly slowed his pace. Faustus Pothecary was the man whose daughter gave the goblet to the Barrow Historical Society. "What about him?" Lewis shrugged, trying not to seem overly interested. "Why would we care?"

"Oh, I don't know," Hereward said softly. "Maybe because of...that goblet you stole?"

Lewis and Moira stopped dead in their tracks.

"You know, the one inside Moira's bag?" Hereward clarified.

Lewis and Moira shared an anxious glance.

"Yeah. I saw it in your hoodie in the car the day we went to the castle," Hereward said knowing he had their attention. "But first, you gotta tell me what's going on, starting with *how* Moira got to Barrow."

"On foot," Moira lied.

"Oh, Moira, Moira, Moira." Hereward shook his head. "You can't expect me to believe that. Really, now. What's all this research about? What's so urgent?"

Moira threw Lewis an uncertain glance, but at this late stage Lewis felt like they'd be foolish not to at least hear Hereward out.

"Moira isn't from now," Lewis began. "She's from another time. And the Barrow Bogwitch, we think she's real. We think she's up to something. And that if we don't stop her, some really terrible things are going to happen. To us."

Hereward stared blankly for a moment.

"You see this is why I don't read fiction." He shook his head. "Overexcites people."

Moira opened her mouth in outrage, but Lewis tactfully interrupted. "I know it sounds absurd. But, Hereward, please," Lewis insisted. "You can't tell *anyone*. Not even your mum."

"Oh, don't you worry, Lewis." Hereward winked patronizingly. "My lips are sealed."

Moira gave Hereward a deathly scowl out of sight. But

Lewis didn't care. Provided Hereward didn't tell anyone he could think whatever he liked.

"When I saw the name 'Pothecary' on that tag round its stem, I knew I'd seen it before," Hereward explained to them as they walked at pace towards the school library. "And then I suddenly thought: railway guides."

In front of the school, Celia's lemon car with the white stripe was parked outside.

Carrying his drone in his outstretched palm like a baby bird, Hereward pushed through the double doors, on the other side of which Cyril was curled up round an umbrella stand.

The Barrow School Library felt pleasantly familiar. The books weren't like the gilded tomes at Elksbridge. They were well thumbed and friendly. Like his library back in Woolham.

"One hundred and sixty-nine doesn't *have* a square root though..." whined the voice of Celia's tutoring student from over near the library tables.

"Well," Celia coughed patiently. "I'm afraid it does."

Hereward tried to sneak them past the furthest shelves, but he could not escape Celia's wily little eye.

"Hereward? Is that you? Oh! You've found some friends!" she chimed, swivelling her chair round. "Good job!"

"You don't have to act *so* surprised," Hereward scowled, ushering Moira and Lewis towards the back of the library.

From behind Celia, a slicked head of jet-black hair poked out.

Leopold Marlow shot out of his seat. His fist balled as he clutched his pencil.

"Wh-what are they doing here?!" he demanded.

"*I'm* a Junior Librarian," Hereward said puffing out his chest.

"S-sorry," Lewis blurted. "We were just—"

Celia put her arm kindly round Leopold, who was glaring venomously, and focused him back on his work.

Hereward rescued a set of keys from behind the library information desk, and led them up a set of narrow stairs that was cordoned off with a rope to a small mezzanine floor. Wedged in the corner was an old computer on a small desk beside some tired-looking sofas and a neat section of textbooks.

"This area is only for teachers and junior librarians," Hereward explained proudly.

"Hereward," Lewis coughed, stepping over a patched-up beanbag. "Not to be rude, but…if you have… information…we're sort of…running out of time."

"It's difficult to explain," Moira added quickly.

"Yes," Hereward said, lifting the key and leading them over to a transparent plastic cabinet, in which a modest assortment of older and more important-looking books were kept. "As I was saying…railway guides."

Unlocking the cabinet, Hereward withdrew a particularly exhausted-looking, red pocket-sized volume with gold lettering and handed it to Lewis.

Babbage's Guide to British Railways

"But what's this got to do with..." Lewis began, and then lowered his voice. "With Faustus Pothecary and the goblet?"

"Let me get there," Hereward said patiently. "There were loads of railway guides in the Victorian era. They told you about different towns you could visit and gave you tips on where to stay, what to do and what to eat. Sort of like an old-timey TripAdvisor."

Moira gave him a puzzled look, but Lewis just shook his head, unsure he'd be able to explain to Moira how internet "reviews" worked.

"*Babbage's Guide to British Railways* went out of print almost immediately because Lucinda Babbage gave too many honest opinions, and lots of people got offended by her. Copies grew scarce. But lucky for you, of the very few books in the restricted section of the Barrow School Library, there happens to be one."

Lewis locked eyes with Moira before slowly lifting the gilded front page.

"What are those spots on your hand?" Hereward asked sharply as he noticed Lewis's palm. "It's not dirt, is it?"

"B-birthmark," Lewis stammered, closing his fingers over the marking.

"I see. Please," Hereward gestured to one of the sofas once he was satisfied.

Moira leaned over Lewis's shoulder as they lowered

themselves between the manky cushions.

"I'd recommend the section on Barrow." Hereward produced a magnifying glass in a felt sleeve from over near the desk. "You'll need this."

"Thanks, Hereward," Lewis smiled softly.

"Don't mention it." Hereward dropped into a beanbag and, hauling his drone towards him, began fiddling with one of its LED lights.

Lewis took a deep breath and turned through the first few pages of delicate binding. The inside cover had been attacked multiple times with an array of crayons, pens and pencils.

It read: *Babbage's Guide to British Railways – complete with local maps and illustrations.* Lewis flicked through the ransacked pages. In some places entire sections of the book were missing.

"Bagwater, Bark-*something*, Barmby, Barnstaple…" he muttered, his finger trailing down the page. "Barrow."

Lifting the book a little he read: "BARROW – *a damp, unremarkable township at the heart of the Snoring Broads. With its lumpy mattresses and inadequate furnishing, accommodations can be found at the Wherryman's Windmill Inn. Prices are moderately affordable, but the author wishes to stress that on no account should the weary rail enthusiast be tempted by the 'surprise pie'. See appendix 16 for train timetables from Great Reedmouth.*"

"Charming," Moira snorted. "I can see why she wasn't exactly a bestseller."

Lewis breathed through his nostrils as he skimmed the

page, hoping there was going to be a point to all of this. His eyes landed on *Places of Possible Interest*.

"Places of Possible Interest," he read. *"There is little to recommend in Barrow for the curious excursionist, but if you are in the market for third-rate examples of Norman architecture and tired old bridges, please see the author's selection of the least tedious attractions below."*

His eyes went on flitting until, beneath Orkley Castle – which said something about it being a *tiresome place not fit for picnicking* – he finally caught sight of the word "Pothecary":

> Nearby for refreshment is the Merry Barnacle Inn, but do not trust the standards of hygiene there, for I found concealed in my soup what I am convinced was a recently deceased moth. This ho nothing compared to the grease-coated tea served coffee in
>
> at the bottom of which was a most alarming residue that I am positively resigned to believe caused me an upset stomach and a night of terrible quaking.
>
> HOGWEED BRIDGE – a feeble stone structure across the Hogweed Quarry on the southern road from the township. Upon visitation of Hogweed Bridge, the author was accosted by a vagrant wh alleged that the stones beneath the bridge ar

site whereon a local folklorist
Faustus Pothecary is said to have
Inscribed a curse

and chisel.

The story is of course apocryphal, but rail enthusiasts can enjoy a respectable view of passing engines on the East Snoring Line.

"*Faustus Pothecary, is said to h have inscribed a curse,*" Lewis read, his cheek twitching. "Moira, do you think tha—"

But Moira had realized something.

"Shhh!" she hissed flipping the page back and forth.

"But Moira," Lewis babbled. "*–arrow* must be *Barrow*, and if there's a cur—"

But Moira smothered one hand over his mouth as she read the reverse side of the page they'd been looking at: "*If you're in Catwick for the purposes of partaking of its culinary delights, steer well clear of the Pig and Porter, where the only thing you're likely to be served is a large helping of disappointment. Instead, try the sustenance on offer at Mrs Maggs's Eatery for Gentlefolk, however this author—*"

Moira looked up at him. Her hand dropped, and the words fell from Lewis's mouth as if he'd said them a thousand times over, "*...wouldn't recommend the quail salad.*"

A pincer-like shiver made his shoulder blades flinch.

Scrambling, he flipped back a page.

"It was from here. Herbert's clipping..."

Moira dived into her bag, ferreting about until she fished it out.

And as it slotted perfectly into place, they read:

was a recently deceased moth. This however was nothing compared to the grease-coated tea cup I was served coffee in at
at Orkley Castle: an artefact brimming with unspeakable secrets, hidden
at the bottom of which was a most alarming residue that I am positively resigned to believe caused me an upset stomach and a night of terrible quaking!

"Hogweed Bridge – a feeble stone structure, built across the Hogweed Quarry on the southern road from the township. Upon visitation of Hogweed Bridge, the author was accosted by a vagrant who alleged that the stones beneath the bridge are the site whereon a local folklorist
Fastus Pothecary is said to have discovered inscribed a curse upon the township's young by a vengeful Barrow local using a smith's hammer and chisel.

Lewis felt his heart begin to drum against his ribcage.

"Lewis," Moira breathed. "Herbert must have found this *exact* book. And quail salad had nothing to do with it!"

"It was about a curse," Lewis murmured, "on the kids of Barrow...inscribed on the stones *beneath* the bridge. We need to find out what it says. This book says the person laying the curse was *vengeful*. The Bogwitch made the curse, so a 'wrong' that must have been done to her. If we know precisely what the curse *is*, maybe what we saw in the goblet will make sense."

"And if we know all that," Moira went on. "Maybe we could put that wrong *right*. And we can stop it, Lewis!"

For the first time since the rook had landed on his windowsill, Lewis felt answers were within their reach. They were close. Very close.

"Useful then?" Hereward asked.

"Hogweed Bridge," he said hurriedly as Hereward replaced the book and locked the cabinet. "Did you say you go train watching there?"

"Train-*spotting*," Hereward corrected him, poking the magnifying glass back into its sleeve. "And yes. I do. Why?"

"Can you show us where it is?" Lewis asked glancing at Moira. "I wouldn't ask...normally. But, it's...it's kind of urgent."

Hereward gave a doubtful grimace and, shuffling his sleeve up, glanced at his watch.

"Hmm. I'm not sure, but if we leave now we should be just in time to see the two-seventeen to Great Reedmouth."

Chapter 23
Hogweed Bridge

As Lewis, Hereward and Moira turned out of the school driveway, Lewis glanced back at Leopold. He had finished his tutoring session with Celia and was sitting on the edge of a flower bed, tossing rocks at a squashed pine cone in the car park as he waited for someone to collect him.

"Wh-what are *you* looking at, *Buckley*?" Leopold snarled. If anything, Lewis had been trying to give him a half smile. But Leopold's tone made him quicken his pace.

"Is he like that all the time?" Lewis asked quietly.

"Mostly," Hereward sighed. "Mum says he's just an unhappy kid and that it's up to *me* to be patient. But nobody's got time for *that*."

Lewis remembered the way Sir Hector had spoken so sharply to Leopold. It must have felt humiliating. And if

Leopold didn't like feeling humiliated, he *definitely* wouldn't have liked Lewis stumbling across him during his tutoring session.

"No wonder he doesn't smile," Moira said softly. "What a grumpy puss."

"Oh he does smile." Hereward turned to her. "Just sometimes. When he finally understands something Mum's trying to teach him…or when he twists your arm with other kids watching."

But Lewis felt his eyebrows crumple a little as, without looking back, he thought about Leopold sitting on the edge of the flower bed. Feeling humiliated, even a little bit, was horrible. Like Dad had made him feel after he'd missed the exam.

Hereward shuffled into a ditch on the roadside and Lewis and Moira followed, clambering up the other side and making their way along the row of brambles until a path opened up in the clump of woodland beside them. As they picked their way between the birch trees Lewis caught sight of a crossing sign up ahead.

"Is-is that Hogweed Bridge – where the East Snoring Line crosses?" Lewis asked as the arch of brick which spanned the gap between the two faces of stone slipped into view.

Moira broke into a run.

"Yes," Hereward told them, clutching his hat and satchel as he tried to keep up. "But there's no need to hurry! There are still three minutes before the two-seventeen!"

The bridge with the railway tracks feeding across it was old and mossy. Cordoned off with a wire fence, it was suspended between two large mounds of rock, at the bottom of which flowed a shallow creek.

"How do we get down there?" Lewis panted as he drew to a halt against the white wooden barrier at the top of the embankment, pointing to below the bridge.

What does a curse even look like? he wondered.

Hereward arrived beside them, carrying his drone as if it were a pet hawk, but before he could catch his breath, Moira was already clambering over the barrier.

She inched down at first, but then broke into a run as the steepness of the slope overcame her, landing with a small splash on the stones at the bottom of the creek.

Lewis followed, skidding to a halt at the bottom beside a clump of plastic bags snared on the banks of the creek.

"Er, shout if you need me," Hereward called down to them with a reluctant wince.

There was a sudden whir and, like a mechanical kite, the drone took to the air buzzing high above them as Hereward guided it on the soft currents of wind.

For a second, Lewis felt like he ought to remind Hereward that flying his drone so close to the tracks could end up with it being smashed to smithereens, or worse. But he had bigger fish.

He gazed beneath the bridge. Somewhere in that dripping, mossy throat a curse was chiselled into the stone. Knowing what the curse said was one thing, but whether there would be a way to lift it, get Moira home and stop him from being transported to some other time altogether, Lewis did not know. And even if there was, they had little more than twenty-four hours to piece together what other parts of the puzzle were yet to be revealed.

"You ready?" he asked, his breathing becoming heavy.

Moira gave an uncertain nod.

The mouth of the tunnel that ran under the bridge swallowed them up as they picked their way upstream.

They scanned the rocks, searching the crevices defeatedly. But even as they tried wiping at the grime with their bare hands, only blackened stone stared back at them.

"Nothing," Lewis choked, peering up at where the bridge met the rock face as hard as he could. "You?"

Moira shook her head.

There can't be nothing, Lewis told himself. *There can't.* And shoving his foot into the nearest crevice, he tried to lift himself up to see if there was anything higher up that they hadn't spotted.

But as he felt along the slimy rock for a crevice, his fingers slipped. And his trainer lost grip. With an awkward tumble he fell, elbows first, into the babbling creek. There was a sharp sting beneath the water as his palm met with something jagged. An irritable flare of frustration caught him off guard and, scrambling to his feet, Lewis kicked the rock as hard as he could. But his other shoelace snagged on a twig and he stumbled backwards over an abandoned tyre.

"Lewis, are you—"

"NO!" he howled.

Snatching up a pebble, he flung it at the rock where it ricocheted into the water with a pathetic plop. He could feel the fearful rage pulsing like bursts of radiation inside of him. How had they come so far and navigated their way through so many clues, only to wind up in a manky underpass with nothing but rocks and a creek that wouldn't SHUT up?!

The crossing signal on the bridge above them began to clang repeatedly.

"Lewis," Moira said softly. "We need to remain cal—"

"So many stupid clues! So many stupid, stupid, stupid half pieces of information with nothing making any sense!" Lewis bellowed. He could feel the waves of electricity welling inside of him. As if somehow his terror was turning them up in powerful prickling bursts. "I'm sick of it! SICK OF IT!"

And with all his might he clenched both his fists as hard as he could and flung them at the rock.

The train flew over the top of them, the bridge aching and clattering.

And from Lewis's fists there was a *green spark*...

He backed away, colliding into Moira as the two of them clung to each other.

Glimmers of green lightning blistered over the rock. Burrowing. Releasing.

Lewis's chest pounded as a shaking weakness filled him.

It had come from him. The sparks. The green

electricity. *He* was somehow making this happen.

The tendrils of light jabbed and cracked into the stone, chiselling. And from beneath their glow, words began to appear. Until, with a fizzle, the lights puttered out, and the curse lay before them.

Lewis felt for Moira's muddy fingers and squeezed.

WHEN FLOODS ARISE A CHILD BE TOOK,
FOR MY PRECIOUS ONE YE STOLE.
AS EACH REPLACE THE NEXT-IN-LINE,
WHEN WATERY MARK COMES WHOLE.

I BIND THIS CURSE WITH IRON RING,
WITH MALICE AND INTENT.
AND CALL UPON THE CURSING GODS,
FOR STORMY STAY UNBENT.

UNTIL WHAT LIES NEATH LINTEL WINGED,
IS BROUGHT TO FORGE AND ME.
FORGOTTEN SHALL THESE CHANGELINGS
WAKE. FORGET FOREVER BE.

A stinging numbness blistered through Lewis as the two-seventeen to Great Reedmouth shot off into the distance. The clanging signal subsided and they were surrounded again by nothing but the creek and the distant buzz of Hereward's drone.

Lewis felt faint as the words babbled from his mouth. "We were right." His voice was scratchy. "*When floods arise a child be took*. Kids were being taken when it flooded. Held until the next flood came. And..."

He reread the words, hoping he'd skipped something. Missed something. "*Each replace the next-in-line*." He pointed, his fingers shaking uncontrollably. "Watery mark. That's the marking. All of them had it. Child number one replaced child number two, two replaced Tea-Chest Tabitha, Tabitha replaced Herbert. Herbert... he-he replaced you. You were living at the Willows, with your family. And he took your place, which is why he had flashes of living in that windmill...with his real family. And now you—"

He stopped. His throat sore. Rasping. Not daring to catch Moira's eyes. "A-and now you'll replace me. In my family. And you'll be stuck here. And I'll be somewhere else, until at some point in the future when there's next a flood I'll wake up. Not knowing who I am. And everyone I ever knew will have forgotten I ever existed. You're a... you're a..."

He searched for the word that the curse had used. Anything not to look at Moira.

"A *changeling*," he breathed. "And tomorrow...I will be too."

Moira's breathing quickened.

The words pierced his chest, a stabbing terror gnawing through him.

Mum. Dad.

Lewis gazed down at his shaking palms, the sixth marking coming steadily into view. The echoing stream became almost deafening in his ears. And through it all he heard a drowning ticking as the two faces of the chess clock counted down in his head.

Tick,

click,

click,

click...

An aimless fury forged inside him. He didn't know where it came from. Just that he could feel a poisonous rage seeping through him. And Moira was there. The only person in the world who understood how he felt.

"Lewis, I—" Moira reached for him.

He jerked away from her, stumbling.

"You're going to steal my life, Moira," Lewis whispered, his mouth contorting as he tried to keep his lips from trembling. "Mum and Dad...they'll probably wake up one morning thinking that they must have always had a daughter. I'll just see their faces...in my dreams. And maybe they'll see mine. But they won't remember who I am."

Moira burst into tears.

"A-and you'll be *here,*" he choked.

"W-what do we do?" she sniffed. "I-I'd never want anything bad to happen to you, Lewis. H-how could I ever want to hurt *you?*"

Lewis felt his eyes becoming hot, and he let out a shuddering sob as Moira ploughed defiantly through the water towards him, wrapping her arms round his shoulders.

"It just..." he began haltingly. "It just struck me. So clearly, that...whatever happens...whether we work to stop the curse or not. Whichever way we look at it. We're never going to...to see each other again. You're the only person who will ever know how this is feels. And I'll never see you again."

He sniffed.

"It hurts, Moira."

Moira was quiet for a moment.

"Everyone makes us feel hurt at some point or another, Lewis," she whispered softly. "But just sometimes you meet someone who's worth feeling hurt for."

Silence fell.

And the creek trickled over the strange forgotten debris around them.

There was a *thwack* from outside the tunnel, followed by a cry of pain.

"You think you can make fun of me? Huh, Train Boy?"

Lewis's gaze shot down to the opening of the tunnel, just in time to see Hereward's battered drone fall from the sky with a *crash* as it landed on the gabbling stones.

There was a grunt. And Hereward toppled down the slope, his remote control clutched in his hand as he landed in a heap beside the shopping trolley.

Leopold stormed down the rise, a gnarled branch in his hand. He waded past the groaning Hereward and began demolishing, whacking, smashing the drone against the rocks.

"Let's. See. How. High. You. Fly. Now!" Leopold seethed.

Hereward heaved himself up on his elbow.

"S-stop," he said faintly. "Please."

But Leopold kept thwacking. And Lewis could feel his humiliation. A blind fury in his eyes as flints of motor and propeller splintered in the air.

"Lewis!" Moira gasped.

But Lewis was already striding down the tunnel. Knowing where he wanted to send his anger flying, as Leopold drew closer, and closer until he was so close Lewis could see the whites of his wild sunken eyes.

Lewis lashed out and shoved him. "Get. LOST!"

Leopold staggered and as he righted himself his gaze drilled into Lewis as a renewed plume of hot anger smoked through him.

"Or what?" Leopold taunted him. "You're going to *fail* that exam, Buckley. You're going to *fail*. Just see how your loser Dad likes it when—"

Lewis felt both hands shoot out in front of him.

There was a jolt through his fingers as they curled.

A green, electric bolt. Like a shard of iridescent lightning that daggered through the air. And Leopold was kicked backwards, the stick flying from his hand as he tumbled over the stones and into a sloshy heap.

Hereward's mouth fell open so wide Lewis was surprised his jaw didn't make a splash in the creek.

"GO!" Lewis shouted, doing his best to sound threatening.

Leopold staggered on the stones, his feet slipping.

"T-t-that was—" he stammered, his eyes swirling with dread as he pointed at Lewis then at Moira. As if he expected the next bolt of electricity to come from either of them. But with a scramble, Leopold scarpered up the embankment as fast as he could, vanishing over the barrier.

Hereward staggered upright, still gasping.

"Would someone, please, please for the love of non-fiction tell me what's going on?" Hereward wheezed cradling the shattered remains of his drone, as they jogged into town.

Lewis glanced at his watch as they hurried back past the school towards Orsman Road.

15:06

Mum would be still waiting for him at the clinic. But it didn't matter. In his heart he knew she'd understand. If he could tell her. If he could explain what was really going on.

"You shoved him." Hereward replayed the scene over to himself. "Lightning. *Kaboom.* He flies backwards."

"But what could this *precious one* from the curse be?" Moira panted. "It must be the *reason* for the curse. Something that was stolen from the Bogwitch? The goblet maybe?"

"I don't think so," Lewis wheezed. "The curse said that it will keep going until whatever lies beneath the *lintel winged* is returned. There must have been something else that was taken from the Bogwitch. Something precious to her."

"But what even *is* a lintel winged?"

"Lintels are stones that sit above a doorway in old buildings," Lewis gasped. How he hated running. "The curse says it's 'winged'. So maybe it's shaped like wings, or has wings on it or something like that. So perhaps we need to find out where there are lintel stones in Barrow. Churches. Castles. Halls. Anywhere. Then, when we've found the right one, maybe we'll be able to bring whatever lies beneath it back to the Bogwitch."

"And the *forge*, the place this thing is supposed to be brought back to, that must be out on the marshes," Moira explained. "In that origin tale of Gretel Murk you told me about, she was found as a girl by an elderly blacksmith, and she bewitched him: a blacksmith who lived in a *forge* on the marshes."

"Exactly," Lewis agreed. "We have until midnight tomorrow. It was exactly midnight when you knocked on our door that night. I remember my watch beeping."

He stopped dead in the street.

His heart was already racing, but suddenly it drew to a painful peak.

Two police cars, their lights flashing, were parked outside the Buckleys' house.

Chapter 24
A Postcard Moment

Lewis broke into a run, his legs dizzyingly light as he pounded down the paving slabs, and burst through the front gate with Moira calling after him.

Three police officers, who were standing in the driveway, unfolded their arms as he flashed past them.

He barged through the open door, flinging down his rucksack as he skidded into the kitchen.

"What is it?!" he blurted out in panic. "Is someone hurt? What's wrong?!"

Mum was staring blankly, her arms folded as she rested against the counter. Dad was leaning against the fridge, playing with his wedding ring. And standing beside the kitchen door he had just flown through was a police officer, who seemed, of all things, to be watching something on Mum's phone.

"Mum?" Lewis croaked, but Mum said nothing. He caught sight of the phone in the officer's hand. A video was playing. Snowcapped peaks. Mountains. And then—

"Juuuuuuuune," Badger yodelled. *"Messages not sending to George. Could you pass on? It's an absolute belter of a day here in the high peaks. Here's Emerald. Say hello, babe."*

"Hiii," Emerald simpered dreamily.

"And theeere's Moira." Badger grinned. *"Say hi, Moira."*

A breathless freeze withered through Lewis, into his fingers, his bones, his feet, as it glued him to the floor.

Moira Wigby-Polkinghorne. The *real* Moira Wigby-Polkinghorne came into view, looking just as ready to clobber someone's finger with a hockey stick as Lewis had remembered her.

"Just to say." Badger rambled on. *"Terrible reception up here so couldn't send this sooner. But got George's message. Decided to bring the little rascal along with us, eh."*

Badger gave the real Moira Wigby-Polkinghorne a nudge with his elbow.

The video ended with a close up of Badger's foot.

Tick,

click,

click,

click.

Stooping, the officer peered out of the kitchen window and handed the phone back to Mum.

"Is that the girl, Dr Buckley?" He pointed towards the driveway.

Mum gave a nervous nod.

Lewis felt his stomach rearrange itself, like a plastic bag being turned inside out.

"I…w—" His throat cracked as a watery taste filled his mouth.

He could hear voices. Soft voices out the front.

"Our job right now is to keep you safe, okay?" he heard someone say. *"We're going to just need to get a little bit more information from you, alright? Can you just give us your real name there, love?"*

They were speaking to Moira.

"No," Lewis croaked, shaking his head. "No, no, no—"

This couldn't be happening. Not now. Not now.

"We're going to issue a police protection order and take her down to the station," the officer in the kitchen said calmly, "check for missing children in the area and get social services to find her somewhere to stay until we've worked out what's going on."

"NO," Lewis spat, louder this time as his legs trembled. "You don't understand. You're not *listening*!"

"Lewis," Dad said. "We need to keep very calm now, okay?"

"CALM?!" Lewis squawked bewilderedly.

"Uh, we're going to need your son to make a statement at some point," the officer said softly. "Whose details should I take?"

"Mine," Dad sighed, reaching for the notepad the officer had produced and beginning to write.

Lewis's face felt numb, as if he'd just been stung. He couldn't think. And the watery feeling in his stomach was building in a gut-wrenching crescendo.

"I'm...so sorry about all this, officer, honestly..." Dad went on. "I'm just...shocked that we didn't realize what was going on. I feel like we're to blame."

"Well at least she's safe," the officer added. "We'll make sure she gets somew—"

"AREN'T YOU LISTENING TO ME?!" Lewis bellowed his arms flailing as he turned to Mum. "WE'VE GOT TO STOP IT FROM HAPPENING. IT'S A CURSE. THERE'S. A. CURSE!"

"Lewis," Mum pleaded in alarm. "Please. I know this is really, *really* hard. But can you just stop with this for a minute and we'll explain what we know."

"YOU DON'T KNOW *ANYTHING*! THERE'S GOING TO BE A FLOOD AND WORSE IF WE DON'T STOP IT!"

He bolted to the window, his heart thudding.

A wreath of arms had surrounded Moira, gently guiding her to the police vehicle as her eyes brimmed with terror. Hereward, who was still clutching his butchered drone, watched on in open-mouthed amazement.

"I just...can't believe that was...a stranger. In our house," Mum murmured. "All this time and we didn't notice. Why *our* house? How did she kno—"

He had to go and help Moira. He had to stop them.

"MOIRA!" Lewis bellowed, his breath hot against the glass.

"*Lew*is!?" Mum gasped, sounding shocked, but he didn't care.

Diving round the table he ducked past the officer and made for the door. But Dad was too quick for him, budging his hand against the door frame, barricading it as Lewis tried to squeeze past him.

"Lewis, this has to be done," Dad said in a strained voice. "This is what's best for her."

Mum's hands were suddenly on his shoulders trying to comfort him as he struggled. But his stomach was churning and his forehead beading with sweat.

He was going to be sick.

He pushed against Dad's arm, catching flashes of Moira through the open door, her terrified gaze searching for him. Waiting for him to help.

"PC Harvey, could you make the car nice and comfortable for us?"

"FIND IT, LEWIS, FIND IT!" she shouted. "THE LINTEL WITH WINGS! FIND IT!"

She sounded utterly crazy, but not to him. "MOIRAAA!" he cried hoarsely back. "MOIRAAAAAAAAA!"

"We'll take it from here, Mr and Mrs Buckley," the officer said grimly, sidestepping them. "You've done the right thing. I'll give you a call a little later, yes?"

Lewis yanked himself free from Dad, skidding into the living room as he slammed against the window.

Moira was inside the car, her hands pressed up against the glass.

"She's...she's going to be okay, isn't she, officer?" he

heard Mum say. "Can you please call if she needs anything, anything at all?"

"Of course," the officer said quietly.

Lewis's eyes became foggy. Thick with tears. He could hear the first police car with Moira in it pulling away but he couldn't see anything.

Mum was suddenly beside him and he felt her hands round his wrists as she led him in a daze to the sofa.

"Y-y-you can't," he choked. "You can't let them take her, Mum."

Mum pushed her hair behind her ears and sat herself next to him.

"We were calling you non-stop? Where's your phone?!"

He said nothing.

"Lewis," Mum began hesitantly "...did you...*know* she wasn't who she said she was? Is that why you've been acting strangely this past week?"

The front door closed and Dad appeared, his arms folded. But Lewis said nothing. He couldn't. Not when no one was listening to him.

"Lewis," Mum sighed raggedly, pinching the bridge of her nose. "You're seriously telling me that you *knew* she was a complete stranger and you didn't say *anything*? I know we let her into the *house*. But...you *knew*? All this time?"

Lewis's body squirmed and a hot feeling returned to his eyes.

"Where are they taking her?!" he croaked weakly. "What have you done?!"

"You have to realize…" Mum sighed. "There's nothing else we *could* do. We've got no idea where she comes from, or who she is. Lewis…you know it could be *dangerous* to have a complete stranger like that in our house? What was she doing?"

"You wouldn't believe me!" Lewis shuddered, feeling cold, and small.

Dad massaged his brow. "This is *so* unlike you, Lewis. What's going on? We trust you. We always have. And I'm not saying we're not to blame as well. But…but how could you be *so* irresponsible that you'd pretend that girl was somebody else?!"

"*Pretending* is all you ever do!" Lewis snapped, flapping his hands at the blotchy peeling wallpaper. "Look at this place: it's a *dump*! Your whole *life* is about pretending! You do it with the houses you sell, you do it with your friends. You even did it on my *scholarship* application!"

Mum frowned. "What's he talking about?"

"Yep." Lewis twitched. "He lied. He put cricket. I *don't* play cricket. And now you've ruined it. You've ruined everything. And if I never see either of you again, it'll be your fault."

He curled up in the corner of the sofa, pulling his knees to his chest. Wanting to sink between the gap in the cushions.

Mum's hand found his forehead.

"He's boiling hot," she whispered to Dad.

"We're gonna talk about all this later," Dad stepped in. "Right now, you need to rest and calm down."

Lewis sniffed, heaving to a sitting position, and hugging himself as he stumbled up the stairs.

When he was little and used to lie on the sofa like that, he always remembered Dad's arms scooping him up, carrying him to bed and then rolling him drowsily beneath the duvet. But now he felt cold and shivery as he passed Moira's empty room. Yanking his duvet off the bunk, he wrapped it round himself and collapsed up against the wardrobe.

Where was Moira? What were they going to do with her?

Mum arrived slowly carrying a steaming mug, which she placed beside him. Pulling his pillow off the bunk, she laid it out beside him. Lewis said nothing. He couldn't see the ticking. He couldn't even hear the clock ticking. He could just feel it. Seconds slipping away.

"Rest. I'm going to go and check on her, make sure she's okay," Mum said softly, running her fingers through his hair. "Then when I'm back, we'll talk."

As she went to leave, her foot clipped the black rook on his chessboard and it toppled, rolling across the board before puttering onto the carpet.

"Huh," she said. "Gramps's chess puzzle?"

And with that she pulled the door to.

Lewis sniffed as he twisted inside the duvet towards the chessboard. Freeing his hand, he wiped his eyes and replaced the fallen rook. The board was now just as he'd left it, the pieces positioned like the seven mills along the river in the formation of the Bogwitch's marking.

His neck prickled as he named the squares where the pieces were positioned.

Bf4, Kg3, Rg2

And then on the white.

Ke1, Rf1, Qg1, Rh1

Lewis gazed down at the board, his eyes reddened and blurry. All the countless times he'd said those letters and numbers over and over in his head to try and imagine the positions. It was Gramps's chess puzzle. Gramps's chess puzzle *was* the Bogwitch's marking.

He collapsed on the softness of the duvet, gazing at the ceiling.

What did Gramps know about the marking?

Dad said himself, they never went to the Peering of the Goblet when he was a kid. And Gramps hated Barrow. He couldn't wait to leave. So why would he have cared enough to make a chess puzzle about it?

Lewis breathed through his nose, his body limp with exhaustion. As sleep took him, the chess puzzle fired over and over in his head. And for the very first time, Lewis could imagine all the pieces at once, as if they were spread out across the board in front of him like a diorama of tiny windmills.

There was a spark beneath his eyelids of electric green.

And Lewis awoke. His throat dry and scratched.

How long had he been asleep?

He twisted onto his stomach. Judging from the light

outside it had been several hours. It was raining, and through the foggy windows of his room the sky had turned a steely shade as evening set in.

Moira's out there. Alone. Waiting for someone to help her. Praying tomorrow and the curse that came with it didn't arrive too quickly.

The thought seemed to hammer like a lightning bolt through his chest.

Lintel winged. He remembered. He needed to find out where "Lintel winged" was and work out a plan to get there. But without his phone he had no way of accessing the internet to research it.

Staggering to his feet, he wriggled out of the duvet, hugging himself as he shivered.

He needed to focus.

Laptops. Mum's or Dad's.

The house was silent as he crept down the stairs. Maybe he was in luck. The kitchen was dark and empty, but as he peered into the living room, the table lamp was on. Dad was sitting there alone. Hunched. And, from the stack of encyclopedias in front of him, he was removing his postcards, one by one.

"I put them in here once they were dry to flatten them out. Water damage," Dad murmured without looking up. "You've been asleep for ages."

Lewis shifted on the spot.

Dad's laptop was on the table beside him.

In the light of the lamp, he didn't look as tall as he normally did. His shoulders seemed narrower and the lines between his eyes more furrowed. "Vintage postcards with pictures of Barrow." Dad held one of them up. "Bought them at a shop in Reedmouth years and years ago. They look like Barrow the way I remember it. When I was a kid. Wanna help?"

Dad pushed one of the volumes across the table.

"Where's Mum?" Lewis rasped hoarsely.

"She's still down at the police station," Dad said flatly. "Making a statement and checking in on Moi— I mean... well...her."

Lewis shuffled across the living room, dropping into the seat opposite Dad and hauling the encyclopedia towards him.

"What's going on, Lewis?" Dad asked gravely, leaning his chin on his tented fingers. "All this...it's...I just don't understand. So, tell me...what is it? Why all this... secrecy? We don't fight. We never fight."

Lewis fell silent as he flipped through the book removing the postcards.

"Do you not like it here?" Dad asked. "Is that it? Or are you worried about...the exam...Elksbridge?"

Lewis picked with his fingernail at the grains of wood on the table.

"Don't...do that," Dad said. "You'll ruin—"

He stopped.

Lewis brushed the spot he'd been picking with the back of his sleeve.

"If you don't talk to me, I can't help you, Lewis."

On the front door there was a sudden jolly little knocking.

Lewis sat bolt upright but Dad shot out of his chair. "*I'll* get it."

He waited until he heard the door open.

"Is Lewis in?"

Lewis edged his chair out and reached for the laptop.

"He's er...he's not really available at the moment, Hereward."

"Oh. Okay," Hereward said softly. "I just wanted to drop these off for him. We were discussing erm...linear interpolated motion...physics stuff...earlier...and I found some books that really helped me during the exam."

Lewis stopped. His hand outstretched.

"Tell him the one on the top was particularly useful," Hereward went on. "Especially chapter six."

Lewis could hear him, but one of the crinkled postcards lodged between the pages of Dad's encyclopedia had caught his eye.

"Chapter six," he heard Hereward say again. "*Really* helpful."

Lewis prised open the encyclopedia and extracted the postcard.

It was three composited photographs, separated by yellow lines with the words *Visit Charming Barrow – the heart of the Broads!* printed at the top.

The largest image was of a long gallery, complete with heavy velvet drapes, oil paintings and an immense grandfather clock. The second was a close-up of some jewellery. And the third was a carving of a bird in stone, its wings outstretched as if it were emblazoned on a coat of arms.

Lewis flipped it over, his eyes running down the scrawled message on the back until he came to the caption in the bottom right-hand corner.

View of Winter Gallery – Marlow Hall

Necklace and rings belonging to Baroness Lucrilla de Marlow

Details of Winter Gallery lintel stone – Marlow Hall

Lewis shot upright, his stomach pulsing as he clutched the postcard. It was a lintel. With wings. *Lintel winged.*

"Hereward brought you these," Dad said, closing the front door and lugging a stack of books back into the living room.

Dad's phone rang.

Lintel winged, Lewis repeated in his head. Just like the curse had said.

The room swayed dizzily.

At Marlow Hall. Where Gramps was the cleaner.

What lay beneath the Winter Gallery lintel stone of Marlow Hall?

"Vandalized?" he heard Dad say as his head came swimming back into the room. "Well, someone must have broken in to the school."

"My keys are just in my safe—" Dad stopped.

Lewis's fingers twitched as the skin of his elbows pinched against the cold wood of the table. He didn't remember locking the gym. Or replacing the keys. That was when Hereward had happened upon them.

"I can assure you this has never happened before," Lewis could hear Dad saying. "I'll personally clean up the mess and pay for a new lock and… Oh…well, I understand, but if you have any other properties you're thinking of sell—"

He stopped and glanced at his phone, whoever was calling having obviously hung up.

"Lewis," Dad said calmly, and Lewis's head became light and dizzy.

"Aside from Mum, you're the only other person who knows the combination for that safe. And this morning, those keys were there."

"Lewis," Dad asked again, "is there something you're not telling me?"

There was a thrashing inside of him as he tried to find the words. But without looking at him, Dad stormed into the kitchen, returning moments later carrying Lewis's rucksack. Lowering it forcefully onto the table, Dad yanked at the zipper and began to fish through it.

There was a tinkling sound and his hand emerged, clasped around the keys to the gym.

"Dad, I—"

"This is my *job*, Lewis," Dad fumed, his eyes strained and hurt. He flung the keys on the table.

"Life isn't a little chess game, Lewis. You can't just… pick up all the pieces and start over again. You make choices, decisions that have effects that last for ever. Everything we do, everything we are *doing* is to give *you* the best life you can possibly have. And for us, it's hard work. It's really hard work. So I'm not going to stand here watching you *throw* everything away just because you're not being mature enough to recognize an opportunity when it is face to face with you!"

Dad swept up Hereward's pile of books, landing them in Lewis's outstretched hands.

"Chapter six." He pointed to the book on top. "That's what you're going to do. You're going to go upstairs, and you are going to study chapter six. You can leave the house to go to the exam tomorrow but after that, you're grounded. I mean *seriously* grounded. Because if you want to have any semblance of the nice life we're trying to give you, you've got to work too. Hard. Now go."

It was like being hit in the stomach with a freight train. Winded, Lewis was unable to muster a single word.

Leave tonight, he told himself slumping to the floor and dumping the textbooks beside him. *Find Moira somehow, break her out, go to Marlow Hall, find the lintel and take whatever lies beneath out to the forge: the marshes. Stop the curse.*

What other choice did he have? Receiving a scholarship didn't mean squat if everyone you'd ever known had completely forgotten you, and you were trapped in another time without any idea who you were, just foggy flashes of your old life.

He'd slip out when Mum and Dad were asleep. And, until then, he wasn't going to give them a single reason to suspect him. Lewis hauled the top textbook into his lap and began flipping irritably through the pages.

Chapter six. Pfft! How could Dad even give a rat's about chapter six when—

Lewis stopped.

Chapter six was entitled: *Electrical Energy and Power.*

And there was a sticky note patted across the page that read:

Lewis
Keep Calm.
And go to exam.
Leave rest to me.
H.

Chapter 25
Day Seven

Lewis awoke to a dark sky; a sky heavy with clouds.

His first instinct was to open his palm. Sure enough, the seventh marking had begun to loom into view.

Mum had cancelled most of her appointments, except for an emergency tooth extraction at noon.

That morning, PC Woodgrove had dropped by with another officer to take Lewis's statement, which they did with a social worker, but without Mum or Dad. Although he knew Mum was listening at the door.

"And why do you think she needed somewhere to stay?" PC Woodgrove asked, making notes. "Did she tell you anything…unusual?"

But as he tried to tell them as little as possible, Lewis's head was elsewhere entirely: *What was Hereward planning? Could he trust him? What if he'd got it wrong, and now he was just wasting time?*

Dad watched him like a hawk, poking his head out of the living room whenever Lewis so much as tiptoed to the bathroom.

And at 11:30, Lewis heard the hiss of the iron downstairs as Dad prepped his things, on top of which Mum had left a note:

Just get through these next few hours. It'll all be over soon, I promise.
We'll talk tonight.
Love you, Mum
xx

"It's a deluge," Dad muttered as they pulled up at the towering school, which was just a turreted outline in the cloudy rain.

Lewis checked his watch, the buttons on his cuffs pinching into his wrist.

14:30

Half an hour before the exam.

Eight-and-a-half hours before it happened. Waking up somewhere else. Not knowing who he was, and erased like a troublesome maths problem from his own life, only to be replaced. By Moira.

Moira. He didn't even want to imagine how scared she'd be. How alone.

Lewis squeezed his rucksack between his legs, hoping he'd thought of everything. *Extra socks. Torch. A pen?*

What *were* you supposed to pack when you were trying to stave off a four-hundred-year-old curse?

"That'll be the invigilator," Dad murmured.

Through the sheets of rain, Lewis could see a woman with a tight bun, cardigan and mean little glasses standing in the double doors at the front of Elksbridge Collegiate School next to a sign that read:

15:00 – Scholarship Examination

They sat silently for a moment, the rain harrying the roof of the car as the wipers counted rhythmically across the windscreen.

"Well, you got everything?" Dad said distantly.

Lewis's hand rested on the door handle.

He didn't want to even contemplate what might happen if it all went wrong. But he had to say something. Just in case.

"Dad, I'm sorry for—"

"Good luck, Lewis," Dad interrupted, dusting something off the dashboard with the side of his hand.

Lewis looked over at him. He looked greyer somehow, his hair less combed and his eyes puffy and tired.

Dad put both his hands on the steering wheel.

What do I say? Something honest. Something that means something.

But before Lewis had the time to muster the courage, Dad's phone rang.

"George Buckley speaking," Dad sighed as the phone connected to the car speaker and, reaching over Lewis's lap, he pushed the door open.

The rain spattered onto the side of his face and, hurt and stung, Lewis felt his legs lift him out of the car.

"No, no *the Willows*, Wherryman's Way, is still on the market," Dad went on cheerily. "Would you like to arrange a viewing?"

The door closed and almost immediately the car pulled off.

"Name?" the invigilator asked as Lewis approached.

"L-Lewis Buckley," he croaked.

"Follow me, Master Buckley," the invigilator said.

Lewis turned, his jaw clenched. Down the driveway, Dad's car became smaller and smaller until it was nothing more than a tiny blob of white that vanished in the thickening rain.

In the enormous Elksbridge assembly hall complete with a stage and tall velvet drapes, a single desk was placed in the very middle.

"Mr Buckley, if you'd like to present your pencil case for inspection?"

Lewis awkwardly crouched, his tie pressing up against his throat.

Where was Hereward? How long would he need to give it before he ought to just make a run for it?

Lewis prised his pencil case out and placed it on the desk. The invigilator ferreted through it with her manicured nails, pausing to examine a pawn-shaped eraser before nodding crisply.

"Pockets?" she said.

Lewis pulled them inside out.

"Hands?" she barked.

"Sorry?" Lewis frowned.

"To make sure you're not *cheating*, Master Buckley. You'd be surprised at the things I've found written on the insides of palms and wrists."

Lewis slowly unclenched his fingers.

"What's this?" the invigilator frowned, looking at the marking.

In the stark light of the assembly hall, Lewis could clearly see the seventh circle, coming ever more clearly into sight.

"B-birth mark," Lewis stammered.

The invigilator gave him an uncertain glance. He lowered himself stiffly into the chair and fumbled with one of his pencils. Through the tall windows of the assembly room the trees of the school grounds creaked in the wind and rain.

Where is Hereward?

On the invigilator's desk, a large clock let out sharp echoing ticks as the seconds clipped down.

Don't listen, he told himself. *Shut it out.*

The ticking grew louder, burrowing into his skull until he heard a voice from the front.

"You may begin."

Lewis flipped the exam paper, leaning his head on his shaking fist. His breathing quickened and pushing both of his fists against his ears to drown out the ticking, Lewis began.

Q1.) Explain in your own words how lightning and nitrogen atoms in the atmosphere help to fertilize plants.

Lewis read the question again, his head feeling like a wet carpet, incapable of soaking up even one tiny thing.

He looked up at the clock.

Fifteen minutes had elapsed.

Why am I waiting? With every passing surge of rain, the flood and midnight with it were drawing nearer.

Shouldn't I just run?

But from behind him there was a clatter as the swinging doors to the assembly hall opened. Lewis stiffened, waiting for Hereward's voice. But instead, a warm buzzing sound followed, accompanied by hissing. Like a bee trying to land on a barbecue steak.

The invigilator looked up, and her tight bun cocked to one side.

From the corner of his eye, he watched as a small drone came bumbling through the assembly hall, a lit sparkler sticky-taped to the top. The drone hovered in mid-air for a moment before doddering on, heading past the invigilator and on to the stage behind her.

Her mouth fell open a little as she gazed at the mechanical insect in utter astonishment. It did a small loop of the stage, as if taking a bow, before drifting off into the wings and down what sounded like a corridor.

The invigilator shot Lewis a wary look and he gave an innocent shrug. Standing up, she marched after the drone, her heels clicking deliberately on the floorboards.

The buzzing grew fainter, as did her footsteps, until,

with a rustle, one of the curtains began to move.

Lewis's heart skipped.

There was a mutter as whatever was concealed beneath the heavy folds of velvet tried to free itself. A flash of curly red hair.

"Hereward!" Lewis hissed.

He leaped off the edge of the stage, his anorak flaring out behind him as he carried a small remote.

"No time to explain, you can tell me all about it later," Hereward panted.

Scooping up Lewis's rucksack, Hereward replaced it with his own and skidded towards him, peeling off his anorak.

Lewis clenched his pencil, a triumphant feeling welling up inside him.

"Tie," Hereward said, holding out his hand and Lewis bewilderedly obeyed. Hereward hung the hood of his anorak on Lewis's head and tossed him the rucksack. He elbowed Lewis out of his chair and looped the tie round the collar of his white shirt.

"You're-you're going to pretend to be me?!" Lewis whispered loudly. "She'll never fall for it!"

"Who cares! It'll buy you some time."

"Marlow Hall," Lewis whispered to him pulling on the anorak. "That's where it is. The winged lintel!"

"I don't really know what you're talking about," Hereward reminded him as he did up his buttons and smoothed back his hair. "But, sure. Great!"

"What about Moira?" Lewis hissed. "The police took her."

"I'll do my best," Hereward insisted, giving Lewis a shove. "But I can't promise anything. Now what are you gawking at?! Go!"

Lewis paused.

"Hereward," he croaked, feeling uncertain he'd ever be able to repay him. "Th-thanks."

"I'm just getting you out of a sticky situation," Hereward told him, seizing the pencil and beginning to write on the exam paper almost immediately. "You did the same for me."

Leopold thrashing wildly as he disintegrated Hereward's drone flicked through Lewis's mind.

The clicking of high-heeled shoes returned as the door in the wings of the stage opened, and Lewis bolted.

He slipped through the double doors, taking the weight of the handle so they didn't clatter and, as his rucksack slipped through after him, the invigilator reappeared.

Lewis peered through the square glass panel, his heart pounding, expecting at any second that she'd clock on. But Hereward kept his head down at an angle, the top of his flaming red hair the only thing visible to her from the front. And adjusting her skirt, the invigilator sat back down, none the wiser of the switch that had occurred.

Lewis punched his fist into his palm. But his enthusiasm was quickly dissipated as he pushed through the front doors of Elksbridge Collegiate School, and the rain bellowed down. He pulled Hereward's anorak closer round him and tightened the straps on his rucksack.

It would take a few hours, but he'd walk back from

Elksbridge into Barrow, across the river and then follow it as far as he could up to Marlow Hall.

He glanced up at the groaning sky, rain droplets peppering his face as the tall avenue of trees wailed.

The flood was coming.

And although the assembly hall was behind him as he set off on the road back towards Barrow, the utterances from the invigilator's clock seemed to grow louder with every passing step.

Tick,

click,

click,

click.

Chapter 26
Marlow Hall

Lewis's legs began to ache as, through the blustering gloom, lights from the first houses of Barrow appeared.

As he passed the Barrow School, water gushed across the gravel driveway, pooling like milky tea in the potholes.

He kept repeating his plan to himself under his breath.

Up this road. Through town. Cross the bridge. Along the river. Marlow Hall.

But as a fresh trickle of water clustered on the anorak and slipped down the front of his shirt, he felt his determination waver.

He was so close to home. Just a few streets away. Maybe he could just walk past the house. Say goodbye to Mum and Dad, even if it was just through the window. Just in case. But he couldn't. Not now. If either of them caught so much as a glimpse of him it would be over.

Hoisting up his sleeve he checked his watch – 17:45.

If Hereward had managed to pull it off, then he'd be finishing the exam shortly and Dad would be getting ready to pick him up.

He had to focus.

Moira.

What if Hereward wasn't able to help her? What if they'd taken her to a different station in another town and now he was going to have to work this out alone? The thought stung him and he tried to pick up his pace to ignore the endless ticking in his ears as the seconds slipped by.

Lewis froze, as a series of ghostly wails went up across Barrow. They pitched up and down, an endless moan that echoed through the driving rain, warning of imminent danger.

The flood sirens.

People were bustling back and forth along the river, which was now level with the town square and sending out great sloshes of murky water over the cobblestones as it thundered past. Shouts rang out as people hurried about, lugging sandbags and laying down traffic cones.

"Keep clear of the river!" came a shout from a man in a fluorescent vest as someone in a long coat tried to cross the town square.

Lewis crouched in Moorings Passage, where he and Moira had found the plaque for Tea-Chest Tabitha, and shoved his fingers into his sodden rucksack. Fishing out the map he'd taken from Orkley Castle, he squinted at it as the rain scoured the corner of the passage.

Marlow Hall was marked as a red symbol in the shape of a spiky-looking manor house on the opposite side of the river. He *had* to cross.

The flood sirens moaning in his ears, he bolted for the drawbridge, praying no one would see him. But as the wooden structure drew closer, its chains groaning in the wind, his stomach sank.

SEVENMILL BRIDGE CLOSED
Due to inclement weather

Lewis glanced back towards the town square, his hood slipping down. From where he was trying to crouch beside the drawbridge, there was another lurch of water around his feet and the two raised segments of the bridge clanged together with a creaking thud as the whole thing swayed.

His fingers gripped the enormous chain to steady himself.

Just at that moment, a flash of yellow beneath the bridge caught his eye, followed by a hollow thud.

A fallen branch scratched past, and then bobbing out of the murk he saw it.

A yellow canoe.

Tethered to the bridge, and filling with water but still visible above the maelstrom.

Lewis leaned out as far as he could, still clinging to the chain.

And edging himself out above the water, he reached.

"HEY!"

Lewis's head swivelled.

A wiry man carrying a sandbag on his forearms had seen him from the town square. Lewis shot into action, gritting his teeth as his fingers flailed hopelessly for the rope until, with a lashing movement, he grasped.

"YOU!" the man shouted again, followed by the thud of a sandbag as he bolted towards the drawbridge.

Lewis tugged. The rope came free and he felt the sudden pull of the current against him.

"OI! THERE'S A FLOOD WARNING IN PLACE, BOY!"

Steadying the thrashing canoe as best he could, Lewis jumped.

A sharp sting shot through his jaw, as he collided with one of the oars, clinging on for his life.

There was another bellow from the sandbag man, but Lewis flipped over onto his back, the water on the bottom of the canoe coming up to his wrists. The town square was speeding by in foggy flashes of warm light as the pub vanished. He was free.

"STOP!" the man roared again, but Lewis could hardly hear him.

Thick branches and loose debris thudded past making the little yellow canoe shudder. Lewis felt for the oar in the murky pool at his feet and plunged it into the raging swirl around him like a paddle.

He was out.

Flying along. Leaving Barrow behind as nothing but the marshy, lightless path of the Broads lay ahead and the haunting cries of the flood sirens grew ever more distant.

For a moment he was filled with a brimming optimism.

I'll find the lintel winged. Hereward will get Moira out. And we'll end this.

But as the wind began to sway the direction of the rain, and the banks of the river feathered out into marshy fingers of reeds and sunken logs, he remembered the Bogwitch's grip round his ankle, how little time he had and how alone he really was.

He checked his watch, a smattering of water gathering on its face almost immediately.

19:07

Dad would have already tried to pick him up.

Did Hereward make it out?

There was a *crack* from under his feet as the canoe struck something submerged beneath the water's surface. Lewis was flung forward. His wrist sprained and the oar slipped from his fingers, vanishing instantly into the torrent.

His fingernails drove into the wood, his teeth grinding as the water carried him, spinning mercilessly as if the canoe was as light as a bath toy.

There was nothing he could do. He'd have to sit. And wait. And pray that somehow in the rising water his course would stay on the Sevenmill River and Moira would be at Marlow Hall, waiting for him.

Moira.

If they were able to successfully return to the Bogwitch this thing that had been stolen, and all went back to how it was, what then? That would be it. Whichever way he cut it, no matter what happened, Moira would be gone. Just a memory somewhere at the back of his head. Like someone you'd once bumped into on a train.

He checked his watch again as the rain tittered down.

19:57

Little more than four hours until midnight.

How can it possibly have been nearly an hour? Had he passed Marlow Hall already or was he being swept in another direction entirely?

The canoe had finally stopped spinning, but to either side of him he could see nothing save for a pale maze of reeds, their ghostly tips flinging back and forth like drowning limbs.

Widening his stance, he stood up as carefully as he could, his legs shaky from clenching as the canoe sped along.

A dark thicket met his eyes. Silvery birch trees meshed together as the water lapped around their trunks, making it impossible to tell what had once been land and what was now a flooded marsh.

There was a sickening scrape that shuddered through his feet, as the canoe collided once more with something lurking beneath the surface.

Lewis was thrown forward as the prow plunged head first into the reeds, burrowing itself between them as the gushing water threatened at any moment to flood the canoe.

Tick,

click,

click,

click.

Gripping the tops of the rushes, he tried to haul himself forward. But they snapped away in his hands.

He was lodged.

Stuck.

With no phone.

No idea where he was. And the minutes slipping away.

Mum. Dad.

An overwhelming heaviness filled him as his whole body quivered with exhaustion. And from the pit of his stomach a guttural burst of frustration welled up, building to a gargling pitch until he let out a great bellowing howl of pure rage.

"AAAAAAAAAAAAARGH!"

A splintering of bottle-green lightning bleached across the sky almost at once, followed by a deafening peal of crackling thunder.

Lewis shrank back into the canoe peering up at the sky. Had he...had he summoned that somehow?

Blink! Blink! Blink!

He squinted as the thunder subsided.

Blink! Blink! Blink!

A tiny dot of flashing red seemed to be heading towards him.

Another drone? The top of a pylon?

The dot drew closer. Larger.

There was a loud *CAW!* And the rook, with Lewis's red bicycle light fastened round its left claw, landed on the prow of the canoe.

A thudding filled his chest.

"GET OUT OF HERE!" he shouted, swiping his hands at it. "GO! WHAT DO YOU WANT? YOU'RE THE ONE THAT STARTED ALL THIS!!"

But the rook didn't budge.

Edging sideways along the canoe, it pecked at a spot in the water and let out a fat croak.

Is it…trying to show me something?

With another warble it pecked again, before there was a flapping of wings and it took to the air, vanishing over the tops of the rushes in flashes of red light.

Lewis reached into the water.

His breathing quickened as a slimy branch just below the surface met his fingers. Adjusting his position in the canoe, he lowered himself to his knees and, wrapping both hands round the branch, he pulled.

At first nothing moved, but as he leaned backwards his fingers slipping on the algae there was a scrape and the canoe slid.

Lewis heaved again, and this time there was a splash from underneath him as the canoe freed itself, drifting out once more to the middle of the river.

"CAW!"

A pulse thundering through his temple, Lewis wedged

his fingers through the zipper of his rucksack and felt around for the torch.

Slapping its side as it flickered, he pointed it across the swell in the direction the rook's croak had come from.

Blink! Blink! Blink! from the edge of the water.

Where he thought the path would continue, it seemed the river was forking off in different directions.

"CAW!"

The pale beam of light from his torch passed over the treetops, piercing through the rain until a fluorescent flash of yellow appeared in the trees to his right where a narrow stretch of water splintered off.

There was a flutter and the rook took off again, landing just a little further up the marshy channel, the bicycle light still clutched in its beak.

"CAW!"

It wants you to follow it, he told himself. *It wants you to go down there.*

The rook let out another fat croak, which echoed over the marshes.

He hesitated as his fingers brushed some reeds. It was risky. What if the rook was leading him out into the marshes? Luring him.

Lewis pointed his light directly at the bird as it waited.

"CAW!"

And as the trees slipped past him, Lewis saw it.

A dark, towering ridge of chimneys and gables that looked like a small, lightless city reaching up into the thundery sky.

Marlow Hall.

Gripping the low-hanging branches above him, Lewis lifted his leg out of the canoe and lowered a foot into the water. It was only knee deep and, leashing the rope round the tree, he stepped round its trunk, making sure to hoist his rucksack as high above the water as he could.

Why had the rook helped him? Was it part of a trap?

But for some reason, despite those piercing yellow eyes being only inches from his, he didn't feel scared of it any more. And reaching out, he placed his finger cautiously on the rook's head.

Its skull felt fragile. And small beneath its oily feathers.

The rook let out a low warble and blinked its yellow eyes.

Lewis squeezed his way through the thicket, his rucksack snaring on twigs and brambles.

Marlow Hall seemed to have been built on the only small hill in all of Barrow. The grounds of the house began to take shape around him, and before long he was creeping through a sweeping garden.

Crouching low, he slipped along to what seemed to be a small gardener's shed and peered out from behind it. He couldn't see any movement or any lights at all. Maybe the Marlows had moved elsewhere when the flood sirens went off.

There was a gentle flapping behind him and the rook followed, this time landing for a moment on his shoulder. Even through the anorak, Lewis could feel its claws as its feathery breast brushed softly against his ear.

He crept up the garden, shifting from hedge to hedge until, with one final dash across the open lawn, he dropped beneath the nearest windowsill.

Lifting his head, he peered cautiously into the darkened glass of the room. Everything was still and draped in long white sheets as if no one had entered that part of the house in a long while. Along the sides of the room, enormous hats with sweeping feathers were crammed into dusty cases, which had to be part of Sir Hector's famous Charles II collection.

How would he get in?

Lewis jiggled his wrist to check his watch. But from out of nowhere, something thudded against his ribcage sending Lewis tumbling. Arms, sopping and strong, wrapped round him.

The rook gave a startled squawk as it was knocked from its perch and, in the darkness, two enormous chestnut eyes appeared.

Moira.

Chapter 27
The Lintel Winged

Lewis scrambled to his knees, threw his arms round Moira's and squeezed.

Moira was there. In front of him.

"How did you get out!?" Lewis whispered. The rain, the wet, even his bleeding fingers that had been clobbered in the boat, none of it seemed to matter. Just that she was there, as a warmth bloomed inside him like a candle's wick slowly puttering into flame.

"I think it was a police station!" she gabbled breathlessly. "Oh it was awful, Lewis. Everyone was being so nice and they gave me a room and a bed. And there was a lady with a very smart jacket who kept checking on me and asking me if I needed anything. I was so scared, because they kept asking me questions, and the only consolation was that I was allowed as much cocoa and biscuits as I wanted. And then I remembered: the goblet. And I asked for some water, looked inside it and I saw *you. You,* Lewis. I saw the postcards. And Marlow Hall. And then Hereward came and he distracted the police with one of his flying contraptions. And I escaped, managed to catch a lift with an old lady. I told her I was Sir Hector's long-lost granddaughter. I couldn't think of anything better. But it worked!"

Lewis grinned in the darkness.

"It was here all along," Lewis said hurriedly, lifting his head above the windowsill again as he caught sight of a silver latch on the inside. "Dad had these postcards, that's what you would have seen. Of a lintel stone above a door in the Winter Gallery of Marlow Hall with a bird on it. That's what we need to look for."

"How are we going to get inside?" Moira whispered, her elation transforming to a squint of determination. "We haven't long."

"Do you think you can manage it?" Lewis asked pointing at the silver latch as Moira's face pressed against the glass beside him.

Moira fixed her gaze through the glass onto the latch and squeezed both her thumbs between her fingers.

Around the metal, there was a sputter of electric green. But the latch didn't budge.

"You try," she panted. "It doesn't feel...as easy this time. I-I think its fading."

Lewis focused his stare on the latch, trying to remember how he'd managed it before. He honed his eyes, pushing from deep in his stomach as a flickering twig of light crackled across the latch.

"Gently," Moira coached him. "Just think of—"

There was an explosive *bang*! Lewis felt a sensation in his arm like he'd just brushed against an electric fence. And the latch flew off the windowsill, crashing into the far wall where it shattered a large vase.

Moira winced as they listened for a moment, praying no one had heard. But silence followed. And pressing his palms against the glass of the window, Lewis slid it open.

"Up you go," Moira whispered, cupping her hands.

Putting his shoe on her hands as lightly as he could, he wrapped his fingers round the sill, hoisted himself up and lowered himself inside.

Reaching back down, Lewis hauled Moira after him.

Lewis scanned the room with his torch. Damp-looking tapestries and towering cabinets stuffed with feathered hats surrounded them as the hulking furniture slept beneath white dust sheets.

Sneaking across the deserted room, they pushed through the door and out onto a landing that seemed to wrap round the entire inside of the house.

"Which way do you think the Winter Gallery is?" Moira whispered as her foot creaked on the misshapen stairs leading down to the main entrance.

Lewis tried to orientate himself for a moment as he thought back to the map of Barrow and the direction the river had wended its way to the hall. "It will be south. Rooms for winter are usually south-facing," Lewis said.

"They get the most sunlight, which makes them the warmest. That's what...what Dad says when he's selling houses."

Dad. It pained him even to hold the word in his head, let alone say it aloud, as he tried to stop himself from imagining what he and Mum would be feeling and thinking as they searched hopelessly for him.

But it was just like Gramps always told him: *Remember what we say to our opponent when we are cornered on the board, the seconds are ticking and we can't see any way out...*

Not now, Lewis forced himself to think. *Not. Now.*

Moira led as they crept across the landing, pausing behind an antique bookcase to make sure the coast was clear.

Lewis gave a confirmatory nod as Moira pointed to a small door to their left and, twisting the handle, she pushed it aside. It opened up onto a narrow hallway broken up with intermittent flights of stairs that wound up and down, as if intersecting the innards of the house. They inched along the corridor, Lewis taking in a small breath to listen every time they met with a corner.

But there was no one and, before long, a large door with a levered latch appeared.

Lewis lifted it with a sharp creak.

He recognized the narrow room almost immediately from the postcard. Nothing seemed to have changed, except for a suit of armour stationed untidily at the opposite end, a sword clutched in its hand. The walls groaned beneath the weight of the heavy oil paintings that cluttered them, and the enormous grandfather clock was still.

Lewis fumbled with his torch, edging from one chequered flagstone to the next, like a chess piece. But there were no other doors in the gallery save for the one they had entered by.

There was a small *clang* from behind him as he caught sight of Moira, wide-eyed, balancing one end of an antique sugar bowl she'd evidently just clattered into with her elbow.

"Quietly!" Lewis mouthed.

Moira slid the sugar bowl back onto the cabinet.

"I can't see *anything,* Lewis," she muttered as they searched. "Do you think—?"

But the beam from Lewis's torch had stopped.

Jutting out of the wallpaper, above a space where it seemed there was no door at all, was a stone beam. A lintel.

Lewis circled it with his torchlight.

"The rook," Moira murmured drawing in closer.

It had been worn away, but the carved bird, its wings splayed across the stone was clearly visible.

"But, Lewis," Moira asked, "where's the *doorway*? You said that lintels were stones above doors!"

Lewis's torchlight wandered lower. And a wooden barometer, larger than either of the ones they had seen before appeared just below the lintel.

The two of them stepped towards it, and the barometer's dusty needle began to flicker manically. Like a scratching seismograph as an earthquake approached.

Lewis positioned his torch on the cabinet and placed his fingers round the dial.

"You ready?" he breathed and then frowned. "Moira?"

But Moira's gaze was fixed on something over Lewis's shoulder.

Lewis slowly turned.

The suit of armour he had spotted as they entered the gallery was no longer standing up against the wall. It had moved. And it was now standing on the long carpet in the middle of the gallery.

Lewis could hear only his breath moving quickly in and out of his lungs as the wind howled beneath the window cracks.

"Lost? Wandering through locked doors once again, eh?" the suit of armour said.

Lewis snatched up his torch, finding the figure almost immediately. It was not made of chain mail and metal at all, and as the light moved up to its face, a hand was lifted.

Lewis flicked off the torch.

"I heard something clang and thought it might be Leopold up to no good." Sir Hector Marlow's voice filled the room as he hobbled towards them. "But it seems I was mistaken. I had a strange feeling I'd be seeing you two again."

"W-w-we..." Lewis began, but Sir Hector cut him off.

"You were two young people curious about this old town, and who can blame you for that? Now I'm not sure breaking into my house when there's a flood warning in place was the *best* course of action, but it does at least give me cause to think I might need to acquire some more fearsome guard dogs."

In the darkness, Lewis saw Sir Hector's twinkly little eyes smile.

"W-w-we didn't mean to break in," Lewis stammered. "We just...didn't think anyone would believe us if we told them... It's about...the Bogwitch."

The old man shifted his weight to his cane.

"Well," Sir Hector sighed mopping his brow with a handkerchief. "I suppose the game, as they say, is up. So, how much *do* you know?"

Lewis flashed his eyes at Moira as the skin round his neck twitched.

"E-everything," Lewis lied.

Sir Hector pursed his lips together as Lewis and Moira waited in the darkness.

"The Barrow Historical Society have kept the goblet safe for many years," he began. "As I'm sure you will have learned, it is quite an extraordinary object that would be highly sought after if its abilities were to come to light. And if people were to try to take it." He raised his eyebrows at them both. "Who knows how long it would be before it fell back into the Bogwitch's hands."

Lewis's breathing quickened as he realized that the goblet must still be in Moira's bag. Was that *really* the answer to all this?

"A-a-and the barometer..." Lewis demanded warily. "The addresses. The dates. I found it in our house."

"You found it?!" Sir Hector gasped. "Oh, thank heavens! Terrence Smythe died rather suddenly, you see, without telling anyone where he'd last hidden the barometer. As Secretary of the Barrow Historical Society, Terrence was in charge of keeping its whereabouts a secret. And the barometer was a record we kept of when and where these strange occurrences happened to the children of Barrow, in the hope that one day we might find a pattern and put an end to it."

"So the *goblet* was what lay beneath the winged lintel then?" Moira clarified.

A look of genuine bewilderment crossed Sir Hector's face.

"Winged lintel?"

Lewis stood back and let his torch beam fall across the dusty stone wings.

"Aah yes. The rook," Sir Hector whispered brushing the carving gently with his cane. "The Bogwitch's bird, flying notably low, just above our heads. What of it?"

Lewis paused, wondering for a moment if telling Sir Hector everything they knew was a bad idea. But the seconds escaping before him seemed to jolt him into action.

"We found a curse," Lewis told him. "Inscribed by the Bogwitch beneath Hogweed Bridge. And it said that it would only be lifted if something beneath the 'lintel winged' was returned to her at the forge. We think the curse was referring to this stone here at Marlow Hall."

Sir Hector looked from one to the other.

"The goblet was *never* kept at Marlow Hall," he sighed gravely. "Which, I think you'll agree with me, leaves us with one course of action."

An almost mischievous smile broke across Sir Hector's papery face as he leaned in: "We must investigate to see what truly lies *beneath*!"

Lewis felt relief flood through him. His questions were far from answered, but time was fast escaping.

He handed Moira the torch as Sir Hector stood back and, reaching out, he pressed his fingers round the barometer's dial as the needle jittered.

"Careful!" Sir Hector warned gently. "Miss Putter would eat me alive if we damaged it."

There was a *click*, like the unsealing of a jar. And the dial twisted off, revealing a patch of unmarked wall with a crude keyhole inside the barometer.

Sir Hector gasped. "I've lived here my whole life and never intend to leave this house. As a boy I explored every crack and every sunken floorboard but never did I lay eyes upon *this* before."

"But we need a key!" Lewis panicked, poking his finger desperately into the keyhole.

"Right ahead of you." Sir Hector winked and lifted a key from round his neck. "The skeleton key of Marlow Hall. Opens every door in the whole house. Try it!"

Lewis took the key and, lining it with the lock, he turned.

There was a metallic *crunch* and Sir Hector stood back, gasping.

Lewis leaned his shoulder against the wallpaper. Moira did the same. And, together, they pushed.

A grinding of stone followed, like the unsealing of a tomb and, with a jagged tear, the invisible door scraped open.

A musty smell caught Lewis's nose.

"Never in a thousand years!" Sir Hector cried out in astonishment, shaking his head. "After all this time!"

Moira shone the torch as a dripping sound echoed up at them.

A set of glistening stone steps had appeared, leading down into inky darkness.

Lewis glanced at Moira, a pulse building in his chest.

"Remind me what it is you expect to find down there?" Sir Hector asked as he peered cautiously over Lewis's shoulder.

"We don't know exactly," Lewis muttered. "But something that was stolen from the Bogwitch. Whatever it is, we have to find it. It's the only way."

He placed his foot on the first grimy step as a strange gust of wind barrelled down the stairs.

"Perhaps," Sir Hector asked his brow wrinkling with concern, "we ought to call someone to investigate it for us?"

"We can't wait," Lewis told him.

"We've got until midnight," Moira added.

"I'll keep watch. In case I need to call for help," Sir Hector told them warily. "Slippery steps and old bones are not the best of friends."

Lewis took the torch and placing his hand on the

mildew-covered walls began to make his way down as the smell of old water surrounded him.

"Careful!" he told Moira, trying his best not to sound panicky as his sneaker slid.

"What do you see?" Sir Hector called down.

"There's water," Lewis called out as his torch illuminated the grey slosh lapping up ahead. "The steps are vanishing into it."

"Do be careful!" Sir Hector's voice wavered.

Gripping the wall as best he could, Lewis tentatively lowered his foot into the murky swill, feeling for the next step. There was a horrid swaying sensation, and his leg dropped into the water, which came up to his knees, as Moira let out a gasp.

"It's okay," he told her, shifting his foot about. "It's... it's flat. I can feel the bottom."

Lewis pointed the torch ahead as Moira stepped down beside him.

"There's a rusty grate," Lewis made out, as torchlight flashed against it. "Like a door. Up ahead."

"Make sure you stay together!" Sir Hector's voice echoed down.

Lewis clenched his fingers as he waded towards it, the water sucking as it spilled through the metal grill of a sewer opening along the passage.

There was something beyond the grate. A room? The rusted padlock round the bolt was unlocked and finding the handle he pulled.

"It's stuck!"

"Here," Moira muttered gripping the iron slats beside him. "Together. Three, two, one."

They heaved. With a *screech* the grate caught for a moment before pulling jaggedly ajar.

And, with his heart pummelling, Lewis stepped through.

"Do you see anything yet?" Sir Hector's voice echoed down again.

The room was round. Stone. The water up to their knees.

Lewis's torchlight travelled up the walls, higher and higher.

"Moira." He squinted as the light caught droplets of water pattering softly downwards. "It's…it's a tower."

The hollow emptiness loomed above them, its only opening a pair of small, barred windows at the tower's peak.

"Lewis," Moira breathed, gripping him by the wrist. "Lewis, look."

He hadn't noticed at first, but growing from every stone surface was a leafy cloak of hooded white flowers. They emerged like limbs of mist from the murky pool at the tower's base, tangling their way up the walls as far as the torchlight allowed them to see.

"They're…beautiful," Moira whispered as she brushed the pale petals. "But how could they grow *here*? In the dark?"

"Did you find it?" came Sir Hector's worried voice. "Do you see anything?"

"It's some kind of…tower," Lewis called back as he

turned on the spot. "And there are flowers. White flowers…hundreds of them."

"Indeed," Sir Hector sighed, his voice seeming to grow closer. "A veritable bower that conjures strange winds inside the walls. Green lights in the night."

There was a creak from behind them.

"Sir Hector?"

Lewis's torch beam found the iron grate, just in time to see it slam shut.

Sir Hector's papery hands appeared on the other side of the door, clutching the padlock. And as he squeezed the rusted mechanism closed, there was a sharp *click*!

Lewis froze as his stomach gave a nauseous thump.

It was locked.

And they were trapped.

Chapter 28
There Never Was a Bogwitch

"What are you doing?!" Lewis called out in panic.

"Lightning in bottles and drinking marshes dry. Ha!" came Sir Hector's slow chuckle from in front of them and Lewis pointed the torch. The old man was standing just down the passage, knee deep in the water as he leaned on his cane.

"What do you mean?" Lewis croaked. He could feel the blood rushing to his ears, as if he was hanging upside down. "Let us out!"

"Stories of ghosts and ghouls," Sir Hector went on with a smirk. "As the weary passage of time creaks on, sometimes they become a little ragged at the edges. Their threads weave themselves together. And before you know it you have all manner of strange tales, the real truth so twisted out of shape that it becomes scarcely recognizable."

Lewis felt a chill thread itself up his spine.

"Wh-what are you doing?" he shouted, his face pressing against the grate as he gave it another hopeless rattle.

"Waiting for the change to take place, my boy," Sir Hector replied. "Once it's complete, my work will be done. And the secret will go on sleeping in the walls of the West Tower of Marlow Hall until the next flood comes to Barrow."

Moira let out a roar and thrust her hand through the grate. There was a feeble flicker of electric green that puttered out almost immediately.

"The change is nearly upon you," Sir Hector said as Moira stared at her fingers. "As your strange abilities fade into nothing more than puzzling memories of another life and the curse is passed on completely."

"I-I don't understand," Lewis murmured, his voice almost a whisper as his throat seemed to close.

Moira gave Lewis a panicked glance in the darkness.

"Well, I suppose there is still a little time to tell you the story of what *truly* happened, before the midnight switch takes place. The story of how there never really was a true Bogwitch of Barrow."

Lewis glanced around the room, hoping for a sewer, a passage, something. But only ghostly white flowers and huddled stones stared back at him.

"Once, long ago, at a forge in the fields just outside Barrow there lived a blacksmith," Sir Hector began.

"The blacksmith was a widower, and a humble man, who made horseshoes and cauldrons out of pig iron. His daughter, on the other hand, was a talented little creature. She was *gifted*."

"Gifted how?" Lewis asked.

"In strange ways," Sir Hector said darkly. "With an unnatural *mastery* of the weather; a dominion over the elements."

The barometers. The floods, Lewis thought.

"She could squeeze the clouds as if they were sponges," Sir Hector went on, "bargain with storms as if they were weary travellers to pass on or to stay. Haul lightning down from the sky and scatter it throughout these lands, bringing rich, fertile soil. And yet, despite all this, she was as gentle a creature as ever breathed. Her name? Gretel *Murk*."

Lewis felt his shoulder blades twitch as Sir Hector continued. "Her parents knew from her very birth that Gretel would be no ordinary child. Even when she was a babe, a highly distinctive bird, prone to sensing changes in the weather, would come and perch itself on her cradle as if, like a barometer, it could sense the stormy magic gathering inside her. Can you guess which bird?"

"A rook," Lewis murmured.

"Indeed," Sir Hector went on. "The girl's mother, a village herbalist, had died when Gretel was small, and as time went by the blacksmith kept his talented little daughter out of sight from their neighbours in Barrow, afraid her gifts might be perceived as the fruits of a dark craft. But as the years passed, and the blacksmith's eyesight grew poorer, and his once-strong arms frailer, they could no longer afford to feed themselves with the small sum he made producing goblets and doorknockers. The time had come for Gretel Murk to put her remarkable talents to use."

Moira's teeth chattered.

Her strength was fading.

And Lewis felt convinced it was a sign that the change would soon occur.

"In that same year, there was a terrible flood that threatened to destroy Barrow's harvest. So, to gain the townsfolk's trust, Gretel carved a marking into a goblet: a symbol of protection for Barrow's seven windmills and their precious grain."

The marking. In the shape of the windmills, Lewis thought.

"And, taking the goblet, she channelled the waters from the town inside it saving Barrow from the rising floods. The townsfolk, seeming to think that such magic could only be a good thing, began to pay her to use her arts. Gretel tempered the rain and lightning, allowing the townsfolk to grow their crops and, over time, Barrow prospered. And grew. Until it was the richest town for miles."

Sir Hector paused for a moment and examined the signet rings on his fingers.

"Curious, the things ordinary people will do when opportunity and wealth are within their grasp," he mused. "Before long, greed seeped into the townsfolk's hearts, their demands exhausting Gretel's bountiful talents to their limit. And wise beyond her years, yet blazing with a foolish, childish indignation, Gretel refused to grow their crops to such excess any more.

"Consumed by anger, the townsfolk rallied behind their baroness, my ancestor Lady Lucrilla de Marlow, and set out to capture Gretel. Gretel ran for her life but, quickly realizing she was cornered, summoned lightning to forge the truth into the iron goblet she had used to save the town. So that any who found it would know what had really happened."

The scrying, Lewis gasped to himself. It was what they'd seen. *Lucrilla chasing Gretel.*

Moira gave a faint groan, leaning against the grate as Lewis put his arm round her.

"Lucrilla imprisoned gentle little Gretel in the unfinished West Tower of Marlow Hall – the very one you find yourselves in now. She bargained with the girl to see reason and restore the fading town of Barrow to its once prosperous and fertile state. But Gretel refused. Until, at midnight on the seventh night, there was a terrible storm. Lucrilla's chambermaid was sent to take a new candle for young Gretel, and happened upon a strange sight."

Lewis waited, his forehead gluey with a cold sweat.

"A bower," Sir Hector said quietly, "of white nettle flowers, seeming to grow from the very stones of the tower."

Lewis listened as the wind whistled through the grates high above them. The truth had been there in those old stories, just like Sir Hector had said, only twisted out of shape.

"A-and what about Gretel?" Moira asked feebly.

"She was never seen again. Trapped inside these stones, away from the natural world, Gretel's magic faded. Leaving nothing more than these last traces of her strange magic," Sir Hector said quietly.

"Every night after, for many years, in the hope that somehow she would escape and find her way back to him, the blacksmith kept a candle burning in the window of the forge in which they had lived. A light to guide her back to him."

"The green light," Lewis rasped. "The one that appeared out on the marshes."

"But, needless to say, no such reunion occurred. And a painful rage entered the blacksmith's soul."

"It was her father then?" Lewis whispered as the hollow realization gripped him. "The blacksmith?"

"He fired up his forge and smelted a *doorknocker* that he bolted to the stones at the entrance of Barrow. And although he was not as talented as his young daughter, a thread of magic, awakened by his sorrow, must have lived inside him. Because he chiselled beneath the doorknocker a curse. A curse which proclaimed that the doorknocker would keep finding itself a home on one of the doors of Barrow. And, until his daughter was returned to him, in each flooding year a child would be taken from within the house the doorknocker had chosen."

Lewis felt his eyelids grow heavy as he remembered Dad pointing out the doorknocker on the day they'd arrived. He'd even said that a lady from the Barrow Historical Society had been round to drop it off.

It's why there's a regulation that every house in Barrow has to have a doorknocker, Lewis realized. *So no one can tell which one is the actual blacksmith's doorknocker.*

Sir Hector placed both hands on his cane.

"Filled with terror from the curse, Lucrilla ordered the townsfolk to take the goblet they had stolen from Gretel to the fields outside of Barrow and destroy it, so that their descendants would never learn the truth. But when the townsfolk's hammers struck the cup, the flood waters Gretel had concealed within it when she'd saved the town burst forth, flooding the fields and giving birth to the marshes. The forge was destroyed, and the blacksmith with it."

The awakening Lewis felt inside of him was almost peaceful. Like a book slotting perfectly into a shelf, a key clicking into a lock and uttering the words "checkmate" all at once. The hand that he'd thought was trying to drown him out on the marshes was actually the blacksmith's; he'd been trying to show Lewis what had happened.

"With the blacksmith and Gretel both gone, and the townsfolk left with a curse that it was now impossible to put an end to, Lucrilla and the elders of the town decided they needed a means by which to avoid their own children being taken. And they quickly realized that, instead of leaving the choice of victim up to the cursed doorknocker, they could elect the house themselves. A secret list of addresses was hidden inside the barometer, shared only among those unfortunate few burdened with the knowledge of the truth."

"Th-that's...what the Barrow Historical Society is for then?" Lewis hissed in disgust.

The dripping and the chatter from Moira's teeth became the only audible sounds for a moment.

"Whilst people sometimes leave Barrow, they seldom move here," Sir Hector went on. "Not without a very good reason. So what better way to lure in unsuspecting candidates than with the promise of success and opportunity for their dearly beloved children."

Lewis froze.

"The...the scholarship," he murmured. "You're trying to bring people to the town so that...you'll have...other kids to choose from."

"Laying vengeful curses, uprooting lives in the search of prestige and wealth, protecting your own young by offering another in their place. Strange isn't it, the things a parent will do for their child?"

And in the dark of the tower, Dad flickered into Lewis's head.

Dad giving up his job and selling their house in Woolham.

Dad fudging his scholarship application.

Dad desperate for him to have the life he hadn't had.

Lewis tried to swat the thought away. *Not now,* he tried to tell himself.

But he couldn't.

"B-but why do you keep doing it?" Lewis quivered, the defeat sinking over him. "Why don't you want it to stop?"

Sir Hector raised his eyebrow sharply. "It's quite

impossible to return something already lost to the passage of time. The curse lives on. Its secret passed to the eldest Marlow. Supported by the members of the Barrow Historical Society," Sir Hector told them. "Leopold hasn't taken too eagerly to the idea. He's far too jumpy. But we'll sort that out. In time."

Leopold's distant, terrified eyes. It wasn't humiliation that made him such a bully. He must have been scared of what he knew. Terrified of making friends with anyone in Barrow in case the curse came for them. It was why he'd gone all strange when Lewis told him where he lived. He *knew* about the doorknocker all along.

"But he will come round," Sir Hector said sternly. "Because he must. He will come to realize, when one day he has a family of his own, that he would do *anything* for them. As the blacksmith did for Gretel, as your grandfather did for your father, as your father has done for you."

Moira leaned up against Lewis in the darkness as she shivered.

And Lewis felt an angry pulse build inside of him.

"Oh yes," Sir Hector simpered. "Your grandfather learned many secrets in his time mopping the floors here at Marlow Hall," Sir Hector smirked. "But he kept his mouth shut. Knowing that if he uttered so much as a single word, a member of the Barrow Historical Society might happen to visit his house in the night to swap the doorknocker on his door."

"He—" Lewis croaked. "H-he just wanted to protect them. His kids."

The memory of Gramps hammering planks over their front door in Woolham glimpsed through his mind's eye.

"Your grandfather saved what money he had and took his family as far away from Barrow as he could. Terrified that his children might one day be forgotten to him. As you will soon be. Single threads pulled from a tapestry."

"There will be more kids! Others who work it out. And they'll come. And they'll stop you," Lewis spat through gritted teeth.

Sir Hector looked down at him as a wry smile drifted across his face. "Oh, they *always* work it out," he chuckled as he began to take the dripping stairs one by one. "But the curse states that only when the blacksmith is reunited with his own dear Gretel will it lose its hold. The blacksmith was drowned when the forge flooded, and Gretel vanished almost four-hundred years ago. Taking whatever hope there was for lifting the curse with her."

Sir Hector vanished, and his voice echoed towards them through the gloom. "I'm not willing to risk the fall of the Marlow family from the town's good grace whilst I'm presiding over it. The curse will sleep again now. Until the next flood."

There was a scraping of stone.

"STOP!" Lewis bellowed hoarsely as a cold suffocating sweat began to grease down his forehead. "STOP!"

He thrust his hand through the air, pointing it towards the grate as he tried to remember how he'd done it before, how he'd sent a shard of triumphant green crackling towards Leopold as he attacked Hereward's drone.

But there was nothing. No deep jolt in his stomach. Just a leaden heaviness.

As if a sinkhole of terror had opened up inside of him, sending everything, even the strange powers he had inherited from the curse, tumbling towards it.

A heavy *clunk* followed. And they were left with nothing but the rain, and the wind heckling on the tower walls high above them.

Lewis desperately paced the room.

There had to be something. Some way of escape. Maybe there was another secret door? A hidden window? Anything.

"Something's h-happening," Moira stammered. "I'm s-so cold."

He rooted around in his rucksack for his spare hoodie. Perching beside her, he pulled the hoodie round her shoulders as she leaned up against him.

"We can't stop, Moira," he said firmly. "We can't let them win. There's *got* to be a way out of this. There's *always* a way."

He checked his watch.

22:15

One hour and forty-five minutes left.

"I don't think...I don't think we *can* win this one, Lewis," Moira croaked softly, pulling the hoodie tighter round her.

An unpleasant calm sank over him. And in the quiet, without pushing them away, he let Dad's and Mum's faces drift inside his head.

"How does it happen?" he whispered. "What's it like?"

"I don't remember," Moira shuddered.

Tucking the torch under his arm he reached inside the rucksack and fished out the chocolate-covered pretzels Zia had given him.

Moira frowned. "I thought you were saving them – for when you made your first friend in Barrow."

"I was," he whispered tearing open the packet. "I did."

Moira reached out with a quivering hand, grasping a few pretzels in her fingers.

The minutes ticked by, as the two of them munched in silence.

"Do-do you really think…" Lewis said presently. "We won't remember each other?"

Moira turned to him, her enormous eyes glinting in the fading torchlight.

"I know almost nothing about you," Lewis went on. "I don't even know your real name. And yet. I don't think I could imagine ever not having known you."

Moira smiled bravely. "It would be completely impossible to forget you…Willis."

Lewis's cheek twitched. It was the closest he could come to smiling as he remembered Moira mishearing his name on the night they first met.

In the torchlight's pale glow he flexed his fingers. The seventh marking was growing darker, more vivid, as the minutes passed them by. Moira scooped up a few more pretzels, cupping them in her palm, and beneath her thumb Lewis could see the single dark spot, like nothing more than a faint bruise as it faded away.

"I'm thirsty," Moira rasped.

"I brought some squash too," Lewis murmured. "I…I know you like it."

The torch gave a flicker.

"Lewis?"

"Yeah?"

Moira swallowed.

"I'm so glad you were…you." She leaned her head on his shoulder. "I'm glad it was Lewis Buckley, and that I got to meet him."

Lewis felt a lump rise up in his throat. "Me too," he whispered.

The torch guttered, illuminating the ghostly white flowers around them, before there was a sputtering burst of light and it went out.

A heaviness seemed to spread inkily through his limbs.

Lewis pressed the button on his watch.

22:47

Just over an hour.

What would it feel like to remember nothing about who you were or where you'd come from? What would Mum and Dad remember? Would all the memories they had with him be memories they now shared with Moira? Would everything just go on in his life as if he'd been plucked out and replaced? Or would they too have the torturous feeling of being torn away from the people they loved with nothing but haunted little traces of them, like the blacksmith had?

Tick,

click,

click,

nothing.

It didn't matter any more. He didn't need to drown out the ticking now he knew it was going to happen.

Lewis felt his eyes droop.

And the two of them leaned against one another.

He closed his eyes sleepily.

Moira was right. There was no one else he would rather have been with.

His watched beeped.

But he didn't look down. He knew.

One hour to go.

Just one hour.

Just one...

Just...

Leeeeeeewis...

There was a gleam of light beneath his eyelids.

"W-wh-at did you do?!" Lewis stammered, sitting upright.

"Hmm?" Moira asked blinking her eyes open.

"You said my name," he blurted out.

Moira frowned. "I did no such thing."

"There was a flash too," Lewis went on. "Of light. I *saw* it."

Was it starting to happen? Was this it?

"Lewis, stop...you're scar—"

But before the words had left her mouth, there was another brilliant glow of green from around them.

The two of them scrambled to their feet, clutching each other.

I'm here, the voice echoed again, louder this time. *I'm here. I'm here.*

"What the—?!" Lewis began but Moira elbowed him.

"SHHH!" she pointed. "The flowers, Lewis! It's coming from the *flowers*. Look!"

From inside their drooping petals, the white flowers were *glowing*. Pulsating silently, like pale fireflies up and down the walls of the dark tower.

"Oh, Lewis..." Moira murmured as she gazed in wonder.

I'm here. I'm here.

There was a sizzle from high above them as sparks of lightning green blistered through the plants. As they disintegrated, a wave of light descended around Lewis and Moira like a starry cloak until the crackles vanished with a hiss into the murky pool.

Almost at once, the water rippled. And an orb of green light appeared beneath it.

"The green light...the one we saw," Lewis swallowed. "Moira, if that was the blacksmith. Then this must be—"

Moira stepped towards it, and crouching down she scooped. The grey water ran through her fingers as the orb appeared in her outstretched hand.

On the walls of the West Tower, the green light glimmered.

And Lewis whispered, his eyes gleaming. "*That's* Gretel Murk."

Chapter 29
Midnight

The light hovering above Moira's hand swayed a little.

"It's Gretel Murk," she breathed. "It's really her."

Lewis suddenly felt as if he'd been shaken awake.

He pressed his watch.

23:21

Almost at once, the defeated calm that had come over him dissipated.

Not. Now.

"HEELLLLP!" Lewis bellowed hoarsely. "HELLLLLP!"

If someone could hear them. If someone was passing. They could take this light. Take Gretel back out to the marshes where her home once was – to the forge. They could *end* it.

"SOMEBODY!?" Moira belted out, stamping on the trapdoor as she cupped the light in her hand. "It's hopeless!

We've come all this way. And now we're stuck. We're *STUCK!*"

From beyond the iron grate above them, there was a loud thud. And immediately, the two of them drew together as the light cowered.

"Do you suppose this is it?" Moira panted. "The change?"

Lewis's bottom lip trembled as he gripped Moira's free hand.

There was a grunt, followed by a hideous scrape.

Sloshing. More grunting.

Lewis waded over to the door and peered into the darkness through the bars.

There was a *clang* and one of the sewer grates exploded off the wall, colliding with the stones.

A matted tangle of grey emerged from the ensuing hole and Lewis froze.

"I *knew* it!" the tangle said. "Historical preservation, my eye!"

Lewis squinted as a pair of silvery, fish-like eyes stared at him.

"Martha *Godwit*?" Lewis shouted down. "What are you doing here!?"

A billowing triumph welled inside him.

"I-I-I was trying to catch the B.H.S. at it!" she blabbered in shock as she surged towards them. "With the floods, I *knew* they'd be up to something tonight of all nights! W-what are you…how…?!"

"There's no time to explain," Lewis blurted out,

checking his watch. "Sir Hector. He locked us in here. Can you get us out?"

23:12

"That beast! I *knew* it! I-I-I..." Martha floundered, and then an idea occurred to her. "My car! My trusty little car."

Untethering the rope from her belt, Martha hooked it onto the latticed rungs of the iron door.

"We'll get you out, little birds," Martha told them, patting Lewis's hand.

"We have to hurry!" Moira said.

"You were right, Martha," Lewis called out as she turned to dive back into the sewer. "About your uncle, the goblet, the Barrow Historical Society. It was all true. They *were* keeping a secret."

"I *knew* it!" Martha said again, and she punched her hand. "Make sure you stand well back!"

"We *need* to keep Gretel somewhere safe," Moira told Lewis as Martha's legs vanished like an eel back the way she'd come. "Somewhere she can't get lost."

Lewis prised open his rucksack, hunting until he snatched out the bottle of squash. Twisting off the lid he emptied it and held it out for Moira.

As if she were coaxing a spider underneath an upturned glass, Moira tipped the light into the squash bottle. It slumped inside, before making terrified little loops around the bottom as if realizing it was trapped.

"I'm sorry about this," Moira apologized as she twisted the lid back on the bottle. "But it's for your own good!"

"STAND BACK!" came an echoey bellow down the sewer.

An engine revved somewhere in the distance. The rope went taut.

Lewis, Moira and the squash bottle huddled at the far side, away from the door.

There was a groan of rusted iron. A high-pitched creak. And, like a cork exploding, the grated door shot off its hinges clattering into the passage.

Lewis punched the air as the two of them surged forward.

"You first," he breathed as they crouched beside the sewer.

Moira's legs vanished into the opening and, pushing his rucksack ahead of him, Lewis followed.

The grime leached along him as they squelched down the narrow tunnel, until he saw glints of torchlight from over Moira's head.

"Quickly, dears! That's it!"

There was a yelp from Moira, and Lewis slid headfirst after her into a puddle of scummy water gushing from a gutter.

They were *out*.

"We need to get to the marshes. Where the forge used to be. Before midnight," Lewis told Martha as she untied the rope from the tow bar at the back of her car. "So we can end this."

"In you get," Martha told them firmly, nodding at her green three-wheeled car as she removed a camouflaging branch from the roof. "She won't get us all the way. The bridges are closed. Flood waters."

Lewis yanked at the handle, then scooched over on the back seat as Moira sidled in next to him.

"SEAT BELTS!" Martha shrieked, dropping into the front seat and seizing what looked like an old sock to wipe the windscreen.

Lewis helped Moira with her belt first, as she clasped the precious squash bottle, and was just in time to tighten his across his chest when Martha revved the car to a deafening level and it shot off, clipping a garden statue as they charged towards the gates.

"We can make it," Lewis assured them. "We just need to—"

But through the foggy windscreen something pale flashed in the headlights. There was a *clang* and the iron gates to Marlow Hall groaned shut.

"I've called the police! They know you're here."

Lewis leaned between the seats his forehead pulsing.

Leopold Marlow in a pair of striped pyjamas had flung himself against the gates, his sunken eyes squinting as the rain came down in torrents.

"What's he *doing*?!" Martha howled.

"GRANDPA!" Leopold bellowed hysterically towards the house.

Lewis fumbled for his seat belt.

Not now. Kicking open the car door he edged in front of the headlights.

"Leopold?" Lewis called out, shielding one side of his

face from the rain. "We *know* he told you about all this. About what happens."

Leopold's eyes twitched in the headlights.

"GRANDPAAA!" he howled again at the top of his lungs, panting wildly as his hair plastered across his panicked face. "You can't go. I-I-I'm not letting you. I c-c-can't."

His lip wobbled.

A door opened behind Lewis at the front of the hall, followed by the click of a cane against the doorstep.

Lewis glanced round as Sir Hector's silhouette appeared in the doorway.

"You're scared," Lewis panted to Leopold. "I know. I am too. But if you let us go, you'll never have to think about this again. We can finish it."

Leopold flinched.

"It'll be over," Lewis blurted out. "And you can be friends with whoever you like. You'll never have to worry if something's going to happen to them or not. Please."

Leopold's forehead tightened.

"Stay where you are, Leopold. There's a good lad." Sir Hector's cool voice rose behind him. "He's lying. They can't end it. It's impossible."

Lewis turned, his anger billowing.

But from where Leopold stood, there was a *click*. And his hand emerged, clutching the unbolted chain.

Sir Hector let out a gasp of desperation as he lunged towards him with his cane.

Martha honked the horn furiously.

And Leopold flung the gates open.

With lightning speed, Lewis dived for the car door and tumbled inside.

"SEAT BELT! SEAT BELT!" Martha bellowed as she hit the pedal.

The dumpy car's engine spluttered as Sir Hector drew nearer.

"Come on, come on, old girl!" Martha snapped.

There was a cough and with a powerful roar of her exhaust the car lurched into action, shooting through the iron gates. Martha hauled the steering wheel, making a jagged turn in the road, and Lewis slid towards Moira as branches snared through the open windows.

He checked his watch.

23:31

The rain picketed down and the car hurtled along, slipping and roaring until, as they came to the bottom of a small slope, Martha bellowed, "Brace! BRACE!"

A jet of water flew up across the windscreen as they collided with the flood waters. There was an exhausted whir from the motor, but the three-wheeled car powered on as the floods surged past, trickling through the gaps in the doors.

23:39

The haunting wails from the sirens swelled. The drawbridge was just ahead.

"Come on, old girl. Come on!" Martha coaxed, but as the car's engine rose to a fever pitch battling against the onslaught, there was an explosive *bang*, this time followed by a hiss of steam that billowed through the air-conditioning vents. The car succumbed to the water, bobbing like a buoy at sea as the engine flooded.

Lewis's fingers dug into the ripped leather seats. With a groan, the olive-green car tilted, floating up against the brambles which lined the road as their tendrils reached in through the windows.

"Abandon ship!" Martha shouted.

Flinging off his seat belt, he reached over to Moira's side and spun the lever to wind down her window.

Moira angled her legs through the opening and, clutching the squash bottle beneath her arm, lowered herself into the water with a gasp.

Lewis followed as Martha clambered over the seats, her silver eyes glazed with terror. "I-I can't," she sobbed. "Not into the water. I'll climb onto the roof and wait for help. I'll be alright. You go. *Go,* you brave, dear things!"

Lewis squeezed her hand and, pulling himself up using the roof of the car, he swung out through the window and plummeted into the surge.

"LEWIS!" Moira shouted.

On the other side of the river, the town square was ablaze, sirens sounding and emergency lights flashing red and blue.

"HOW CAN WE CROSS?" she shouted, gripping the bottle with one hand and the chain from the drawbridge with the other. The two halves of the drawbridge jutted out of the scummy river as branches and litter gathered around it.

Lunging forward, Lewis's fingers slammed against one half of the drawbridge, the surge pushing him to one side as he hauled himself up.

It's just a jump, he whispered, clambering to his feet and steadying himself on the wooden frame of the drawbridge.

With a lunge Lewis tumbled across, rolling down the raised half as the water swept him.

"MOIRA!" he yelled as he pulled himself up. "JUMP!"

Moira steadied herself on the creaking wooden frame, the squash bottle tucked into her arm.

Lewis glanced down the river. A tree, snapped as if it were no more than a pencil, was thundering towards them.

23:51

"One."

The enormous branch bumped its way nearer.

"Two."

She poised ready for launch.

"Three!"

Right at the moment she leaped there was a sickening crunch as the branch collided with the drawbridge.

The two halves clanged.

Moira was knocked sideways, and she toppled into the water.

"MOIRA!"

She grasped, snatching at a chain with one hand, the other clutched round the bottle.

"L-LEWIS!" she spluttered, clinging on as her bare

knuckles squeezed and the river hauled her sideways in a muddy torrent.

Her grip on the chain was loosening.

Lewis dropped to his stomach, his hand shooting out and his eyes catching sight of the seventh mark. Vivid and dark beneath his thumb as his fingers wrapped round her forearm.

He heaved his weight backwards as he let out a roar. And Moira slid over the edge, collapsing against the wooden slats, the bottle clutched heroically beneath her arm.

Barrow was flickering with torchlight as the blades of the Wherryman's Windmill Inn blustered about.

"HELP!" Lewis shouted, wallowing through the knee-deep water. "PLEASE!"

A worker in a hard hat turned.

"Th-there's someone in a car," Lewis panted. "Over near the drawbridge. She needs help."

The worker nodded firmly, heading in the direction Lewis pointed.

23:54

"Come on!" Lewis shouted as they headed towards two inflatable rescue boats which bobbed beside the Wherryman's Windmill Inn.

An old man pushing a dinghy piled high with belongings swung past them. And clamours went up as the flood sirens wailed and the rain pummelled the gritty water.

"HEY!" A whistle rang out. "YOU TWO!"

A short distance away amid the throng, a police officer was pointing directly at them.

She spoke into her radio as another officer joined her side.

"LEWIS! MOIRA!"

Lewis's eyes shot up.

Hereward Winski was standing on one of the rescue boats, soaked to his bones, a *There's No I in Steam* T-shirt clinging to his gangly frame.

Lewis felt a kick of triumph in his chest.

The officers chugged furiously in their direction, the first speaking firmly into her radio.

"Two kids matching the descriptions of those missing. One male, sandy hair; one female, dark hair. I've got eyes on them. Town square."

Hereward yanked at the rope, mooring the rescue boat to a bicycle rack, hurling his legs over the edge.

Moira barrelled after him, slinging herself over the side and landing on the seat.

The officers were so close now.

Hereward thumped into the driver's seat, Lewis tumbling in sideways next to Moira.

"The recoil starter!" Hereward shouted to Lewis as he fumbled with the power lever.

"THE WHAT?!" Lewis bellowed hoarsely feeling his way around the outboard motor.

"The *recoil* starter!" Hereward repeated.

23:56

"WHAT ARE YOU *TALKING* ABOUT?!"

The officers closed in.

"The recoil—"

"LEWIS!" Moira shouted grabbing Lewis's hand. "TOGETHER. One, two, *THREE*!"

Moira slammed her fist, clenched round Lewis's fingers onto the motor.

There was a *spark*.

And a snare of green electricity crackled across the boat as the propeller puttered into action.

Hereward pulled the power lever.

The first officer lunged.

And in a jet of water the boat shot forward as the constable landed face down in the drink, her fingers slipping off the rubber edge.

"WHERE ARE WE GOING?" Hereward called back.

"THE MARSHES!" Lewis shouted, collapsing on the thwart of the boat beside Moira, who was still gripping her precious cargo with both hands. They had minutes.

With a sharp twist, Hereward turned the steering wheel as they surged up the high street, past the darkened shopfronts, the water swilling at their windows as they cracked beneath its weight.

"They're in pursuit!" Moira shouted over the motor. Lewis swung round, squinting through the hammering rain as lights, blue and red, flashed behind them, and a second rescue boat gave chase.

23:57

"STOP THE VEHICLE!" echoed a voice from a loudspeaker.

"Faster, Hereward!" Moira ordered. "Faster!"

"We're at full tilt!" he hollered, forcing the lever down as far as it would go.

"LEFT!" Lewis coughed.

Hereward swerved as they slid along the thwart, gripping anything they could.

The bottle glowed brighter as Moira huddled.

Nearing the edge of town, Lewis scanned the houses and his eyes latched on to a sign jutting from the swilling stew.

Dowsing Road.

Through the gloom, the stile leading out to the boardwalk slipped into view.

"They've gone!" Moira frowned. "The police!"

Lewis swivelled.

The second boat had vanished from behind. Maybe they'd lost them?

But in a split second, there was a deafening *beep* and a flare of a flashlight as the boat came barrelling out from the road to their right, scraping narrowly past them.

They were side by side.

"I REPEAT, STOP THE VEHICLE," the loudspeaker blared again as the officers waved emphatically.

Lewis ignored them.

The marshes were in sight.

23:58

"Hold ON!" Hereward shouted, yanking the lever down hard. They skidded to a halt. There was a soft *bump*. And the boat smooshed against the wooden posts at the corner of the road.

Lewis jumped, not daring to look back as, through the thicket, the seconds like iron hammer strikes.

Tick,

click,

click,

"LEWIS!"

He turned, his stomach twisting.

Dad.

Just his outline. But it was still Dad, surging towards the boat clutching a torch. His shirt was soaked and his hair plastered down the side of his face as a small group of people in raincoats followed after him.

"He's here! We've found him!"

What he wouldn't do to go and hug Dad. To tell him he loved him in case it all went wrong. But he battled on. To reunite Gretel with her father. To get Moira home. To see Mum and Dad again. The swell ploughed across him, thrusting him sideways.

Not now, Lewis told himself. *Not. Now.*

Moira dropped like a plumb into the water beside him.

"LEWIS!" Dad shouted again.

The second boat arrived.

Lewis's palms slapped against the stile, heaving himself over as his thighs, his chest, his whole body burned with exhaustion.

23:59

A sting of brambles snatched across his fingers. And through the wooden posts beneath him, the frothy marsh water spewed, twisting into whirling pools as it was carried in a torrent down the road.

He could see the boardwalk, and a sea of rushes poking above the choking marshes.

He turned.

Moira clambered out of the water, and up onto the stile. Pivoting with one hand as she gripped the squash bottle.

The first officer dropped off the police boat, wading.

They had seconds.

"MOVE!"

Hereward was shoved aside as the officer clawed her way up to the stile and barrelled past him. A hand lashed out, gripping Moira by the wrist.

She resisted. And the bottle slipped.

Moira snatched.

There was a glimmer as it was hauled by the torrent.

A glint of green.

And the bottle disappeared in the great dark sea as the water carried it down the road. Away from the forge. Away from the marshes.

Moira let out a howl of despair, her eyes locking painfully on Lewis as she howled.

Lewis felt his heart thud to a halt. But a blink of red light caught the wind in his lungs. And from over his shoulder—

"CAW!"

The rook, ragged yet majestic, glided past them with a powerful beat of its wings.

It swooped over Moira's head and Lewis backed onto

the boardwalk, trying to get a better view as it creaked and swayed beneath him.

The rook glided high in the air to a spectacular arching peak, before diving, falling from the sky like a dark star. There was a surge of water as the street leading to the marshes was swallowed up and the bird vanished.

Nothing.

Lewis waited. His head squirming. His eyes glued to the spot he had seen it disappear. He could feel the seconds passing. His thumping heart drawing to a steady, echoing beat in his ears, slower and slower as his vision honed in.

There was a flicker.

And shooting from the waves the rook reappeared, the glowing bottle clutched in its wily claws.

Almost at once, Lewis's heart began to bolt again.

The rook soared high above them.

And the bottle dropped, dogged by the wind but falling straight towards him.

He reached for the sky, his wrist outstretched as his watch glowed.

23:59:55

23:59:56

23:59:57

23:59:58

The marshes became perfectly silent.

Nothing save for his breathing, slow and certain, until with a clatter the bottle landed in his fingers.

Lewis twisted, the lid toppled onto the boardwalk. And dropping to his knees he placed the mouth of the bottle beneath the dark waters of the Dowsing Marshes, as if he was releasing a fish back into a pond.

Beep. Beep.

Midnight.

The light emerged, from the bottle, turning and flickering as if uncertain of its newfound freedom.

Moira was suddenly pounding along the wooden slats towards him. And her fingers laced themselves through his as she squeezed.

Amongst the small group of police at the edge of the boardwalk, Lewis could now see Dad, and those other people who'd been searching with him. A volley of gasps went up as from the middle of the water, there was a *second* bottle-green glow. The glow he had seen beneath the marshes.

"It's him," Moira whispered. "The blacksmith."

The two lights danced towards each other.

One lost. One found.

And as they met, a sting of jagged lightning, green and brilliant, thrust down into the water and the marshes were bleached in its pale glow.

A wind murmured through the tops of the rushes.

And, with a flicker, the two lights silently vanished.

There was a deafening *crack* of thunder, followed by a volley of caws high above them, as a cloud of rooks circled, their wings dark and ragged against the night sky as it crackled with green stings.

Lewis turned to Moira as the wind blustered. Her dark bob of soaking hair was whipped from side to side.

And suddenly it was all before him.

Nothing uncertain.

Now.

The hurricane of rooks grew around them, twisting the rain into a scorching whirlwind of feathers and shrieks as they seemed to descend around Moira.

As if taking her home.

She was leaving.

Lewis tried to hold back his panic. He needed to say something before the moment was gone. Something big.

Because he knew this was it. This was goodbye.

"W-what if I just forget you?" he croaked, a lump rising in his throat. "What if you just forget me?"

"Impossible," Moira insisted, squeezing his wet fingers. "And if ever I feel like I'm forgetting, I'll just think about home. Not houses or bedrooms or hallways. Just the feeling. Because that's what home is. And you'll always be there. A little piece of you."

The rain scattered through his eyes and he squinted.

"I-I wish…I wish you could stay," Lewis gulped, his eyes filling with hot, bleary tears. "I wish there was a way."

Moira's eyelids fluttered, the blizzard of wings drawing closer still, surrounding the two of them in a feathery shrieking hurricane as the boardwalk groaned and creaked in the windswept marshes.

Her grip became loose on his hand. "Everyone makes you feel rubbish at one point or another. I think you just need to know which ones are worth feeling rubbish for."

Lewis's bottom lip trembled.

Her eyes closed.

And a smile crossed her face.

"I remember it, Lewis. My name. I just remembered it."

He could feel the rook's wings battering against his cheeks as the spray from the marshes roared around them.

"What is it? Moira? Tell me your name."

But she shook her head.

"Don't come looking for me, Lewis. Will you promise?" she grasped his fingers. "You might see how I looked when I was grown and old. And you must remember me as I am. As we are now."

Her voice grew faint and her grip seemed to become just a memory as the haze of water and wings flashing around them thickened.

And the last word he heard before everything went black was the girl with chestnut eyes from the marshes saying his name.

He remembered falling. And darkness.

Then there was a distant memory. Of Mum's voice. Of arms. Dad picking him up and carrying him whilst he slept, like when he was small, followed by a warm glow on his cheeks, soft pillows meeting the back of his head, and nothing.

Chapter 30
A Letter

There was light. And it was warm. He flung his eyes open and immediately regretted it. A sharp pain pierced his forehead as he shielded his vision from the impossibly brilliant sunlight. Lewis opened his eyes again, slowly this time. He was on a sofa, a blanket stretched across him.

What am I doing on a sofa?

He scanned the room.

Boxes. Postcards. Tacky tooth ornament. Dry carpets. This is my house. My living room.

It all came back to him, in a blinding flash.

The flood. The marshes. The rooks.

He could remember all of it.

Moira.

The name sounded strange.

As if it no longer belonged to the person he could so clearly imagine.

"And he's up." Mum appeared, carrying a hot mug of steaming chocolate.

Lewis leaned on his fists as he lifted himself up. He was stiff. His back and legs ached as a sting shot across the back of his head from where he must have hit the boardwalk.

How much did Mum and Dad know? What did they think had happened?

Mum placed the mug on the coffee table and, nudging his legs, she scooched onto one end of the sofa. "It's good to have you back," she said quietly, playing with the corner of the blanket.

Lewis felt his back stiffen.

"You were scared, weren't you? About everything changing." She swallowed as Lewis waited, pressing his neck back against the cushions.

"You've always known best, Lewis. Ever since you were small, you know that? When we bought our first house in Woolham, Gramps would come over to pick you up and walk you to the park in your little pram." She smiled. "He thought it was so funny when he gave you a little bag of oats to feed the ducks, you'd divide them into piles so they could all have the same amount."

Lewis felt the corner of his mouth twitch as Mum gazed at the floor.

"We shouldn't have put so much pressure on you. Moving here. On the whim that you'd get into some ridiculous school. It wasn't right. Not even if you'd wanted to go to Elksbridge would that have been right."

And then Lewis realized.

They have no idea what happened.

As if the girl he called Moira had never existed.

Mum folded her arms across the top of the sofa, leaning her cheek on her forearm. "You know," she said softly. "After Gramps passed away, even though they didn't get on, Dad was really sad."

An image of Gramps sitting in his chair in the retirement home with a blanket tucked across his legs flickered through Lewis's mind.

"I think Dad felt like there were so many things they never got to say to one another. And in the end, because they were too scared to speak honestly with each other, Dad just felt resentful and Gramps felt as if he'd been forgotten."

She reached out and played with the edge of Lewis's blanket. "They were so different. Dad with his cricket. Gramps with his chess. And…I think Dad really wants to make sure he doesn't make the same mistake…with you."

Lewis lay motionless as a single tear made its lonely journey across his cheek.

"W-where is he?" he croaked.

"Down at the old school gym," Mum said.

"He didn't…he didn't lose the sale?" Lewis asked.

"Sale? No. There was just some damage in the storm and he's clearing it up."

"From the flooding?" Lewis asked.

"Hardly flooding!" Mum frowned. "Just a bit of heavy wind and rain. The garden's a mess, but nothing damp old Barrow isn't accustomed to. Must have given poor Sir Hector a bit of a fright though."

Lewis's forehead wrinkled. "What do you mean?"

"He passed away. Very suddenly. In the early hours of the morning. Very sad for his grandson."

Lewis thought back to Leopold's sunken, frightened face. How alone he must be feeling now.

Mum reached out and squeezed his hand, turning it in hers.

The marking was gone. Nothing but a clear patch of skin.

"Dad left that for you." Mum nodded.

Lewis turned his neck stiffly.

The orange gift bag with a note clipped to the top was perched on the coffee table. Reaching across, she hoisted it over and placed it on his lap. Then, kissing him on the forehead, she slipped out of the room pulling the door to.

Lewis's fingers investigated the tissue paper. Gramps's chess clock lay in the centre, plus a tiny screwdriver and something called ammoniated clock-cleaning concentrate.

Unfolding the note, Lewis read Dad's messy script:

Lewis,

I've wanted to fix Gramps's old chess clock for some time. And I wasn't going to give it to you until I could. But I've driven all over Woolham and the

Snoring Broads trying to find someone who could fix it and I've had no luck. But the lady at the hardware shop in Great Reedmouth told me that all it might need is to be taken apart and cleaned. So I'm returning it to you here with accompanying supplies so we can do just that.

As I watch you sleep on the sofa, I've been thinking all night about what you said. About being truthful and honest. It's never come very easily to me to say things just as they are. It didn't come very easily to my dad either. I guess that's the one thing we really had in common.

I always thought it was because we were so different. Gramps would get frustrated when I couldn't learn his chess puzzle off by heart and I'd be disappointed when he wouldn't come to my cricket games.

But when he passed away, I felt really guilty. Guilty that I hadn't visited him more in the home and guilty that he might have felt as if I'd forgotten about him. It scared me so much to think that the same thing might happen to me and you. And I tried to push you to do things you didn't want, in the hope that we'd have more in common.

But I know seeing you now, watching you sleep, that I never had to worry. Because you're you. You're not your gramps. And you're most certainly not me.

I'll never forget on the day you were born when

Mum handed you to me in Woolham Hospital I thought, "I can't believe I'm his dad."

And every time I see you playing chess, or being the kind, clever person you're growing up to be I think the same.

I'm so lucky to be your dad, Lewis.

Please keep talking to me. Honestly. Tell me what you're feeling. And I'll try do the same. I promise.

Your Dad

Lewis scanned the room for his trainers. Wedging them on, his heart thumping, he bolted down Orsman Road, the letter clutched in his hand. And he didn't stop running until the school gym slipped into sight.

One of the large dusty windowpanes had smashed and leafy debris was strewn across the playing fields. The door was ajar as the sounds of glass scraping across the floor echoed from within. Dad was sweeping the window shards and leaves into a pile at one end of the gym.

Lewis knocked and Dad looked up.

"You know," Dad chuckled, tapping the end of the broom on the floor, "maybe it's true about apples never falling too far from the tree. Being an estate agent involves a lot more cleaning than I ever expected."

He leaned the broom up against the wall and sat himself down on the edge of one of the school chairs as Lewis stood in the doorway.

"I'm..." He swallowed. "I'm sorry, Lewis. For all the...

I know now Elksbridge wasn't something you wanted. You were just doing it to humour me."

Lewis stared at the mud drying on the scuffed floor, not knowing how he could say what he wanted.

"When I was your age, Lewis, *I* applied for a scholarship at Elksbridge."

Lewis looked up.

"You did?" he rasped.

Dad nodded.

"Filled in the application myself and went to the interview without Gramps knowing. I even borrowed one of Badger's ties. When Gramps found out, he was livid. He thought it was charity. And shortly after, one night in the summer, he told Jean and me that we were leaving Barrow. For ever. For good."

Lewis's memory drifted back to what Sir Hector had said about the scholarship. *Gramps must have known about that too.*

"He didn't tell us why. Just that we'd be better off in Woolham. And we arrived late one night. To a dingy flat in an apartment complex. And I was so angry with him for letting his pride get in the way of an opportunity. But then I wondered if he was embarrassed by me. Embarrassed that even though my grades were rubbish and I barely scraped through school, I'd somehow thought there was a chance I'd get in."

Lewis wished he could tell Dad everything. That he could make him understand why Gramps had done it. Because he'd been afraid he'd lose him. Afraid his son would forget all about him. But now Dad, the events of the night before completely forgotten to him, was further away than ever from really understanding.

"I'm sorry about your application, Lewis," Dad murmured. "About what I did. I was just…scared for you, if you didn't get in. I want you to have everything in the world."

He sifted through the words in his head. Trying to find ones that were important. Honest enough.

"Y-you and Gramps." Lewis sniffed, his voice thin and trembling. "You weren't really that different at all. You were both doing things to protect the people you love. The ones worth hurting for."

Dad's eyes grew red and watery.

And Lewis told the truth. Wrapped in a lie, but the truth nonetheless.

"When I used to visit Gramps. At his home," Lewis said. "Whenever he'd see the ads for Buckley's Estate Agents in the paper. He'd point to your picture, and he'd tell the nurses bringing him his food that that was his son. That he was your dad."

Dad's shoulders collapsed as he broke and Lewis ran across the gym. He threw his arms around Dad's shoulders and hugged him. Feeling safe.

Dad sniffed, wiping his eye on Lewis's shoulder as he gazed around the stormswept gym.

"Look at the mess I've got us in, huh?" he chuckled. "Pushed you to the point of running out on a scholarship exam. Relocated the three of us to a town nobody wants to move to, where there's no properties to sell, and now we're stuck with a damp old house that's about as homely as a bus shelter."

"Home's not a place," Lewis told him softly. "It's just a feeling you get."

The summer wind murmured through the cracked window. And they sat, a frail memory of the girl from the marshes, her hair swept across those chestnut eyes, dancing through Lewis's head.

Chapter 31
The Black Rook

"Now are you both *positive* this is a good idea?" Celia asked uncertainly as the car pulled up.

Hereward shrugged.

"Lewis?"

A few days had passed, and Lewis gazed up at Marlow Hall as the Winskis' lemon-coloured car with the white stripe drew to a halt outside the imposing iron gates.

The hall was draped in ivy, withered from the summer sun, as faded droops of honeysuckle flaked from its walls.

"Yep," Lewis said, scruffling the head of Cyril the puli dog and hoisting on his rucksack.

The gravel crunched beneath their feet.

"He's quite...odd, you know," Hereward said uncertainly as Celia puttered off. "Doesn't really talk much."

Hereward was wearing a bright blue jumper with criss-crossing railway lines on it and the words *Stay on Track* printed across it in daffodil yellow.

"All the more reason then," said Lewis as he pulled the bell. There was a clanging from inside the ancient house.

With a shudder, the door opened and a lady in a tweed suit skirt with jet-black hair answered. She was on a call, her phone against her shoulder.

"Yes?"

"Is Leopold in?" Lewis asked.

The lady gave a surprised frown and called back into the house.

"Leopold! Visitors!"

She went back to her call.

There was a padding of footsteps and a dark head of hair, followed by a pair of eyes, peered out.

He was timid and mouselike. As if any sudden movement might send him flying for a hole in the skirting boards.

"Hey," Lewis said awkwardly.

A blank stare followed.

"We heard about your grandfather," Lewis went on. "We're really sorry. Just...thought you might like some company."

Leopold watched them suspiciously.

Does he remember any of it? Lewis thought. *The curse? The changelings? The flood?*

Hereward had. A couple of days after it all, Lewis had casually asked him if he had any experience steering boats.

And Hereward had nearly choked on the slushie he was slurping as he tried to blurt out that, yes, yes, he *did* remember. But Celia, like Mum and Dad, didn't. And nor, it seemed, did anyone else.

Maybe it was because they were kids that they remembered. As potential victims of the curse.

But both decided not to tell anyone about it. It would be easier that way. And, as Hereward pointed out, being part of a joint delusion which involved a girl from one hundred years ago and a conspiracy to make children disappear was NOT a good look when you were starting at a new school.

With a creak, the door pulled back, revealing the flagstone atrium, its contents cloaked in white dust sheets.

"Who's that lady?" Lewis asked as Leopold led them silently to a room at the back of the house.

"She's my aunt," Leopold murmured arranging himself on the sofa. "She's moving here. From London. We're gonna live together."

Lewis nodded, gazing out of the window he and Moira had climbed through on that stormy night.

Lewis sat on the sofa opposite Leopold. And an uncomfortable silence followed.

A clock chimed.

"This lady has a *massive* chin," Hereward said loudly as he peered at a large portrait in a gilt frame.

Leopold looked up. "That's my great-great-grandmother."

There was silence.

Had Hereward offended him?

But then Leopold let out a sudden snort of laughter. He tried to stifle it, as if he'd been holding in laughing at that painting his whole life.

Hereward began to grin, growing a little more confident. "Looks more like a turnip than a chin. You're lucky you didn't inherit her looks."

The three of them gradually chuckled to a halt.

"I-I brought my chessboard by the way." Lewis hurriedly tried to fill the silence, as he pulled it out of his rucksack. "You know how to play?"

Leopold shook his head as behind him Hereward inspected a suit of armour.

"Wanna learn?"

Leopold nodded eagerly.

"These are the pieces," Lewis explained, tipping them out and crouching beside a velvet ottoman. "There's the king. That's the one you need to protect most. And it can only move one square at a time in any direction."

Leopold watched carefully, kneeling beside the board placing both elbows on its soft edge.

"Then there's the queen." Lewis went on slotting both the black and the white pieces to either side of the board. "That's the most powerful piece. The queen can move as many squares in any one direction she wants."

Leopold nodded slowly. There was a *clang* and a chain-mail helmet displayed on a cabinet snapped shut, narrowly missing Hereward's fingers.

"And there's the rooks." Lewis found the two white pieces. "Do you wanna put them on the board?"

Lewis held out the pieces in his hand. But as Leopold reached forward to take them he did the most uncharacteristic thing Lewis had seen him do yet. He brushed the pad of his finger, ever so softly over the skin beneath Lewis's thumb on the very spot where the marking had been just a few days ago. As if to make sure it definitely wasn't there any more.

He remembers, Lewis realized.

Leopold looked up, and for a split second there was a panicked flicker in his eyes. A fearful flicker. A strange memory that Lewis was quite sure Leopold wanted to just pretend was all a bad dream.

"Here," Lewis said tactfully, taking the two pieces and placing them on the board.

Leopold gave him a small, but grateful smile. And Lewis smiled back as he continued with his explanation.

"Rooks can move as many squares as they want, but only in straight lines. And they can do this thing called 'castling', which is where they switch out—"

He stopped, his hands raking through the pieces.

But in the pile, he could only find one black rook.

The other was missing.

"I'll pick you up after school once I've finished up at the Open House," Dad told him as he dumped a stack of For Sale signs in the back seat of the car. "Mum's working late. But we can get a takeaway tonight. Watch a film maybe?"

Lewis grinned, waving to Dad as he set off along the street.

It was the first day of school and autumn seemed to have come early to Barrow. The gardens on either side of the houses on Orsman Road had already become faded and thin, and the sun had a tired apricot glow that signalled the start of school books and classrooms.

Not a day had gone by where he hadn't thought of Moira. Hoping beyond hope that she wouldn't have forgotten him. But as the summer holidays had drawn to a close, the heavy, leaden feeling that that door had closed for ever settled over him.

He'd pondered going to the library and searching amongst the archives. But even if he'd wanted to break the promise he'd made to Moira, he couldn't face it. He never had learned her real name. And the thought of finding out what might have really happened to her was too painful.

Hoisting up his rucksack, he made his way along Saltmarsh Road towards Barrow School. People bustled out of the fronts of their houses as leaves drifted and lunches were stuffed into rucksacks.

"Lewis!" came a shout.

There was a yapping from Cyril as Hereward's gangly legs swung out of the Winskis' car and Celia shot off again with a merry little *toot*.

"Mr Wirrel said, if there's enough interest this year,

he'll start a robotics club," Hereward told him as they walked along Wherryman's Way. "Apparently Cressida Laws built a robot last year that could stir sugar into tea. But Caspar told me that. And he once fell into the stingray tank at Reedmouth Aquarium."

Up ahead Lewis could see the Barrow School gates, bustling with life as cars flocked towards it.

Lewis stopped, a hollow sensation filling out inside of him as they passed number six.

The Willows was low, with dark criss-cross windows and purple lavender bushes at the front, faded to an ash grey.

Hereward turned. "Lewis?"

"You go ahead," Lewis told him. "I just need to check something."

"See you in form." Hereward shrugged and set off in the direction of the gates.

Making sure no one was looking, Lewis ducked beneath the bushes.

On the lawn was a large canary yellow sign:

BUCKLEY'S ESTATE AGENTS
ANOTHER ONE SOLD!

Where the bins were kept to the side, there was a narrow gap, and making sure he didn't clatter into anything he crept into the garden and hid himself behind one of the conker trees.

The roof of the shed seemed to groan beneath the weight of the withered ivy, and the walls looked faded and sunken as he darted across the empty flower beds towards it.

Pushing with his shoulder up against the door, he wedged it open and slipped inside the musty-smelling room, filled with compost and flowerpots.

Spiders had gathered in their hundreds and the cobwebbed mess of rakes and seed packets looked as if had been undisturbed for years.

How strange it was to think that Moira had once been in here.

He'd tried to imagine her. Hugging her knees as she leaned against the wall in his room. Or cycling across the boardwalk. But none of it had felt very real, and the person he pictured inside his head was more of a stranger than the Moira he'd once known.

He checked his watch. There were a few minutes before he had to be at school and, sitting himself cross-legged on the ground, he let out a slow breath.

A spider needled its way across the tiny windowsill and lowered itself down to the cracked weatherboards in the corner.

A rogue thought glanced through Lewis's head.

Getting to his knees, he hauled aside the sacks of soil that were spilling out in front of the wall and wedging his fingers into the gap he yanked at one of the weatherboards, which prised away with a *prang* of rusty nail.

Rolling up his sleeve, he reached inside.

No, he thought as nothing but wood and wafting cobwebs met his fingers. *She made you promise not to go look—*

Lewis stopped. Something soft that felt as if it were hung by a string knocked gently against his knuckles.

Unhooking it, Lewis lifted the object delicately out.

An embroidered bag. So familiar to him and yet now it was faded and thread-worn.

This was hers, he whispered to himself, squeezing it. And through the fabric he felt something small, and hard. Gently poking out the button that clasped it together Lewis held out his palm and tipped the bag sideways.

It was a rook. The black rook from his chess set. His missing piece.

The varnish had worn at the edges, as if it had been turned many times in the hands of its captor.

A smile twitched at the corners of his mouth.

Lewis squinted.

There was a tiny slip of paper wrapped round its stem.

Picking at it with his nail, Lewis unfurled the note in his fingers.

Moira had kept her promise never to forget him.

Her face was foggy. But her voice so very clear as Lewis read, hopeful of what was to come, knowing that Moira would not be his only true friend, merely his first:

Told you I'd never forget you, Willis

The Tricking of the Bogwitch
Words by Eugenia Bilge

LUCRILLA:
"Can you make yourself to fly,
As before you now I cower.
Oh, mistress of the stormy sky,
Show to me your power!"

GRETEL MURK:
"Bah and bees, and glibberty gleeze!
That's easy as mere clapping.
I can ride the southern breeze
Without so much as flapping!"

LUCRILLA:
"Can you bottle thunderbolts,
On dark and stormy nights?
Snare their glinting gleaming volts,
And show to me your might!"

GRETEL MURK:
"Pish and fie and tom-tiddle-tie,
That's easy as mere talking!
I can bottle lightning, why,
Like ale ripe for corking!"

LUCRILLA:

"But can you drink these floods here,
With your goblet, iron made?
Show folk why they ought to fear,
And your wish shall be obeyed!"

GRETEL MURK:

"Snort and bat and diddly-pat!
That's easy as a flea!
I'll quaff it down in two ticks flat,
Like a cup of goodly tea!"

ACKNOWLEDGEMENTS

Never was the old proverb that no one achieves anything alone more true than with this story. It would still be a murky, marshy lump of an idea if it weren't for all the people below and many more – whether they have given patient words of encouragement, kindness, or cups of steadfastening tea.

To my brilliant agent, Silvia Molteni – thank you for helping me carry this idea, in its many varied forms, through to completion.

To Jo Briggs for very generously taking the time to give me some research advice for the penultimate passage in this story.

Thanks to Rebecca Hill, Becky Walker, Alice Moloney and the Usborne team for their story and design acumen. Thanks to Helen Greathead for her considered copyediting, and Gareth Collinson and Anne Finnis for their uncannily perceptive proofreads. And to Laura Borio for her lovely cover and design trimmings.

To Darren Simpson, Serena Patel and Ann-Marie Howell for being my story friends and for their open-armed words of encouragement – hugely, hugely valued coming from three such dab hands.

To Emily Priestnall for reading this book I don't know how many times and tirelessly feeding back with enthusiasm and razor-sharp editorial prowess. Thank you, thank you, thank you, extraordinary friend.

Mum and Dad, siblings, inlaws – those in Poland, Australia and beyond – I will never get over how lucky I am to have such an incredible collection of people to call my family. Thank you for your care and for just being the people you are.

A most particular thank you to my sister Micky (Mackerel, Mackie, Michaelmas-Broadway) for being a constant source of inspiration – whether its sending photos of unusual shapes in the floorboards or having sudden and magical epiphanies about the sorts of mischievous things children get up to in books like this.

To my husband, Wojciech, who I quite simply cannot even begin to thank enough for his patience, selfless care and sheer belief that I can and I will. Has it been ten minutes yet, since I told you?

And finally to my nephews and nieces whose names are in the front of this book – I can't tell you just how much you make my mind glimmer with inspiration every single day with your acts of kindness, delight and untiring curiosity. I hope you will all find true friends you are able to love and to miss as much as Lewis did with Moira.